# WAKING

## HELEN RICHARDSON

Published by Accent Press Ltd 2017
Octavo House
West Bute Street
Cardiff
CF10 5LJ

www.accentpress.co.uk

ISBN 9781786153449
eISBN 9781786153227

Printed and bound in Great Britain by Clays, St Ives Ltd

*For my brother, Mark.*

I see plainly that there are never any sure signs by means of which being awake can be distinguished from being asleep.

The result is that I begin to feel dazed, and this very feeling only reinforces the notion that I may be asleep.

René Descartes

# PART 1

PART 1

# EAST LONDON, 2015:

It was six in the evening on moving day by the time they finished. Anna had weightlifted her life in boxes up the awkward narrow little staircase to her new room at the top of the house. She dropped the last item on the pile and stood still, her upper arm muscles heavy and sore. She waited for someone downstairs to call her name. A few blissful seconds of silence answered and Anna closed her eyes and sank backwards onto the bed, hoping to steal a quiet minute for herself.

Anna had moved to London because she was going mad. If she replanted herself, pulled up her roots from the coast where they had grown soft and waterlogged beside the Brighton sea, and set them down in hard city soil, they would hold firmer, stand straighter. The gradual unravelling of her mind was a truth she didn't much want to look at. She burrowed deeper into the unmade pillows and sheets beneath her, pressing hot fingers into her temples.

Anna dreamt things. Sometimes she could feel things creeping around in the shadowy corners of her room as she woke up. She was even starting to believe the kind of nonsense that came out of the mouths of those sad, depleted people you saw talking to themselves in low twisted voices in the bad parts of town. Soon she would turn ashen, nicotine-yellow, the colour of insanity, and lose all her friends. Maybe going mad was a bit like getting fat: it came on gradually without you really noticing, and nobody would tell you it was happening because they didn't want to offend you, or they assumed you already knew. Then one day you'd laugh in sympathy at the crazy person mumbling at nothing in the supermarket car park, and people would look awkwardly the other way because you'd lost the plot months ago.

'The girls want to take us out for a drink. Are you ready?' Holly asked from the doorway.

'Would you tell me if I got fat?'

# CHAPTER ONE

'Having seriously fucked up nightmares is meant to be a good thing: it shows you're working through your issues.' Libby returned to her drink, nodding insistently to the bemused looks she was getting from the rest of the group. 'It's true.'

Anna laughed. 'I'll use that excuse in future, thank you.'

'You're most welcome.'

Holly protested. 'Libby, she once fell out of bed shouting while she was still fast asleep. Is that what "working through your issues" looks like?'

Anna sighed. 'I can't even remember what that dream was about. Holly looked so scared when she woke me up.'

'We can handle a few night terrors.' Sophie jumped in. 'We'll look after you.'

'It's not as if you don't do the washing up, or you have weird sex with the door open.' Libby paused. 'You don't, do you?'

'I definitely don't.'

'Your turn then, Anna. What's the worst thing about living with Holly? What should we be on high alert for?'

Anna was sitting on a roof terrace, high up above the city with her closest friend Holly, settling in to unfamiliar surroundings after moving house. Their new flatmates had taken them for a drink, an alcoholic christening of their newborn life in London; they had been residents for about five hours. Anna's face was flushed rose pink in a permanent blush from tequila, humid summer air, and the heat of the strangers that surrounded them. It was a funny, prickly sensation, to be a tourist at a bar that was so crowded with locals. Every few minutes one of the conversations nearby sped up in an excitable flurry as people bumped into friends and neighbours, the air boozy from the careless uninhibited drinking of those who didn't have far to go to climb safely into bed.

They had arrived in the city in the middle of a June heatwave, and the atmosphere on the terrace was heavy with hazy, purple summer dusk. Barbecue smoke and traffic smog floated as thick dusty clouds through the evening. The breeze gathering around them blew in warm, sticky gusts over the concrete, hot instead of refreshing. The bar was high up on a flat roof at the top of a ten-floor industrial building.

From where Anna sat, with her elbow propped up on the railings, she could see the lights of the London skyline glittering like a necklace along the horizon, shining jewelled beads that traced a line between land and sky.

'What's the worst thing about living with Holly?' Anna pretended to think for a moment. 'It's difficult to know where to start ... ow!' She probably deserved the elbow in the ribs.

Anna and Holly had met at university in Sussex, lived together ever since, and had recently agreed to move to London. It was Holly's idea; she had been working there since they'd graduated and was growing weary of the commute. She persuaded Anna over a period of weeks, spotting the perfect job for her at the Whitechapel Gallery and telling her about it on condition that, if she were offered it, they would leave their seaside apartment and move to 'The Smoke'.

So Anna went to the selection meeting, half hoping to put Holly's idea to bed when she didn't get asked back, and half hoping to surprise herself with her own success. That attitude, less precious and more throwaway than it should have been, must have sharpened her interview technique. It left her free to be honest, to challenge and question, to avoid the dreaded embarrassment of finding herself blank-minded and star-struck in front of one of her heroes, a curator whose exhibitions she had attended with her dad when she was a much younger, much greener art student.

She got the job and held up her end of the bargain. It was a good thing, finally, to leave Brighton. In conversation Anna supported all the more socially palatable explanations: it was the perfect time to move; she had an exciting new job; she had the chance to live somewhere new. Privately though, Anna hoped, wished and prayed that a change of scene would bring with it a peaceful night's sleep, carrying her far away from the nightmare that had haunted her for nearly fifteen years. Moving house could be the catalyst for a new life, one where she burrowed down beneath her duvet each evening and stayed soundly asleep until dawn.

'I'm glad Holly's told you about my unsociable sleep patterns. I was going to make up something trivial about her: "she's so noisy" or "she never washes up". But she's reminded me that the worst thing about living with Holly is her inability to keep a secret.'

Holly bristled. 'That is so unfair. Name one secret that I haven't kept – the sleep stuff doesn't count because I didn't realise it was a secret.'

Anna snorted. Holly had told the others about Anna's sleepwalking, sleep-talking, and even occasional wide-eyed sleep-shouting. She had shared one particular episode when a sleeping Anna had tripped over in the kitchen and smashed the window near the sink, narrowly avoiding a nasty injury to her right arm. Holly had even described being woken up in the small hours of the morning to find Anna standing, still as a statue in the bedroom doorway, speaking the strange disconnected sentences of the sleepwalker; words and phrases loaded with apparent hidden meaning from deep within her dream-world.

'That's exactly my point: most people would understand that this was all sensitive information.' Anna turned to the others. 'If there is anything you don't want everybody knowing – and I mean everybody in London – then just don't tell Holly. That's all. Apart from that: cooking, cleaning, having fun, she's ace.' The girls were laughing again.

'No need to tell us. We've known Holly since we were seven.'

'Her nickname at school used to be "Radio Holly".'

Anna choked on her drink. 'No way.'

'If you told Holly something in confidence but you forgot to say, for example, "by the way could you please promise me that you won't repeat that thing I just told you about Joe and I accidentally having sex", you would wake up the next morning to see it on the local news.'

'It was so bad, people stopped having sympathy for you if something got out. They just shrugged and said "Oh dear, did you put it on Radio Holly?"'

Fran closed her eyes and sighed with mock solemnity, 'Nothing was sacred.'

Holly's face darkened like a thundercloud, sulkily pouted lips above defensive, folded arms.

'It's OK, Hols. We know there's no malice in it.'

'And you don't have double standards. You share your own shit just as freely.'

'Holly prefers her closet to remain firmly open, skeletons dancing around in the middle of the room.'

They were moving in with Holly's oldest friends from school, friends from long before she and Anna had met. Anna had played host to them regularly throughout her time at Sussex, welcoming them all into their little university flat down near the seafront. They filled the rooms with high-pitched laughter and speedy conversations that were delivered in riddles but quickly understood. Anna tended towards quieter more exclusive friendships, like the one she thought she had signed up for when she met Holly, sitting shyly in the student union, a timid first year separated from her gaggle of high-volume girlfriends back home.

Holly took Anna to stay with them all in London every few months, for wild weekends of strobe lights and sticky dance floors, waking up on sofas and bedroom floors with sore eyes and dry mouths. They spent nauseous Sunday afternoons winding their way back home to Brighton on the train, towards the shadowy prospect of Monday morning lectures. The others still lived in the same place as they had then, a tall terraced house in Hackney that Anna had just spent the long hot summer afternoon hauling her belongings into.

Libby reached out and laid a hand lightly on Anna's forearm. 'I wouldn't worry about the night-time stuff, honestly. I used to have terrible insomnia, the others will tell you. I know how hard it is when you can't sleep properly.'

Fran was looking out at the sea of people surrounding them, but she nodded at the mention of Libby's insomnia. 'This is different though, right?' She looked at Anna. 'You do get to sleep, but then you have bad dreams.'

'I guess it *is* different, although I'm sure it still leaves me more exhausted than a restful night's sleep would.'

'In ancient times people would have thought you were a saint or something, like a dream oracle. Everyone would have come to see you each morning for spiritual guidance.'

'See, Holly,' Libby jabbed a finger in Anna's direction. 'Not weird: visionary.'

Anna laughed, but all the dream talk was making her feel squirmy and uncomfortable. She changed the cross of her legs and lifted her drink to take another sip. She was looking for things to do with her hands, with her body, while her heart steadied its quickening flutter in her chest.

'You can see why though, can't you?' Fran added, thoughtfully.

'Frankly, Fran, I'd advise anybody against approaching me for guidance of any kind.'

Fran smiled, shaking her head. 'Why people believed dreams were important?'

'True,' Holly joined in. 'Every now and then you have one that just feels ...' she searched for the appropriate word.

'Profound?'

'Maybe. Something that makes you see your bedroom differently, suspiciously even, when you finally wake up, as though the dream is still there, hovering around you.'

'Yet they mean nothing at all.' Libby held her hand up in the air, her fingers springing open mimicking a puff of smoke disappearing, a dream being swallowed up by the dusty atmosphere.

Anna watched the line of fairy lights above them bob in and out of view, as her head nodded automatically along with the others. Something clenched inside her stomach. Recently, that sense of meaning had started chasing her, running with her from dream to dream, snapping at her heels from night-time to daylight. In her maddest moments of weary sleep deprivation, Anna could believe that something was trying to communicate with her through her dreams. There was so much repetition in them, so many recurring experiences and memories interwoven amongst the nonsense and randomness. Her dreams all had a bewildering order to them, deep beneath the surface, that she could never quite get at. She would wake up and see how close it had all been to making sense, and then she would lie in the darkness and worry about the messages wrapped up inside them that she must be missing.

Anna was sure that she was rational, sensible, and down-to-earth. The straightforward, uncomplicated part of her knew that the idea of a higher meaning behind her nightmares was improbable, laughable. But some mornings she felt ready to be converted, to embrace the sort of wobbly, gullible, supernatural beliefs she never thought herself capable of.

When people told ghost stories, relaying terrifying paranormal events that had happened to a friend of a friend, somebody they once met, or themselves, they so often began by assuring the listener: 'I don't even believe in ghosts.' Did scepticism make the evidence of strange and unexplained happenings stronger, that something weird *must* be going on if it was powerful enough even to convince somebody like her? Or did it just show how far she had travelled past her normal boundaries and deep down into insanity? If there was an order or agenda to the terrors that assaulted her mind night after night, then swapping beds and moving up to London was hardly going to fix things. Anna bit her lip. She was starting to feel cold, even with the concrete floor radiating a day's worth of sunny heat at her.

# CHAPTER TWO

She didn't get a single night's respite. Lying in the strange darkness of an unfamiliar bedroom, a storm brewed. Anna's thoughts spun like a whirlpool while she slept. They dragged her insistently, reluctantly, down into the cold wet depths of their circular current. Often a busy evening, especially one involving physical exercise or alcohol, would silence the noise. Something about the damaging nocturnal effects of drinking on a restful night's sleep prevented her from sinking deep enough to enter her dream-world. Not tonight.

Anna was standing on the vertiginous roof terrace, surrounded by the people from the previous evening, now twisted until they were crooked and wrong. The thick still pools of summer air were a nuclear smog, climbing into the sky in muddy streams of smoke that spurted from black holes in the barren concrete ground below them. The smoke tasted dangerous, and clung to the walls of her lungs like a poisonous condensation, every time her grip on life spurred her to take another painful inhale. London was threatening and aggressive, a city with its teeth bared and fists clenched ready for a fight. The sirens of emergency services battled it out in a chorus of loud wails and red lights, and those beautiful glowing beads on the horizon had changed to beetles' eyes, glinting at her like a line of crawling black spiders.

The girls she was with were not her friends. They had the same faces, but their voices had shifted slightly and their mannerisms were all wrong. Anna knew that they were out to do her harm.

'I'm afraid if you wake any of us up in the night we'll have to think about you not living with us. Does that seem fair?' Libby's voice was coming out from her mouth, but it sounded sharp and tinny like an electronic recording. Anna could hear the knobs and dials being twisted, little pulses of interference as whoever was controlling Libby's speech tried to tune it to a more accurate human tone.

'Completely,' Anna smiled, sweetly. It was lucky she had spotted that they had all changed. She shouldn't let on that she had noticed anything unusual. She should keep chatting away, seeming relaxed and unconcerned in their company, but all the while remaining vigilant and alert. They probably thought their disguises were impeccable, but she knew that something was different, inside each one of them. Perhaps their bodies were being used by her enemies in order to get to her. That would make sense.

Anna checked that nobody was tampering with her drink, enjoying the intense sense of clarity, high on her own crystal paranoia. She was sitting too close to the railings, so she slid along her bench slightly, away from the edge, in case one of them tried to tip her over the side of the terrace and smash her brittle skeleton on the hard tarmac of the street below.

'I think that's a bit mean.' Fran tilted her head to one side, eyeing Anna up and down. She was trying, inexpertly, to look friendly and welcoming, not realising that parts of her usually beautiful face were pixelated. 'Why don't we give her three chances? Girls?' The others nodded.

'Agreed. If you slip up a couple of times we'll let you off, but third time unlucky and you're out. I think three times qualifies as something becoming problematic for us. And we're not prepared to put up with that.'

'Absolutely, I understand.' Anna took a sip of the margarita, sickly sweet like an alcoholic Slush Puppie. She closed her eyes briefly and swallowed, straining her taste buds to see if she could detect any poison in the glass. She wanted to Google *What does hemlock taste like?'* but she couldn't find her phone and it would have looked too suspicious.

Somebody screamed from the street below, and the girls jumped up to lean over the sides of the roof terrace. They hung themselves out over the railings that ran underneath the fairy lights, staring at what was happening on the ground.

This was it: the moment that appeared in all of Anna's nightmares. However varied the narrative, however bizarre the content, part-way through they all began to take on an intense darkness, to move towards something unbearable. It was a tipping point. The centre of gravity in the world that she was imagining shifted and everything tilted for a moment, before tumbling down to become a twisted variation of the same scene. It was usually then, with the familiar sense of danger taking hold, that Anna grew lucid, aware of her own sleeping self. She was conscious that she was lying alone and unprotected in her bed. She tried to cling on to the knowledge that she wasn't really seeing any of this, it wasn't really happening. She tried to become brave.

Anna had always been able to dream lucidly. Back when she was younger, lucidity had involved hours of sleep spent manipulating her dad to take her clothes-shopping in glittering palatial complexes, her childhood imagination of an American mall, where everything was free and everything would fit. She would engineer the vivid plastic landscape around them, like a precocious conductor with her own baton, leading her father through the wide marble corridors towards towering walls crammed full of those magic trainers she saw other children wearing, the kind that lit up when you walked. Anna could remember crying when she was woken up prematurely from some of the more exciting visions, having to get dressed and go to school, instead of being able to jump through silver puddles in her shiny new shoes. The skill had grown darker over the years.

Down in the street below, a boy was standing in the road. It was never clear why he was there, or whether he was confused or hurt, but Anna could see that he was in the middle of harm's way. There was a car speeding across the junction opposite, on a collision course with his tiny young frame. By this point, Anna was aware of every little thing that happened before it did. Sometimes she was in the car. Sometimes she even realised that her parents were driving it, or somebody she knew, but on nights like tonight, she didn't know and it didn't matter. She knew that the boy was going to turn and look up at her, his eyes finding hers from where she watched over the side of the towering building. His stare pulled her down into his disaster.

Every single time, Anna had a strong sense of being marked out, of being chosen to save him if only she concentrated hard enough. She would use her force of will, screwing up her face to make the car swerve off course and avoid him. She could never really tell whether she knew it was about to happen, or whether she was making it happen. This was her world, after all. It was then, when the car's course changed, curling in an arc across the centre of the road and over the pavement behind the boy, that Anna would suddenly realise what she had done: she had sent whoever was in that car speeding to their death. She knew, with the same surety that she had known how everything else would happen, that they were going to be killed instantly.

Then the space between her and the boy would evaporate, and she was speeding towards him on an invisible zip-wire. His face grew bigger in her sights until his aghast expression became everything that she could see and she was trapped in front of the terrified bloodshot whites of his eyes. By now Anna was always fighting to wake up, thrashing from the depths of it all and struggling to inject life and movement into her paralysed, bed-bound limbs. She had tried to find courage, but she could never hold his stare past this point. Everything in front of her started to buzz with a dull thudding pressure as blood filled her ears. A terrible darkness was falling and she needed to get out.

The boy's face contorted as the accident spiralled out around him. Anna, lost in his eyes, knew that although she had saved his life, she had loaded an eternity of guilt and grief onto his young shoulders. Even more strange, a kind of dream memory would kick in: she would remember doing this all before, would remember this very realisation, cursing herself for having forgotten that it was better not to get involved. Could she have turned away when he fixed her with that stare? Dropped down on her hands and knees behind the railings on the terrace so that he couldn't see her?

Bits of body, bone, and blood had sprayed out into the road. Here, surrounded by the smell of death, Anna always got out.

She forced herself to wake up with a lurch that sent nausea flowing in waves through her body. The echoes from the noises of the crash filled the room around her and, for a few long seconds, she was completely unable to move. With wide eyes she stared around in panic, trying to work out where she was, unable to spur her muscles out of lethargy. She couldn't even breathe. The weight of what she had seen, of the air in the room and of her ribcage, was pressing down on her lungs. It was like being underwater and so desperate to inhale that her throat began to constrict, searching for scraps of air behind closed lips.

Anna gasped when eventually the weight lifted, scraping breath hungrily down the inside of her body, her ribs spreading up and open towards the ceiling in relief. She was in London. She remembered now. She tried to recreate that sensation of being chosen, the most powerful quality of her dreams. In each world she was dropped into, in every environment, she was a messenger of some kind, a person with privileged access to the workings of that particular universe and an ability to control it. It was a bit like consciousness was, for all of us. Each person felt so many things inside their own mind and body every second of every day, but none of it meant anything to anybody else. Existence was just billions of unique, private dreams playing out inside each of our heads. Maybe dying was a bit like waking up. Would lucid dreaming always feel this wretched? Hope sunk like a stone in her churning stomach; the nightmare had followed her to London.

# CHAPTER THREE

Anna managed to get back to sleep. When she woke up, disappointment settled in the room around her. Nothing had changed. She showered in streams of water that glowed golden in the morning light and got dressed, hoping that she would emerge from her bedroom looking more organised than the chaos of unpacked suitcases spread across her floor.

Today was Monday, the first day of her new job at the Whitechapel Gallery. She was joining the exhibitions team as one of their assistant curators. She walked across town, not wanting to go underground after the dark trauma of what she had watched in her sleep last night. For the first ten minutes, the walk to work retraced her steps back to the industrial building from the night before, crossing the road at the same junction where the car had crashed just a few hours ago in her dream. There was no police tape, no broken barriers, no dented traffic lights, no deep red blood stains curving in gruesome arcs across the tarmac. Anna blinked at the scene a few times but didn't slow down. She looked up at the railings surrounding the top of the building. The strings of fairy lights were switched off now, hanging between the corners of the roof like ropes covered with little shards of dull glass.

The gallery was closed to the public on Mondays, and all the staff were sitting downstairs in the empty café when Anna arrived. Numbed by the constant barrage of new sights, smells, places, and now people, Anna didn't feel the expected cluster of nerves tingling in her fingertips as she said 'hello' and sat down. She had only met Alexei Sharpe once before, in her interview. His clean-shaven jaw, neat haircut, and crisply conservative suit made him look more like a City worker than a revered and often radical curator. He greeted her warmly, shaking her hand and clasping her by the shoulder, though he still looked bleary-eyed, his face creasing in gratitude as somebody handed him a coffee.

'Anna, welcome. We're so happy to have you. I'm fairly new here myself, of course, and one of our other assistants, Poppy, only started a few weeks ago. We're all still getting to know each other.' The girl sitting by the door in a blue dress raised her hand in greeting at the mention of her name.

'Good morning, everyone.'

Alexei stood while the others sat, cradling his drink with both hands. He had presence and authority, but gave the impression that he didn't naturally take to speaking in front of a room of people which, given his impressive status in the art community, Anna liked.

'Anna has joined us today,' he nodded in her direction, 'from Brighton, where she has been involved with a number of galleries including the Brighton Museum and Art Gallery, but more recently, and perhaps most notably, the rather exciting White Walls. If you haven't visited it yet, I urge you to go – a precious little piece of anarchic beauty tucked behind Brighton's Lanes and boasting something to inspire almost anybody.'

Anna inclined her head in gratitude, her cheeks reddening slightly.

'At last, for the first time since I arrived three months ago, I have a full team in front of me! I'll leave you all to introduce yourselves to Anna this morning, in particular Poppy, as you'll be working closely together on *Automatism*.' He turned to address Anna directly. 'Poppy is aware that you both have to decide how you'd like to split the workload, and which artists you'd each like to handle. Everything you need to look at is upstairs, ready and waiting for you. Any questions, let me know.'

Anna was joining at an unusual time of year,

taking on an exhibition that was already developed and in motion. As time went on, she would begin research for new projects, but for now she had agreed to start by fostering a list of artists that had already been confirmed for exhibition. They were preparing to open a headline show later that year, *Automatism and other states of consciousness*, a title that had seduced Anna and been part of the reason she was keen to go for the job. There must be so many ways of interpreting that subject.

*Automatism* was the name of the central work, a series of portraits by Hannah Truss. After blowing away the Turner Prize competition in 2008 with a project that featured decoratively arranged vials of bodily fluids, an homage to the confrontational Britart movement, Truss had become the British art world's young rebel, known more for her utter indifference during interviews than for any of the works she had produced following her shock win. Now more mature, her work softer and richer, Truss had begun working in traditional fine art mediums, rediscovering a love and, it turned out, an impressive skill for painting. The spotlight would certainly be on her return, heading up the summer exhibition at the Whitechapel Gallery.

Working delicately with oils, Truss had captured murderers from all over the world who had each pleaded 'insane' or 'non-insane' automatism in mitigation of a guilty plea. Her collection of killers raised questions around insanity, accountability and effective punishment. Upstairs in the office, surrounded by weeks of Poppy's thorough research and correspondence, Anna leafed through the blurb for each of Truss's images. There were case notes on criminals who claimed to have no recollection of the violence carried out by their own hands, and notes on people who had handed themselves in to the police after discovering weapons and blood-soaked clothing in their own houses. There were prisoners who had long and complex histories of mental illness, who had stopped taking their medication and spiralled out of control. Anna found photocopies of records that Truss had been poring over, each paper a sea of black type, spotted with highlighted neon blocks covering anything she considered significant. Connecting every case was that each prisoner claimed a complete disengagement from all conscious thought while the crimes were being committed.

The portraits were not dark, grainy, full-frontal stares as one might expect. It was the unusually sensitive treatment of her subjects that Anna loved about the work. Truss had taken full creative advantage of the fact that she was painting rather than photographing, and reimagined each criminal in happier times. Each portrait felt like the painting of a loved one, or a family member. She depicted the criminals with incredible sensitivity: talking, laughing, sleeping, even dancing.

Anna reached for a stack of thickly stuffed plastic envelopes. Each one was labelled with the name of a prisoner, and filled with photocopied images. To accompany the paintings, in cases where it had not been possible to get access to the prison or where the criminal was no longer alive, Truss had contacted the families and been sent photographs including school portraits, beach holidays, engagement parties and parachute jumps. In one, a man now jailed on seven counts of murder was icing a chocolate cake for his son's third birthday. A blond twenty-something, now on death row for stabbing both his young daughters in the middle of the night, was suspended in mid-air, grinning as he jumped from a rope swing into a bright blue lake below.

Anna felt tears prick the back of her eyelids, and a strange hot pressure build up in her cheeks. Poppy had photocopied a page from Truss's notebook. Questions were scrawled in a list diagonally across the page, ignoring the direction of the printed lines beneath. *Is it possible to commit a violent act, an aggressive crime, and not to be conscious that you have done so? If prison can only access a conscious part of your mind, can only punish that part of you, then is it not punishing an innocent person? Is it possible*

*to be guilty, but psychologically to be untainted?*
Anna thumbed through the stack of small-scale prints of the portraits.

'They're being delivered in about three weeks. The originals are incredible.' Poppy looked up from her computer and Anna thought she must have noticed the moisture glistening on the surfaces of her eyes. 'It's heavy, isn't it?'

Anna let out a sigh. It whistled through her teeth. Tension had built up in her chest while she looked through everything. She shook her head.

'It's seeing it all together like this, catalogued. When you read about it in a blurb or description, you don't get a sense of the fullness of all these people's lives before their crimes were committed.'

'Or of everything they lost, by what they did.'

'I don't know how she didn't go a bit mad working on it.'

Poppy grimaced. 'Between you and me, I think she did. Have a look at the other artists; I don't think we had them on board when you interviewed. They're a bit lighter.' She leant over the space between their desks, tucking her scarf against her chest so it didn't fall into her coffee, and handed Anna another folder bulging with research. 'This is Whitstone. It's fun.'

The folder was presented like a brochure for a commercial product, a colourful advert for 'Unreason by Charles Whitstone', a computer

28

programme that promised to make sense of your emotions. *Unreason* constructed narratives from random disconnected memories or thoughts. It was meant to recreate the way Whitstone thought our dreams might be threaded together, but also to give a sense of commonality to everybody's individual dream-worlds, reassuring its users that there were many similar tropes or moods that different people shared while asleep.

Anna looked through the instructions. The full, computerised programme was still being coded, but there was a basic analogue-style example included in the pamphlet, a bit like a flowchart. The visitor chose a series of objects, words, thoughts, or emotions from a vast selection of options, and *Unreason* generated a 'subconsciously formed narrative'. For example, Anna selected 'anxiety', 'running late', and 'green bicycle'. *Unreason* generated the narrative: *You are hours late for a meeting. You keep looking at your watch and you know you are not going to make it. You are not very far away, but you cannot climb on to your green bicycle no matter how hard you try. The saddle is too high and the handlebars are too far away.*

Anna laughed. In a gallery environment, where each visitor would probably only try it out a couple of times, it would work well and it did do a good job of recreating the strange combination of nonsense and normality that

29

dreams often had. She read through Whitstone's notes, including some of his most recent emails to Poppy that she had printed out; he seemed to have grown more conflicted, or confused, about the idea of his own dream narratives since finishing the piece and explaining his initial intentions. In his latest contact with the gallery, he had made a comment that Anna understood, after so many of her own mornings spent piecing together the nightmare before: *I have started to wonder whether the narrative, or the linear sense of a dream, is actually something that we impose upon a series of disconnected visions or images, after we have awoken. Perhaps what our mind experiences while we are asleep really is as basic as the first stage of the computer programme: a simple list of selected thoughts and ideas.*

'Do you like it?' Poppy saw she had got to the very last page. She was already getting together something else for Anna to look at.

'I do. I like that it's presented as a bit of a gimmick, when really it's far from it.'

'Exactly.'

'I'd be interested to speak to him. He seems to have changed his mind about the thing he's trying to say, to a certain extent, since he started making it.'

'Well, this one's certainly *interesting*. A local artist called Joe Denning.' Poppy stacked a few files together and passed them across to Anna. 'I don't know what I think of it, except that it is definitely very Whitechapel Gallery.' She raised her eyebrows.

Anna wanted to ask where Poppy had been working before, but she read the title *A Year of Dreaming* and forgot the thought instantly, looking through the photographs, open-mouthed and glassy-eyed.

Denning's work spoke to a deep and central part of her, inside her chest right in front of her heart. It was like a curled finger, beckoning her to come closer. She had been attracted to the title of the exhibition because she feared she was losing grip and control on the workings of her own mind, and Truss's series had fascinated her with the sheer terribleness of what we might all be capable of, given the right, or wrong, circumstances. But Anna had never expected that any piece of art would, or could, reflect her own nightlife with such accuracy as Denning's series of three hundred and sixty-five photographs. He introduced his project briefly and with simple language, describing his fascination with a fact he had come across, that women remember more of their dreams than men do. Denning felt short-changed by his gender, cheated by his inability to remember any of his nocturnal wanderings. He started setting alarms in the middle of the night and, over a period of a few weeks, worked out what time was usually best to ensure he was roused from dream-filled R.E.M sleep. By waking mid-hallucination, he stood a better chance of remembering the events he had just witnessed, or subconsciously crafted.

Every photo was almost identical: the opposite wall of his bedroom in half-darkness, tenebrous shadows casting shapes across the white paint, his bed sheets filling the bottom of frame in varying states of twisted disarray. Occasionally a foot was visible in the bottom corner of the frame, and in one particularly haunting image, the whites of his eyes could be glimpsed, reflected in the mirror in front of him. The only significant difference between each image were their titles: '*A dog wearing a denim jacket cuts down all the trees in my back garden with a chainsaw*', '*I am walking home from work in the afternoon but I can only see out of my left eye*', or '*Something about a fish*'.

Anna loved Truss's work, was amused by Whitstone's, but was physically drawn towards Denning's dream photographs as though to a powerful magnet. They had found her; they had found each other. She looked up. Poppy was smiling at her rapt attention, her sudden descent into total silence and concentration. She clapped her hands and Anna jumped. 'You love it. Great.'

Anna wanted to get Denning on the phone right now, or write him an email. She wanted to get closer to anybody who was trying to make sense of where they went and who they became when they were asleep.

'We can split this up however you prefer,' Poppy said later. They went next door to a coffee shop, a narrow little café filled with colourful macaroons, thick slabs of cake, and chunky fruit-stuffed bricks of honeyed granola. They needed a rest from the gallery. Anna had read until her eyes hurt. 'But I've got a suggestion.'

'Go on.'

Poppy took a bite of brownie. She broke a corner off and handed it to Anna. 'I've exhibited Truss before, less than a year ago, and I've been speaking to her ever since. For the past four weeks we've been getting *Automatism* into shape.'

Anna knew what Poppy was going to say, and she understood. It was normal to be a bit protective over a relationship with an artist, especially one that you'd been working with for months.

'You want to focus on Truss, and give me the other works?'

'Only if you don't mind. It makes more sense. Apart from choosing the key projects from Whitstone and Denning, we really haven't done much else. You'll be able to get more involved, and there's a lot that still needs doing. They've also had much less contact with me. I think it would be easier to hand those over.'

33

'I was going to suggest the same thing.' Anna wasn't interested in fighting for the headline piece, not when she had only been an employee of the gallery for four hours, and when Poppy knew so much about it already. Poring over criminal records and homicides every day would test her nerves, and she was excited to know more about the dream photographs.

Poppy sighed. 'There are a lot of other photos of the prisoners that we're trying to source, collating information for every single one. All the legal issues associated with it are proving to be very time-consuming. There's a lot of paperwork required, and almost all of it is completely new to me, to anyone who's from an art gallery instead of a law court.'

'Have you worked for Alexei before?'

Poppy shook her head. 'Never. You?'

Anna shook her head. 'What about layout?'

'The main exhibition usually spreads across the two gallery spaces downstairs, and runs through the linking corridor between them.'

'Who do we talk to about how we want to use the rooms, or about setting things up?'

'Alexei, and then Tish helps manages the overall layout, and organises any construction work, which needs to be minor – additional display walls, for example. We still need to know exactly which works we have available to us before we can do that.' Poppy stopped speaking to take a breath. She beamed at Anna with relief. 'Last week it started getting a bit impossible – I'm *so* glad you're here.'

Anna looked down at the cover picture of Denning's *A Year of Dreaming* catalogue that she had brought with her. It was just a black and white photocopy on A4 paper, but the atmosphere of his bedroom at witching hour reminded her of the strange in-between space where she lay alone for hours every night.

# CHAPTER FOUR

Anna walked back home down Brick Lane. Her attention was pulled from one side to the other by the rows of bakeries, boutiques and curry houses. They had been quiet and sleepy on her journey in that morning; now everything was enlivened and colourful. Working somewhere new had filled her with nervous energy, a pulse of excitement that propelled her past window displays piled high with traditional Turkish cakes, clothing stalls pumping their booming bass over rails of aggressively studded clothing, and pavement restaurant touts waving discounted menus at her with a smile. The area was similar to parts of Brighton, its edgy atmosphere of subversive rebellion diluted by the traditional tourist tat that was on sale.

The vividness of the environment should have reassured Anna that she was awake, but often the same technicolour realness filled her dreams. It wasn't colour, or sensory experience, that convinced Anna she was waking rather than dreaming; it was sequence and logic. She could trace her way back through the previous day, from getting up and going to work, through all the tiny experiences, events and conversations that had filled the time in between then and now. She knew where she was, how she had got there, and where she was going. These were all things which disappeared, or whose absence she never thought to question, when she was about to plunge headfirst into the heavy waters of a nightmare. Dreams rarely had context.

Before she knew it, Anna had crossed the road underneath the roof terrace a few minutes from home, realising just in time to look back at it over her shoulder. She craned her neck to see the fairy lights blowing in the breeze, illuminated once again in the shadowy air of evening. She hesitated part-way across the road. A car sounded its horn, its engine revving in angry impatience. Anna twitched, raised a hand in apology, and jumped up onto the curb.

Halfway across the park she paused; she wasn't quite ready to plunge back into the noisy conversations that might be waiting for her behind the front door. She imagined all the girls at home, filling up the space with their busy lives. Libby with the television on in the front room, while Holly cooked something for dinner down in the kitchen, raising her voice over the sounds of sizzling frying pans and boiling water to speak to Fran or Sophie, forgotten streams of music floating through their bedroom doors, colliding in the corridor and tumbling down the stairs. If Anna stayed here on this wide patch of green grass for half an hour or so, she could carve out a little window of privacy before she got home.

She meandered around London Fields in slow circles, watching the summer haze fall from the sky and settle like a fog around the treetops. A big triangular-shaped section of the park, behind the green wire-fenced basketball courts, had been turned into a wildflower meadow. It was an incongruously pretty section of countryside, a tiny pastoral escape from the big city that crowded around its edges. There was a clear patch of ground at its centre where Anna sank down onto her knees to sit level with the sea of red poppies, yellow buttercups, daisies and delicate grasses. It reminded her of pressing flowers as a child, pinning petals and paper between heavy books weighed down by stones and then distracting herself with something for a few hours, knowing that a beautiful image was developing like a photographic negative in the dark unseen space beneath her huge hardback encyclopaedia.

Anna snapped a few of the stems nearest her,

collecting a handful of colour between her fingers, looking around quickly to check nobody walking past had seen her vandalism. She folded a stiff piece of cartridge paper from her bag around the delicate petals and slid them flat, between two pages of her hefty A4 work diary. She would have to wedge them underneath something bigger when she got home, to make sure it worked, and then she would have a little slice of meadow for her bedroom wall, something to help her remember this summer when winter set in.

She stood up, pushed the diary carefully down into her bag and headed off in the direction of home. People crowded along each path and across the grass, some walking purposefully with their heads down, desperate to get to their own front door after a long day at work, while others puffed their way through their evening jog in neon running trainers, water bottles swinging from their sweaty hands. At the bottom of the cricket field, Anna watched a dog walker unclip the lead from a fluffy white terrier at his feet. The dog launched itself immediately over the grass, bounding joyfully in the direction of someone they evidently knew. The owner shouted 'Jack!' after the dog, but it was the sloping figure in black, the target of the dog's frantic approach, who turned his head, his messy hair blowing in the breeze. He waved a hand in greeting and slowed down, waiting for his friend to catch up.

As soon as she got through the door, Anna slid her flowers inside one of the heavier books on the coffee table and collapsed on the sofa, staring out of the front window. She sighed into the unexpected quiet of the room around her, energy leaking out on her breath. Above the rooftops on the other side of the street, the sun was setting. She was still there, the motionless 'L' shape of her body sagging into the soft cushions on the big sofa, when Libby got back from work. She dropped down beside Anna and held out a bag of sweets.

'You're not eating Haribo for dinner, are you?'

Libby shrugged. 'I am eating Haribo, but not for dinner. I don't know what meal I'm on now. I didn't get lunch until five o'clock today. My body's all confused.'

'Cola bottles probably won't help.'

'Is that why you're helping me out? To save me from myself?' Libby laughed as Anna tipped a handful of the gummy sweets into her mouth.

'This *is* my dinner.'

Libby checked her watch. 'Come on,' she slapped Anna's leg, 'I'll help you unpack. You can't go to sleep in that mess again tonight.'

'Are you sure? It's late.'

'Yes, I'm sure, and it's not that late. You can tell me all about your first day at work.'

They climbed up from the first floor to Anna's attic room. It spread across the entire top floor of the house, the largest bedroom by far. The others were glad she wanted it; it was too much space for one person to fill completely and the rent was much higher, but Anna loved to paint. Oils and canvases were not a practical hobby in a flatshare. Anna told them she didn't mind, that it would have been unfair to insist on the smaller, cheaper room, and then have to fill up the living room and hallways with half-finished and often abandoned art projects. Her strongest reason for choosing it, though, was that it gave her privacy. Up the stairs and away from everybody else, she was less self-conscious about her irregular sleep patterns, less likely to wake the others up if she shouted at an imagined intruder in the night.

'That's pretty.' Libby pointed at the postcard Anna had pinned up next to her bed, the only mark she had made on the room so far. It was a thick black circle painted over a sea of blurry colours. It looked like two different paintings, one superimposed on top of the other, the crisp black shape lying

41

across a rich wash of blues and greens.

'Thanks. It's by my dad. The original is at his house. I keep asking him to paint another version for me. That postcard is like my lucky charm.'

'I didn't know he was an artist. It's beautiful.'

'He was mostly an art *teacher*, although he does more of his own work now he's retired. He's not famous or anything. He manages to sell most of it, though, back home in Sussex. That one's called *Circles*.'

'Why's it called *Circles* when there's only one circle?'

Anna was stumped. How had she never asked that question herself? 'I have no idea.'

'Did you never want to be an artist, professionally?' Libby was unwrapping the canvases Anna had stacked up on one wall, pulling masking tape and cling film from their frames and looking at each one carefully.

Anna stopped folding clothes and smiled. 'I'm not sure I'm good enough. Whatever that means. No. I love working with art, being around it every day. And I like painting in my spare time, for myself. Although I hope I'm a better curator than I am a painter.'

With the two of them unpacking suitcases and boxes it didn't take too long, and once the sea of clothes was stashed neatly inside Anna's chest of drawers, the room felt nicely bare and clean. Libby yawned, with her arms stretched overhead, and peered out of the window.

'I think I've lost my Haribo buzz.' It was dark outside. 'I'll leave you in peace.' She shuffled downstairs, and Anna could hear a friendly little chorus of 'goodnight' being shared around the landing from each bedroom door.

Her canvases were all unwrapped, including a bright white new one. She stared at its blankness with tired eyes. Anna had tried painting her nightmares before, so many times, but the paintings always looked too much like part of a film or a play. She tried to pack too much detail in, to make sure that each scene made sense. She would include everything that she could remember; the faces of the people around her, the detail of the environment, the colour of the sky, even the expression on her own face as she fought to control it all from a distance with her stare. Yet they were always lacking the most potent thing of all: that hot liquid sense of dread. Maybe she should simplify it, like Whitstone's *Unreason* programme but going backwards, removing the narrative and stripping it down to a single image or thought. She was trying to make it all too linear, too complete. Anna moved her fingertip across the canvas's fresh chalky surface, tracing an imagined outline of the boy's eyes she had seen the night before, a bright line of colour in a ring around the black dilated hole of his pupil.

She would try to paint it again, this time without filling in the gaps that had been there while she was dreaming it, the black holes that hovered in between the abstract floating separate parts. She would just show the boy's eyes, without any of the disconnected scenes that had preceded the disaster. If she could pull all that fear and anguish out into the waking world in paint, maybe it would lose some of its power.

# CHAPTER FIVE

The first week at work was a busy one. Anna frequently caught herself regretting their late night drinks on Sunday. The constant nightmares and broken nights' sleep meant that she was used to being tired, but it was amplified by the relentless newness of every little thing she did or saw. Her muscles were weaker, less capable of propelling her body around the place and up and down the stairs. Holly usually tried to reassure her by saying that it was probably making her stronger, or joking that she was being well prepared for the sleeplessness of motherhood. Anna worried that the opposite was true, that she was stacking up such an insane sleep debt, that if life decided to take any further toll on her body she might just expire, disappear on the wind in a tired puff of smoke.

At five o'clock on Friday she still had a lot to do. With no plans for the evening, she took her work downstairs to finish some emails in a corner of the gallery, while the last few visitors weaved their way around. She sat in Gallery 2 with her favourite piece in the building, Kader Attia's *Jacob's Ladder: Continuum of Repair*. It remained enchanting no matter how many times she had stood inside it that week. Stacks and shelves of books, the accumulation of all human knowledge, were arranged in four walls around the warmly lit glow of a honey-coloured wooden cabinet at their centre. Above it all, a vast mirror reflected a horizontal beam of light a thousand times over, transforming it into the shining rungs of a ladder rising up to infinity in its reflective surface.

Anna climbed up the wooden ladder inside and sat on the top step with her laptop balanced on her knees. The effect of sitting still and trying to concentrate in the quiet room was so soporific that Anna's eyes closed almost instantly, and she dozed, cocooned from the bustle of people finishing off their week's work upstairs. Occasionally the rhythmic footsteps of somebody's heeled shoes tapped against the hard floor in the next room, as they moved from painting to painting, lulling Anna further behind her closing eyelids. The last thing she saw as she lay back on the mirrored top of the large cabinet, was an image of herself reflected again and again in the mirrors above her, like the ever-diminishing versions of a Russian doll.

When she next opened her eyes, it was in sleep. Anna climbed her way up into the sky, pulling her work-weary limbs from step to step up a sunlit ladder into the blue space above her. Something caught her eye. On the right-hand side of the ladder inscribed in the metal just below her hand were the words *Jack's Ladder*.

She carried on climbing, knowing that it was important she reached the top. She was full of excitement. Below her, gliding along on a conveyor belt of light in the sky, was a line of glass orbs with a different scene playing out inside each one of them. They reminded her of crystal balls laid out like prizes at the end of a game show. Inside the first one she could see a series of shapes turning around in a circle like a theme-park Ferris wheel. She looked closer. At the top of the circle a couple was kissing, but as they descended one side of the glass, they shrank until one of them was a white Yorkshire terrier and the other one was a cat. As they ascended again they became a man and a woman once more, standing with their backs to each other, before meeting near the top and beginning to kiss all over again. It was ceaseless, mesmerising. On the rectangular wooden base of the orb was a gold plaque with the words *Lovers in a past life* etched onto it in neat, precise lettering. Perhaps the turning circle was some kind of reincarnation, showing the couple in their previous lives as animals, and then as strangers. Each time they kissed, the air inside the orb turned pink like a sunset.

As the second globe passed by, Anna peered into its swirling interior and blinked as she watched herself in miniature, ordering a drink from the bar she had visited with the girls on Sunday night. The barman was twirling the bottles around, trying to look flashy, but when Anna looked closer she couldn't make out his face. The small gold plaque on this one read *He was your waiter on Sunday night*.

The third scene showed Anna as a young child, lying on her belly on the rug in the TV room, propped up on her elbows with her chin cupped in her hands. The flickering lights from whatever programme she was watching flashed across her wide-eyed face, and the plaque read *He was on television when you were younger*.

Anna scanned the next two plaques just long enough to make out *He is a long-lost relative* and *You went to school with him* before alighting on the fifth and final globe. She frowned at its misty contents. It was a view of London Fields park, the grass soft and golden in the last light of the day. She could see the dog walker letting his terrier loose to bound across the greenery towards the man who had turned at the sound of his name, and raised his hand to wave. It was the moment exactly as it had happened, with nothing added or taken away. It simply resurfaced from her memory like a creature bobbing up for air, announcing itself as a question that Anna hadn't been aware needed answering.

*He is just a stranger.* Anna read the final plaque as many times as she could before the line of crystal balls glided off into the distance and disappeared into heavy cloud.

After a few more minutes of difficult climbing, Anna saw the shape of somebody sitting high above her, casting a shadow over the clouds she was passing through, the way a plane does when the sun hits it at the perfect angle. The sky was so bright blue it almost hurt her eyes. The clouds were so dense and thick that she wanted to reach out and climb onto one of them, to ride it through the air like a pillowy white horse. But the closer Anna climbed to the seated figure, the louder the voice at the bottom of the ladder sounded, way back down on Earth. It was calling for her, shouting at her to come down, 'Anna! Anna!' She tried to close her ears to the sound and forge ahead, but her hands had started to slip on the rungs of light that glowed fiercely in between her fingers. Her foot missed one, her grip slackened in shock, and for a few sickening seconds she was falling at speed.

'Anna.' Poppy was holding her hand and moving it gently, squeezing her palm to try and wake her up without frightening her. Anna opened her eyes, staring directly above at the same million multiples of her own body, reflected from where she was lying with her back against the mirror. Poppy bent over her, shaking a bit of life down her arm and back into her body.

'I'm sorry. I knew that was going to happen.' Anna rubbed her eyes, pulling herself up to sitting.

'The security guard came and asked me to wake you up. He was too embarrassed to do it himself.'

Anna fired up her laptop to see how far she had got through the work she had been in the middle of, disappointed to see the relatively small dent she had made. She snapped the computer shut. 'I love this,' she nodded at the installation surrounding them.

'I just wish it didn't remind me so much of being forced to go to Sunday school when I was younger.' Poppy grimaced, as she climbed back down the steps. 'I remember this story featuring heavily in Bible study.'

Anna spun her legs over the side and down the short wooden stepladder to join Poppy on the solid ground of the gallery floor. They walked back up to the office.

'I never went to Sunday school or church. Wasn't Jacob's Ladder a pathway from Earth to Heaven? Or the other way around?'

'It was sort of both. It was a vision – or a dream. Jacob was a prophet and travelling somewhere; I think his brother was angry with him. He stopped to rest and had this incredible dream that there was a golden ladder between Earth and Heaven, with angels standing on every step.'

'I remember. So that's the connection between man and God? A message?'

'Sure. Like a lot of those dreams in the Old Testament, God speaks to man in his sleep.'

'Well, anything's possible when you're dreaming really, isn't it? Even the existence of God.'

Poppy had packed her rucksack up and had her bicycle helmet and the key to her lock in her hand. 'I would suggest having a drink as it's your first Friday, but we're going to a wedding tomorrow down in Cornwall and we're leaving tonight. The plan is to get halfway there, stay in a hotel, and do the rest in the morning.'

Anna was relieved. She was still tired and didn't want to drink. Her stomach felt sticky and nauseous with the jet lag of an unplanned nap. She walked home to clear her head so she could make a second more successful attempt at finishing her work, traipsing the two and a half miles north into Hackney along the pretty quietness of Columbia Road, through Broadway Market and across the park.

She passed the pub at the corner of her street, scanning the evening drinkers on the pavement outside to see if any of the girls had taken a diversion on their way back. One man stood separated from the crowd, further towards the edge of the pavement, with his eyes closed and his face tilted back to receive the warm evening sunshine. For a few slow seconds as Anna approached, she stared at his face, taking in his features. She didn't notice how close she had got until his eyes sprang open and he caught her looking at him from a few feet away. He gave her a polite nod. Perhaps it was the sun, flooding his face like a stage spotlight, that had drawn Anna's attention to him, or the fact he was standing at a slight distance from the merriment beside him, but the jolt of his eye contact sent Anna back to the dream she had just had. She could still see that metal *Jack's Ladder* etching she had climbed doggedly past, to the friendly greeting she had overheard in the park yesterday, and to those strange floating crystal ball scenes she had been poring over somewhere high in the sky. Was this the man from the park? She scanned the pavement around them, half expecting to see that same fluffy white terrier bounding towards him with its cheerfully wagging tail. The details of her strange stairway into the sky settled in the air around her, as though cold water was being poured over her skin. Anna's stomach dropped, her focus sliding down to the ground at his feet. His familiarity was unsettling.

She walked past, fighting an urge that made no sense, to stop and say 'hello'. She could feel her muscles preparing to stop walking, her throat warming up to speak to him. The scene played out in front of her so vividly that her heart raced and her mouth went dry. She went far enough towards doing it that she got the same nervous thrill as if she had stopped and spoken to him. But her feet didn't slow down and her lips didn't part. She looked back before she turned the corner. A couple had joined him, stepping out of the pub with drinks in their hands. The man handed him a beer, before introducing him to the woman he was with.

The last thing Anna heard before she was out of earshot was, 'This is Jack.'

# CHAPTER SIX

Anna walked east along the canal towpath on Monday morning, between the bold bright graffiti walls on her left and a steady stream of cyclists to her right. She was visiting Joe Denning's studio in Hackney Wick to introduce herself and to take a closer look at his work. He was standing out on the street when she arrived, so that she would know which one out of the identical row of black doors along the front of the warehouse was his.

'I can see why you told me to bring a jumper.' Anna wrapped her arms around herself, the temperature plummeting as they walked inside the building. The studio was one of a series of cavernous brick spaces inside a warehouse that hadn't been properly refurbished, except for a few new window panes here and there where the previous ones must have been smashed. The thick concrete walls were keeping the heat out. Anna looked out at the sunny warm day in the courtyard at the back, and breathed in the smell of chilled damp that surrounded them inside. There was a small electric heater plugged in at the end of the studio, doing its noisy best to heat the air up a little.

'Would a cup of tea help?' Joe said, looking concerned. 'I'll make you one.'

Anna followed him into a communal kitchen at the end of the corridor. The smells of clay, paint, and turpentine, took her back to her dad's studio at home.

'Thanks for coming.' Joe sneezed, and shook his head at himself. 'Well, of course I'm getting a cold in June, spending all my time inside this fridge.'

They walked back down the corridor to the main room and Joe pushed a door open to a storage space on their left, nodding inside at the piles of rolled-up papers, and the stacks of canvases slotted into purpose-built wooden racks along each wall.

'I keep everything here, you see. It would be quite a job to transport it all somewhere new.' He sneezed again. 'Besides, there are rumours that our landlord is going to install proper radiators next year. So I live in hope. What do you want to see first?'

'Let's start with *A Year of Dreaming*. I'd love to look through it again, but also to ask how you had envisaged it being displayed, if you had.'

Joe nodded. 'I held a private view for it here in this room, just to a few friends and some of my family. I'll show you what we did.'

He handed her some photographs from a table below the window. Anna set her mug down, judging from the dark Spirograph of cup stains covering the table's surface that she didn't need to ask for a coaster. Joe talked her through the photographs, pointing out the projection screen they had suspended from the ceiling to show a rolling slideshow of all 365 images. The walls they were standing beside now had been covered in rows and rows of the original smaller Polaroids.

'I don't get the originals out very often. I've got them all as slides and digital images, so I suppose it wouldn't be too difficult to reproduce Polaroids of each one, but in the exhibition I just really need them to be the *original* originals.' He looked at her seriously. 'Otherwise it doesn't make sense.'

'Of course. The original Polaroids were developed in the darkness of your bedroom, by the aftermath of the dream.'

'Precisely.' He pulled himself up to sit on one of the brick window sills, the palms of his hands sending chalky white dust into the air as he gesticulated. 'But is it too overwhelming to have a huge slideshow like that, as well as every single photograph laid out on the wall?'

'It's an overwhelming project, so I think that's how it should feel to the viewer. I'd go further actually: you could have two projectors. Let's assume we're in Gallery 8, for now. It's quite a long space – we could hang one at either end of the room, so that they sort of contain people when they walk in. They could both be showing the slides at the same speed, or one of them could be moving much faster than the other, so you have a three-second hold per photo at one end where you walk in, for example, while up at the other end the screen is flickering through them like strobe lighting.'

Joe smiled. 'You wouldn't actually notice much change, or obvious movement between a lot of them, since they're so similar. That might work well.'

'Then, you could have all 365 Polaroids lining both the right and left walls – so you have the full year of the originals on the right-hand side, beneath glass, but on the left, you have a full year of reproductions that we could just tape to the wall, as though you've taped them there yourself. They'd still be Polaroids, but copies. So people can have a closer look at each one.' Anna took a mouthful of tea and watched Joe absorb her suggestions.

'It would be quite an intense, focussed display. No other works, just this?'

'We don't have to decide that now, but I think it's a strong option.' Anna hoped she had gauged the appeal of the work correctly. Sometimes it was difficult, when you loved a piece so much, to tell objectively whether it really needed to be presented on such a grand scale. There was nothing quite so dissatisfying for a gallery goer, as viewing a piece of art that had been arranged and displayed in a commanding way, while feeling that it really should have been just one part of a larger collection, or worse, an interesting afterthought.

Joe jumped back down onto the concrete floor. 'I've never wanted to get rid of a piece of work so much – as in, just have it out of the studio for a while.' He paced around the room. 'There's something really dark about the whole thing.'

'Dark? Did you have bad dreams? I didn't spot anything particularly nightmarish.'

'No, not that so much. I just realised that there's this second mind whirring away inside our heads that we're barely aware of, living its own life every night when we've gone to bed. Once I'd tuned into it, it became difficult to tune it out. Is it a part of you, or isn't it?'

Anna didn't say anything. She wasn't sure he was expecting an answer, or that she had one. After three more cups of warming tea, a full examination of every single Polaroid, pored over within their protective plastic pouches, and a good look through Denning's vast art cupboard, Anna blinked her way back into the hot sunlight beating down on the street outside. Joe followed her out onto the pavement, his eyes wrinkling in the afternoon light, wiping the dust that had settled in his hair, and locking up the black door with a heavy padlock. He waved her off at the main road, and she walked down towards the river.

On her walk home, Anna noticed a makeshift bar overlooking the canal locks, its terrace a home-made jetty sticking out over the green water. She phoned Holly, who she knew would only be a few hundred yards away in her production office.

'Are you busy or could you finish a bit early today? I'm at that brewery place on the river, by your work.'

'Now? It's half three.'

'I know.'

'It's Monday!'

'I reckon I can keep myself amused for at least an hour. Can you get down here any time soon?'

'I'll do my very best.'

Anna found the sunniest seat on the deck, ordered a large glass of chilled white wine and a plate of home-made chicken tacos. She worked her way through both of them in smiling silence, examining her work emails carefully to make sure she hadn't missed anything important. Before she had ordered a second glass, Holly slumped down in the seat opposite her.

'That was quick.'

'I couldn't concentrate after you called,' she frowned.

'Don't feel guilty. I've been thinking that Monday is actually a really good day to finish early, because you haven't really had enough time to get busy; that usually kicks in around eleven on a Tuesday.'

'I like how you've justified this to yourself in such detail.'

'Also,' Anna continued, 'Monday is such a shock to the system after the weekend that it's probably good for your health to make it a light working day.'

'Another good point.'

'*And* I'm sure I read about an economic study that proved that a four-day week is surprisingly more beneficial, and ultimately more productive.'

'They do say "less is more". You can use all these to sell it to Libby when she gets here. She's going to try and leave work at five. You're a terrible influence on us all.'

'I think I'm going to start running,' Libby said, pulling a spare chair from a neighbouring table towards Anna when she arrived.

'Hello to you too. What's brought this on?'

'I've just puffed and panted my way along the canal for half an hour, *walking*, watching all these rosy-cheeked, bright-eyed women in rainbow-coloured Lycra speeding effortlessly past me, flicking their ponytails from side to side with joy. They all looked so ... disciplined.'

'It's true you do lack discipline,' Anna teased. 'Who would you rather be though? Her?' she pointed at Holly, who pulled her sunglasses on, pouted and raised her glass in the air. 'Or her?' Anna pointed at a particularly out-of-breath jogger who had stopped a few metres up the canal to stretch out her hamstrings on a fence.

'I take your point.'

'Aha!'

'What?'

'That wasn't "a point". It was a genuine question. The fact you assumed the answer was so obvious is just proof that you are not yet there my friend.'

'Not yet where?'

'At the gateway to the Land of Lycra. Besides, you just came halfway across London to have a drink on a Monday afternoon.'

'Are you saying I'm an alcoholic now?'

'Speaking of alcoholics,' Holly looked up and down the river, 'isn't Gemma's houseboat near here?'

'Yes!'

'Who's Gemma?' Anna asked.

'She lived with us for a few months, years ago. Now she lives on a boat and, yeah, I think it is around here. Shall we try and find her?'

Anna looked at her watch. 'We could. Or we could head back home and watch a film or something.'

'No way. You started this. It's happening.'

Holly levelled with her. 'Let's walk in the direction of home—'

Libby started complaining '—I've just got here!'

'In the *direction* of home,' Holly held a hand up and carried on speaking, 'which coincidentally is, I think, the direction that Gemma's houseboat is in. And if she happens to be there, we stop off for a drink or two, OK?'

Libby nodded. 'She makes an excellent rum and coke, Anna.'

'How do you make a not-excellent rum and coke?'

'White rum.'

'Forget the fresh lime.'

'Flat coke.'

'No ice.'

'OK, OK. I'm in.'

It was evident as they approached Gemma's houseboat, that the girls had known it was highly likely she would be home. She didn't look like she had a particularly rigorous schedule. She was lying in a bikini on a half-flattened deckchair on the roof, watering a large collection of pot plants in a line beside her from an old milk bottle.

'Climb aboard.' She welcomed the three of them onto the deck, leaning over the side to twist her long wet yellow hair into a rope. She squeezed it until it dripped. 'I've just put lemon juice in it. Trying to make the most of the sun. I'm heading out in a sec, I'm afraid.

Ah, here he is now.'

The girls turned in the direction of the boat that was approaching.

'I don't really move this one from its mooring,' Gemma explained. 'Simon can just slow his boat down and then we can jump on. He's going down to the market, so we can take you most of the way home.'

It all happened very quickly. The girls didn't have enough time to do much more than agree to the lift, and watch while Gemma pulled a dress over her head and jumped lightly across to the other barge as it drew level. She beckoned for them to follow. Libby and Holly threw their bags onto Simon's boat and followed. Anna started to step over the slowly-widening gap, but the coordination required to estimate the distance between the boats and then make the leap over two feet of open water suddenly felt like too much for her brain. It was as though there was a huge blurry distance between her head and her feet. The combination of white wine, summer sun and a heavy meal made her clumsier and less nimble than she usually was. She faltered halfway across, lost her footing and plunged into the canal below.

The water was freezing. And much deeper than she would have expected. Her feet

64

kicked into blank watery space, her head breaking the surface to find her ears filled with weeds, water and raucous unsympathetic laughter. Anna opened her eyes. Libby and Holly were standing safely over on the other boat, Libby wheezing with laughter and holding onto Holly for support. They weren't moving fast, but Anna had to launch herself quickly through the water to get close enough to grab onto a rope hanging from one side.

'I'm fine, by the way.' She splashed her way around to the front of the boat. 'Thanks for your concern.'

Holly was flapping her hand in front of her face, trying to get the words out. 'Good. Great.' She laughed, regaining control of her breathing. 'That's exactly what I was about to ask.' They hauled Anna out of the water and onto the deck, flapping like a fish as she pulled her legs up behind her.

'As elegant as a mermaid,' Holly reassured her.

Anna thanked Gemma as she handed over a towel, and sat wrapped up while they floated home, occasionally indulging any mocking passers-by with a cheerful little wave.

'They don't know for definite that you've fallen in.' Holly tried to make her feel better.

'You could live here, on the boat, and have just had a shower.'

'And I didn't have time to take any of my clothes off first?'

'This is the time-starved West.' Holly shrugged.

Anna squelched her way home from the canal, sandwiched between Holly and Libby in an effort to shield her sodden clothes and bedraggled twig-tangled hair from fellow commuters.

Anna closed her eyes in the steam of the shower, the water turned up as hot as she could bear, and beamed when she stepped out of the bathroom to find Holly handing her a mug of honey and lemon.

'You started to shiver on the way back. Do you want me to tuck you up under a blanket?' She was joking but Anna accepted, and as she burrowed down under the scratchy tartan blanket that Holly had thrown over her thin summer duvet upstairs, she realised she was looking forward to going to sleep for the first time in ages.

'I love Mondays.' She yawned, as Holly turned out the light.

# CHAPTER SEVEN

Anna sunk into bed. Her duvet still smelt of the Brighton flat. She never noticed how different the air sounded when you lived next to the sea. It was like your ears could tell that the land stopped a few hundred yards away. There were fewer echoes, less street noise; the sea swallowed sound like thick snow. She breathed in the smell of the old flat in the fabric pulled up around her nose, and travelled down into sleep, to her childhood friend Natasha's seventh birthday party.

Natasha grew up in a nearby village over the Downs, further inland from Brighton. She used to come to Anna's house before and after school three days a week because her parents worked long hours. Anna sometimes fantasised that they were sisters, pleading with her mum for the family to keep her. Anna hated being an only child. Consciousness hovered along the surface of the dream so that Anna was slightly lucid throughout, remembering the party at the same time she was dreaming of it. She had looked through her mum's photographs from that day many times, indulging in the nostalgia of party bags, pin the tail on the donkey, and floury sweet Victoria sponge cake with its stiff fondant icing thick with sugar crystals. She remembered those photos so well that, for much of the time she slept, she simply enjoyed flicking through the still images from her childhood.

Then the memory-entangled dream whirred into motion. Anna had on the dress that she always wore for birthday parties when she was little. She loved it so much that twice she cried until her mum gave in, or gave up, and let her go to sleep in it. Each time, she woke up in the middle of the night, hot and sweaty, the scratchy seams digging in under her armpits. It was black velvet with puffy pink chiffon sleeves, and a pink satin ribbon knotted around her seven-year-old tummy. Anna had a fringe, a thick wedge of dark hair that shadowed her eyes and made her look comical, and slightly clumsy, as she darted from one side of the room to the other during a game of musical statues.

It was a big party. All the children in the school year had been invited. The guests sat down in a wide circle in Natasha's front room. Sofas, chairs and the coffee table were pushed out to the sides to make space. They were building funny cartoon balloon characters. Natasha's dad had bought a kit where you could turn each colourful inflated shape into a person by sticking plastic feet onto the bottom for the balloon to balance on. There were hats and wigs, eyes and noses, and little hands fixed onto the sides of each balloon that stuck out like they were waving. They looked like the people Anna used to draw with thick waxy crayons when she was tiny, all their limbs extending directly from their swollen heads.

In a fog of sugary hysteria and birthday excitement, the children were being gathered together on one side of the room with their new balloon creatures, to pose for a photo. The adults all looked tired, resigned to the traumatic sugar lows that would play out tearfully at home later that evening. Anna could remember looking at the picture afterwards. For a while it had been up in the hallway at home, before her parents separated and she had two houses to flit between. Jack was there in the group, much younger, of course, but recognisable as the child who would grow up to be the man she had passed yesterday outside the pub. Anna's eyes opened wider when she saw him. He beamed and scrunched his face up at the camera in an exaggerated smile for the adults around them. She had never noticed him being there before. Never. It didn't bring the satisfying click of a puzzle completed. Instead, a sense of dread crept into the innocent noisiness of the party proceedings around her. Everything was distorted, like looking the wrong way through a pair of binoculars. As soon as the camera had flashed, Jack stood up and left the living room, walking down Natasha's hallway and out of the front door to the street outside. The scene, woven from the fabric of a real memory, was being altered: the pattern changed, the wrong-coloured thread incorporated, a stitch dropped along the way.

Anna ran after Jack, shouting for him to stop. He didn't even turn around. He shut the door in her face. She sped up, pumping her little arms and legs down the length of the house, half-tripping over the corner of the hall rug and sliding in her frilly white ankle socks across the final few feet of shiny wooden floor, to pull the front door open again. She watched Jack run up the steep slope of the front garden and out onto the street.

'I don't want to. I don't want to.'

It was her own adult voice she could hear moaning from the other side of the sleep line. The air hovered, the wind falling still as Anna strained her ears for the sound of a car engine.

For a few seconds nothing moved. Even her breath had stopped. And then, sure enough, she heard it. Everything sped up again. A car careered around the corner at the far end of the road, heading straight for where Jack was standing, facing back towards the house, watching Anna frozen in the open doorway. This foresight was exhausting. She needed to wake up.

'I don't want to.'

Her voice grew louder in her own ears. She forced the car to swerve off course, to save Jack's life as he stared back at her. The horror of his brush with death filled his green eyes. In the balloon menagerie behind her, an unlucky inflatable character was popped with an almighty bang. It chimed with the smash of the car on the brick wall of a house opposite, and Anna woke up in bed.

Next door a gate was swinging in the wind, slamming shut and flying open again. There was a flash of lightning. Anna lay still, waiting for the crack of thunder. Silence hovered, a rumble eventually rolling in from far away. She tried to remember whether she had screamed. Nobody stirred downstairs.

She crept down to the kitchen and drank a bottle of cold water so fast it made her chest hurt. Then she took her house keys from the bowl in the hallway and went outside to shut

71

the gate next door. She stepped barefoot around a pile of broken glass on the pavement. The atmosphere outside was weird. The air was all churned up from the storm, hanging in unsettled patches of warm and cold. A dog barked relentlessly into the darkness. It was a relief to clamber back up to the safety of her bedroom and cover herself completely with the duvet, throwing it right up and over her head. Her breath hit the cotton in front of her face, still cold from the water she had drunk.

It was early the next morning when the summer sun woke her. She scrunched a pillow up over her head, wishing she had curtains, before remembering the strangeness of the night. She climbed out of bed and rifled through a box of photographs that she had stashed underneath her desk. If she hadn't recently finished unpacking and organising her room she wouldn't have known where it was. The last time she visited her mum, Anna had taken their favourite photos away with her, intending to fill an album with them at some point and give it back to her as a present. It was such a shame for them all to be crushed on top of one another, unseen.

In just a few seconds, she found it. Its glossy surface was stuck slightly to the remnants of glue at the back corners of the photograph in front of it. She prized them apart carefully. Perhaps that strange sensation when she had passed Jack at the pub yesterday was just dim recognition. Maybe they had known each other as children. Maybe it was even vaguer than that, and they had simply met once or twice, had spoken to each other briefly for some reason, some minor exchange. She certainly couldn't recall his name from her childhood. It was only passing him twice in a short space of time that had made her sense of recognition mysterious.

There was the photo from the balloon party: Anna smiled from the centre of the picture next to the birthday girl, Natasha. She was clutching her purple sausage-shaped balloon, which was wearing its miniature trainers and a felt beret. Her black and pink dress looked cheap and flouncy, compared to her romantic memories of its exquisite, ebony velvet softness. She stared down at the cluster of young faces, sitting cross-legged and proudly squeezing their new perishable pets. But the child that was standing where Jack should be was in fact a girl called Liliana, with short straight dark hair. Anna remembered Liliana bursting into tears later in the party when her parents were late to collect her. Jack was not there.

He had definitely waited for the camera to flash before he ran out of the house; he would have been in the photo. She cast her mind back to what she had seen in sleep, like watching a goal on slow-motion replay during a football match. She realised that in her dream Jack had not been a child: he had looked exactly as he had outside the pub. In her dream she had felt that she was imagining him as a young boy, when in fact she had watched a man in his late twenties, sit on the floor in a leather jacket and stick googly eyes on a round green balloon.

It was a hot bright day. Her mum would be awake by now; parents got up early. As she waited for the phone to be answered she imagined Elizabeth coming in from the garden with her morning coffee, wondering who it could be. Questions lined up in Anna's mind, each one shouting for attention: had she just inserted Jack into an existing memory, had she invented his presence, or had she met him back in Brighton? Was he the older brother of Natasha, or another friend? Did she know him from swimming club? From art class?

She could hear a smile in her mum's voice, relaxed and sunny, and wondered if she was there with somebody.

'Are you OK, Annie? You sound stressed.'

'I am a bit. I haven't slept well. I had an odd dream and I wanted to ask you about something.'

Elizabeth was used to the occasional random

or unexpected question as a result of her daughter's dream life. She sometimes teased Anna about the half-forgotten childhood moments that they brought up, minor embarrassments, mistakes and tantrums. Usually though, she was tactful and patient. Every now and then her concern veered towards worry, anxious that Anna was so affected in the day by the things she saw at night. That's when Anna backed off, stopped telling her things for a while until something like this happened, and she was convinced that no one else would have the answer.

'I was dreaming about Natasha's birthday party, the one where we all made those balloons into weird characters.'

'I remember. You drank too much Sprite and then danced really fast to *Cotton Eye Joe*. You cried all the way home because you felt sick.'

Anna laughed.

'We got back quite late and I had the temerity to utter the words "bed time". All hell broke loose.'

'Was I awful?'

'Terrible. What did you want to ask? Why was the dream weird?'

'It's nothing much. There was just a boy there, who I don't remember being at the party, called Jack. Everybody else in my dream I do actually remember, and they're in the photo that I have. But not him.'

Anna had imagined that a strange dark pall might settle over the conversation as soon as she mentioned his name, but nothing shifted, nothing changed. Her mum answered, breezy and upbeat.

'I'm one hundred per cent sure there was no Jack at that party. That was always the boy's name your dad and I had in mind, if we ever had another child. I'd remember if it had already been taken by somebody in your class.'

'What about in the other years at school then? Or someone's older brother? Family friend? School clubs?'

'So is this about Natasha's birthday party, or just anybody we might have known who had a child called Jack?'

'Anybody.'

'Well, that's a trickier question, love. I don't *remember* a Jack, but that's not to say there wasn't one, on the fringes somewhere. Sorry, that's not very helpful.'

Anna smiled at her mum's kindness, humouring her without needing to know why she was asking. She decided not to test her patience any further by telling her that she was dreaming about a man who seemed to live nearby, whom she had barely met but saw almost every time she closed her eyes.

'Do you think I'm going mad? I think I'm

going mad. How would I know?'

'You'd know because everything would make perfect sense and you would be utterly convinced of your own sanity: that's madness.'

'Thanks, Mum.'

'Don't worry. You're just a bad sleeper. I'm sorry, you probably get it from me. Chin up, love. If I remember a Jack, I'll give you a call.'

# CHAPTER EIGHT

On Saturday morning, Anna dropped the biggest knife in the kitchen when she was cutting up strawberries for breakfast. She hadn't had enough sleep; she wasn't concentrating properly. It was too big to slice fruit with anyway. The long blade clanged like a tuning fork on the flagstone floor as it landed on its point, millimetres from her foot. It took a few seconds for Anna to realise that the sharp edge had caught her skin on the way down to the ground, a deep red cut bursting open like a blossoming flower on her ankle, spotting blood onto the tiles. Her fingers sprang apart in shock, losing grip on the glass she was holding. The smashing noise of shattered smithereens added to the chaos, while she tried to work out which accident to deal with first.

'Don't come in if you don't like blood,' she shouted at whoever was running downstairs towards the commotion. Holly stuck her head round the door, her hair messy from sleep, still waking up as she processed the scene in front of her.

'Stay there. I've got a first-aid kit from work upstairs somewhere.'

She was back almost immediately, picking her way over the shards of glass to where Anna had pulled herself up to sit on the worktop. Holly cleaned the cut for her with an antiseptic wipe, biting her lip when Anna cried out in pain.

'Sorry. Is it from the glass?'

'No, I dropped the knife. Then I dropped the glass. That's the first time it's hurt though.'

Holly looked down to where the kitchen knife was still rocking slightly on its side, a smudge of blood on its tip. She whistled through her teeth and picked it up, dropping it in the sink. She held a plaster over Anna's ankle, a heavy-duty thick white fabric one that she had to stick down with medical tape. The whole square turned red almost instantly, blood creeping to each corner. Holly peeled it straight off and put a fresh one on. They both watched for a few seconds, waiting for it to soak crimson; a few small bright spots appeared, but nothing more.

'I don't think it will need stitches, but see what happens to this second one. If it doesn't hold we might need to go to hospital. Try sitting down with your leg raised for a bit so the bleeding stops completely.'

79

She manoeuvred Anna over to the kitchen table and sat her down, pulling another chair out for her to put her foot on. Anna rested her elbow on the table and dropped her head on to her hand, trying not to think about what it had looked like, that thin red line splitting open on her leg.

Holly swept up the glass, getting down on her hands and knees to check for tiny pieces under the table and behind the fridge. She wrapped it all up in an old newspaper, tied it in a plastic bag and put it in the bin.

'What were you trying to eat before you maimed yourself? I can make you something.'

Anna pointed at the chopping board covered in strawberry juice. Holly laughed and let out a sigh of relief.

'I thought that was blood too. You're going to be fine. Food will help.' She made them each a bowl of muesli, yoghurt, and strawberries, and sat down opposite Anna, holding a hand out across the table to squeeze hers.

'Are you still not sleeping well? You look tired.'

'Tired and apparently very clumsy. Somehow I don't think our move to London has cured me. The nightmares definitely didn't evaporate on the drive here.'

'Oh dear.'

'Is my whole life going to be like this?'

Holly looked a bit helpless. 'Of course not.' She swirled the yoghurt around in her bowl, peering over at Anna's foot to check that the new plaster was still clear of bloodstains, trying to move the conversation away from questions they both knew she had no answer to. 'How's the job? Are you enjoying London?'

'I'm enjoying it. The job's ...' She stopped, hesitating, searching her foggy head for the right words.

In Brighton, with no danger of anybody else walking in or overhearing, Anna might have shared things. She might have talked Holly through Joe Denning's dream photographs, perhaps made a joke about the mystical predestination that she fancied could have placed her on that exhibition team.

She would even have enjoyed the teasing that followed, the demystifying, her superstitions dressed down by Holly's matter-of-fact interpretation of things.

Would she have mentioned Jack? It would be difficult to voice a thought that she didn't yet have an explanation for, one she hadn't put into words. She only knew that there was something there, tugging insistently at the back of her mind. It would sound ridiculous if she tried to talk about it. Holly would laugh at her, reveal it to be a complete fantasy.

'It's ...?' Holly stared at her.

'What?'

'You're not saying anything. You started a sentence and you didn't finish it.'

'My brain's not working properly yet.' She chewed on her muesli and changed the subject again. 'When I first stopped sleeping, when my parents were splitting up, the doctor gave me these pills. I had to come off them after a couple of months, but I swear I remember those weeks now like they were the golden days: I slept right through every single night.'

'You said you slept right through the days too.'

'True. But I'm doing that at the moment anyway. I fell asleep at work on Friday, on top of one of the artworks.' She looked up. 'That's not nearly as bad as it sounds.'

'You've not been back to a doctor since then?'

'No, I haven't. I just feel like it's something I need to deal with by myself. It's complicated.'

'You don't think anyone will be able to solve the problem, but what if they can? What if a doctor could help you, really quickly?'

Anna shrugged. 'You might be right. I should probably try it.'

Holly looked pleased, taking it as promising commitment from Anna that she would get help, but Anna squirmed in her seat: she didn't like the idea of this becoming a medical issue.

***

It was the first weekend that all the girls had managed to clear their diaries, and the first chance to show Holly and Anna around. They went for a walk across the park and down the canal, sun flaring off the crested waves that trailed behind the barges as they chugged past. Some of the boats were moored up along the towpath, selling second-handbooks or serving Pimm's off the deck to passers-by.

'Careful, Anna,' Holly joked. 'Don't drink and boat.'

They found their way back towards the park for lunch, the market now a sea of people strolling up and down in the shade of the striped blue and white awnings that covered the stalls. They bought fresh, fragrant Vietnamese food from Libby's favourite tent. They ate it lying on the grass in the afternoon sun until the light began to dip, their shadows lengthening, their hands and feet cooling down. Anna was on holiday in a foreign country, not yet settled in enough to have rediscovered those lazy routines that swallow your time when you grow comfortable somewhere: the accidental stolen hours spent idly flicking through the television with no real idea of what to watch; an evening lost when you get sidetracked on the way home, bumping into friends outside your local pub.

She winced when she put her sandals on later, sliding the strap past the fresh knife cut on her ankle. They drank cocktails on Kingsland Road and queued up in a squashed line of excitable students to get into a dirty basement club, with a thumping sound system that made the walls shake and a security set-up akin to an international airport. Frustrated by an interminable argument between the surly barman and an insistent girl whose card refused to work, Anna offered to help by buying the drink herself so that she could at least finish her own order. The girl exploded in a shower of gratitude, hugging and kissing Anna and handing her a slightly bent cigarette from her purse in thanks. It was a relief to have an excuse to leave the sweaty darkness of the dance floor and head out upstairs to street level, to enjoy a moment's smoky peace.

It was three-thirty in the morning. Anna leant back against the warm brick wall outside, watching people on the other side of the road stumble home, and realised she was already wishing for a quiet weekend. She was looking down at the unlit gift when Jack appeared beside her, holding the burning end of his own cigarette out for her to use. Anna's chest constricted, squeezing tight with a breathless excitement that made the tips of her fingers tingle. She was happy to see him.

'Thank you.'

Jack watched her light the cigarette.

She had dreamt about him twice. She had telephoned her mum about him that morning. She fantasized briefly about an intense, romantic *Chrysalids*-like connection between their minds, a precious thread of telepathy running from her soul to his that no one else would ever know about. She choked on her cigarette, mostly because he was standing next to her oblivious to the nonsense flying around her head, and Jack laughed.

'I'm not really a smoker either.'

She waved it in front of her face, fanning away the wispy white nicotine clouds with her fingers. 'I just got given this downstairs for helping someone out.'

'And you felt it would be ungrateful not to smoke it?'

'Yes. What's your excuse?'

'My friend is trying to quit. I'm helping him finish his last packet.'

'That's good of you.'

He smiled. 'Do I know you?'

He could easily have been referring to his friendly nod outside the pub, but Anna knew that he was talking about a time before that, before all this. From another man in this situation, the question would have sounded

85

transparent and obvious, a clumsy gateway to flirtation. Anna decided it was genuine curiosity; he was trying to place her too. She tested her theory.

'I saw you outside the pub the other day.'

'I know. I meant from before then.'

'I moved here recently. Maybe you've just seen me around.'

'Before that.' He smiled. 'Before here.' He swung his hand around through the air, his fingers making circles in the smoke. Anna met his gaze and they looked at each other without saying anything.

'I don't know,' she swallowed eventually. 'I think so. Maybe.'

'I really think I do.'

'I'm Anna.' She held out her hand.

'Jack.' His skin was soft.

Somebody tapped Jack on the shoulder and a couple of other people emerged from the nightclub with a few 'thank you's and 'goodnight's to the doormen standing on the pavement; they were all ready to leave.

'Come on, Jack.' The friend flashed Anna a smile, noticing her. 'Sorry, we're interrupting. Hello.'

Anna raised a hand in greeting. The group exchanged glances, weighing up the situation. They were trying to work out whether they should offer to go without

Jack, to leave him here with Anna, or if that would make things awkward.

'You're not interrupting. I should be heading home soon anyway,' she said.

For a second she saw disappointment on Jack's face, but then he laughed and checked his watch with a grimace.

'Sounds about right. Some of us have to work tomorrow unfortunately.' He glanced past her, over her shoulder. 'Looks like your family has arrived too.'

Anna turned around. The girls were all standing goofily behind her in a line, like teenagers outside a school disco. They were clutching their bags in front of their colourful dresses, their jackets collected from the cloakroom and slung over their shoulders, unnecessary in the summer heat. Anna gave them a look and Libby started laughing nervously.

'See you around.' Jack kissed her on the cheek. He turned back when he was further down the street, almost at the corner. 'Goodnight!'

Anna waved. She reached down and punched Holly gently on the arm to stop the cooing noises that the girls were quietly making behind her. 'Shut up. You sound like a flock of pigeons.'

# CHAPTER NINE

A few hours later the sun rose and Sunday slipped more fully into view. Over a very late breakfast, the girls mustered up enough energy to tease Anna about her early morning nightclub encounter. According to their expert calculations, made in the few short seconds they had drunkenly assessed the scene last night, Jack definitely liked her. Anna was too tired to rise to the provocation, too distracted by the memory of what Jack had said to her, by his hand turning long-fingered through the night air as he had tried to place her. After a bit, the girls gave up and settled into silence. It was no fun teasing someone who didn't react.

Morning, afternoon and evening merged into one, a thick chunk of time lost in a lazy Sunday lethargy. Anna lolled around between the garden and the front room, reading a book. She only spent a few hours dressed in proper clothes before she surrendered to her pounding head and climbed back into her pyjamas, flashing a quick self-pitying frown at her pale face in the bedroom mirror. By sunset they were all squashed up on the sofa and the armchairs, small cardboard boxes of takeaway dim sum scattered empty across the coffee table, watching television and laughing maniacally with the hysteria of their shared exhaustion.

Anna could trace the stages of her life through how it felt to sit on the sofa and watch films. On early childhood home-cinema nights, her dad would borrow a television and video player from their next-door neighbours because he refused to buy either. He claimed it would make it less special, less of a treat to watch a film, if they could do it any time. He hated the idea of them becoming the kind of family that just put on the TV with no plan of what to watch, just 'because'. Anna would burrow in between her parents, waiting until her mum predictably fell asleep, waking up and having to ask what was going on every five minutes for the rest of the film. Each question would send Anna and her dad into a fit of laughter. Elizabeth would never quite manage to re-engage with the plot, eventually picking up the Sunday papers, trying to read alongside them. Anna would complain that the crumpling of oversized broadsheet pages turning beside her was too loud to hear the television over, but they never let her mum leave, tugging her back down into the fold when she sighed and tried to get up to go and sit in the study instead. Afterwards came the post-cinema evaluation, Anna and her dad ruminating over plot and character development, soundtrack and costume design, before she was sent to bed. On film nights she always went straight up when she was asked, no arguments.

Later on, things changed of course. They did get their own television in the end, with more than five channels and a DVD player. After a while even her dad welcomed the colourful background noise as a crutch, a foil to the silence that had developed between him and his distant wife. On those evenings, Anna sat tense on the edge of the sofa, too unrelaxed to sink back into the cushions, glancing from parent to parent. They never argued, but they barely spoke. After a few hours of channel skimming, one of them would feign tiredness and head upstairs to bed. They rarely went at the same time. After a couple of years her dad moved into the spare room – just because of the snoring, they said.

Then one weekend Anna lied, said she was going to a friend's house, and went shopping with a group of girls from the year above instead. None of them had any money, and Anna wasn't meant to be old enough to go into town without adults, but she and the older girls moped up and down the high streets looking through the windows and called it 'shopping'. And there was her mum, in another man's house, its windows looking out onto the street as the girls walked home. She was sitting on his lap, wearing a bright green dress that Anna had never seen before, tied tightly around her waist. She was laughing, a stranger's arms around her, her head thrown back in happiness, her mouth open too wide, her eyes blissfully closed.

After that it all fell apart, not that Anna didn't help to ruin it. Some thirteen-year-old moralistic part of her wanted them to suffer for not being good at marriage, at being with each other, or at being her parents. Evenings in front of the television changed again, became what they still were today: an hour or so to distract her mind before she went to sleep and dreamt of terrible things. It kept her feeling like a child, no matter how much time had passed.

Even now, crammed in between Libby and Fran, Anna was scared of going upstairs to sleep, like a frightened toddler who thinks there's a monster in the cupboard. When they each eventually gave in to the Sunday night blues and went to bed, she tried to convince herself that she wasn't tired, not yet. She sat up at her desk in the safety of the light from her computer screen, reading her book, but her eyelids kept closing and she kept losing her place on the page. Eventually it fell from her sleepy weak-fingered grasp, the spine landing on her big toe and making her jump.

Anna met her dad in sleep. He was sitting in the driving seat of their old family car. She was in the passenger seat beside him picking Liquorice Allsorts from a bag in the glove compartment. Every now and then he gave her a pleading look, tensing the muscles in his arm to make it look like his hands were stuck to the steering wheel, and she popped a sweet into his mouth. He was driving her up to London for a summer arts and crafts course, a weekend thing. They were going to stay in a posh hotel near Covent Garden, which Anna thought sounded very regal, and they had tickets to go to Drury Lane theatre in the evening. She was almost as excited about the breakfast at the hotel as she was about the course. Apparently they cooked you whatever kind of pancakes you wanted while you watched. Anna was going to ask for plain vanilla ones with crispy bacon and maple syrup on top.

'Looks like there's a storm a-coming.' Her dad said it with a southern American accent, as if they were driving down Tornado Alley.

Anna looked outside. The sky had darkened, weighed down by heavy grey clouds that were swollen with rain. The fronts of the buildings they passed still shone bright yellow in the sunlight. It was that strange unnatural mix of weather systems that happens just before a sudden storm in midsummer, where dogs bark and cats hide under the sofa, ears flattened against the sides of their heads in fright.

'Here we are.' Her dad pulled up outside a big 1960s building, all hard angles and grey concrete. The sign above the murky, tinted glass doors read '*Seminar*' in those moveable black and white letters that old-fashioned cinemas or theatres use.

The light of lucidity was growing in Anna's mind, a shift that brought a fresh, unwelcome awareness with it. She knew she was dreaming because of the gaping black hole in time between stopping the car and finding themselves sitting at desks near the front of a huge lecture theatre. Anna looked down at the notebook and pen laid out in front of her. There was a title '*Some Questions*' written in her own handwriting and neatly underlined twice with a ruler. Hannah Truss, the artist, was standing on stage behind a wooden lectern, seemingly coming to the end of a complex speech. She lifted her reading glasses from her face and folded them up carefully, popping them into a small square pocket in her floral shirt, before looking up at her audience again.

'And now we come to my favourite part of the seminar: Some Questions. I know some of you have come a very long way, just for this little bit.' She shot Anna a knowing wink. Anna jumped, turning to her dad beside her to look for an explanation, but he was gone. She thought she remembered him saying that he was going to pick her up after it had finished, but perhaps she had just imagined it.

'Question number one,' Truss continued, 'is a question I know many of you have been considering. If I may ...'

She walked a few paces to her left towards a rickety old acetate projector and switched it on, so that the blank white screen behind her was suddenly filled with a page from her notebook, the same photocopied page Anna had studied in Poppy's exhibition notes.

'Who would like to read this out for me?' Truss scanned the audience. 'Yes, you.'

Anna swivelled in her chair to see Jack standing up out of his seat towards the back of the hall.

'Follow my pen.' Truss instructed, hovering her biro beneath each word on the screen as Jack started to read the question aloud.

'Is it possible—' he stopped, coughing. His voice was very quiet, and an usher or assistant from the back of the hall ran forward obediently with a microphone, holding it under Jack's mouth so that when he next spoke it was booming, amplified to a volume that made the bones in Anna's skull shake.

'Is it possible to commit a violent act, an aggressive crime, and not to be conscious that you have done so?'

'Bravo!' Truss shouted, applauding and signalling for the whole audience to do the same. 'That was wonderful.'

After a few moments the clapping and cheering died down.

'I wonder,' Truss continued, 'would you like to read out the final question too? It's my favourite.'

Jack nodded, taking the microphone from the grasp of the officious steward so he could hold it more directly in front of himself.

'Is it possible to be guilty, but psychologically to be untainted?'

Anna caught Jack's eye from across the hall, and the room started buzzing angrily. At first, Anna thought it was a swarm of wasps approaching outside, or some terrible mechanical failure rising from the bowels of the building beneath them. But then she realised it was the muttering of the people around them. All eyes were now on her. People were shaking their heads in distaste. One man even spat contemptuously on the floor beside her. Something terrible was going to happen if she didn't leave immediately. Anna could see it in Jack's face but she couldn't tear her eyes away from him. She pulled herself up and edged her way to the nearest aisle, trying to put one foot in front of the other, down the stairs and out of the door at the front of the hall. Halfway down, she tripped and fell, briefly aware of a line of people standing up to point and jeer at her as she hit the floor.

Anna woke up at the bottom of the steep twisted stairs from her bedroom down to the landing below. She waited on the floor in anxious silence to find out if she had woken anyone else. Nobody appeared, and she noticed with a small nauseous gasp that the cut on her ankle had opened up again, the plaster nowhere to be seen. She flexed her foot gently and the wound gaped open and shut, like a red mouth talking to her.

She swore violently under her breath as a shock of pain flooded up her whole leg and deep into her stomach. She washed the cut in the bathroom, her leg stretched awkwardly into the sink so she could get the wound underneath the tap. The skin flapped open with the force of the streaming water and she jumped, falling backwards onto the lid of the toilet, cradling her ankle in her hands and leaning back against the cold porcelain, the cistern gurgling away behind her. She closed her eyes, struggling not to vomit on the shiny chequered linoleum floor. She exhaled slowly, keeping her foot elevated the way Holly had showed her, resting it out on the edge of the bath. After a few seconds tears crept into the corners of her eyes; things seemed to be getting worse here, not better.

In the thin air of midnight it all suddenly felt very clear. Of course Jack had been flirting with her, giving her looks outside the pub because he fancied her, found her attractive. On Saturday he had just been drunk, out with friends at the weekend, trying to sound mysterious and enigmatic, trying to pique her interest. He probably didn't recognise her at all, not in the intense, fate-led way that she imagined she knew him. Maybe the girls' dovecote cooing was entirely the right way to read all this. She tried to conjure up the little pulse of electricity that had flickered at the bottom of her stomach, so low it had travelled down her abdomen and between her legs when he had appeared beside her on the pavement, his hand touching hers as she bent over to light the cigarette. Why shouldn't he appear in her dreams? So many waking moments or experiences were recycled, spun around at high-speed until they were nonsense. It didn't have to mean anything. She was becoming the sort of creepy, mentally unstable girl that everybody wanted to stay away from, the ones that got referred to as 'a psycho' with disdainful no-hope looks from women who were happily settled in stable long-term relationships. Holly was right: she needed a doctor.

# CHAPTER TEN

Anna's sleep didn't settle down over the following days. The feeling that had hit her as she woke up disorientated on the hard-polished wood of the second-floor landing, one of madness and of being out of control, had stayed with her. It had started to worry her. She registered at the local doctor's surgery, filling in her details in faded black biro, wondering whether her lack of previous medical complaints would possibly make the doctor take her more seriously. She was terrified of being laughed out of the surgery.

If she booked an appointment in advance she would have time to think about it, to change her mind and cancel. So she went to morning walk-in instead, a decision she immediately regretted when she arrived at the back of a very long line of the chronically unwell, trailing all the way out of the surgery and onto the pavement where passers-by had to weave around them on their way to work. A pale aggressive-looking woman asked if she could go in front of Anna.

'My boy's had a cough for a month now,' she insisted, looking pointedly down at her son where he slumped against her, holding her hand. She raised her eyebrows at him and he coughed obediently. Anna didn't give up her place and spent the next thirty minutes paranoid they were going to create some kind of scene.

As soon as she moved far enough up the line to be inside the building, the air in the waiting room made her long to be outside again. At least the majority of people signing in were being advised to speak to a nurse or to book an appointment. By the time she sat down on one of the sticky plastic seats, there were only six other people waiting. She skimmed the noticeboards on the walls around her. The words that jumped out jumbled in her head in a macabre muddle: Ebola, HIV, influenza, ectopic pregnancy. There was nothing physically wrong with her. Why was she here?

She waited for her name to appear on the screen accompanied by the piercing buzzer. Another box of those magic sleeping pills from when she was a child would be a suitable victory for her to walk out with, progress of some kind. Maybe they would help her to learn how to sleep again, remind her body what it felt like to sink into nothing and wake up hours later with everything in between just a delicious fuzz of warm darkness. It would be like learning to ride a bike with the stabilisers clipped on at first, a little wobbly for a few weeks afterwards, but soon she would be flying along in a perfect straight line.

It didn't happen that way. From the moment she stepped into Doctor Jacobs' room she felt her confidence dripping away as if there was a leak in her somewhere, her ability to control a conversation drying up fast. He was old, in a dignified way, with white hair and tiny wire-rimmed spectacles, a starched white shirt, casual trousers and a beautiful gold watch with a thick soft brown leather strap. He smiled kindly as she sat down and a web of lines appeared at the outer corner of each eye.

Anna knew instantly that she would tell him the truth. Whatever he asked her, she would be honest. At least then she would know that she had got something out of coming here, that his responses really applied to her and were worth listening to.

'What have you come to see me about today then, Anna?'

He didn't say hello or indulge in any introductory questions like 'How are you?' or 'I'm Doctor Jacobs,' yet all those pleasantries were contained within the kind look he gave her, as she put her bag down at her feet and troubled over how to begin.

'I haven't been to the doctor's in years.' He nodded in acknowledgment. 'Does everybody say that?'

He smiled again. 'Not everybody, no. Go on.'

'I've not been sleeping well.' She realised this wasn't quite right. 'Sorry, I don't have any trouble getting to sleep, I just have terrible nightmares. I wake up a lot. I sleepwalk sometimes, although not too often. I don't know how to make the nightmares go away. I'm not sure this is something people come to the doctor for.' She was adding sentence after stilted sentence, anxious for him to say something. She stopped so that he could.

'How long have you had this sort of disturbed sleep?' He busied himself preparing an ear thermometer and connecting the blood pressure machine. It wasn't enough activity to give the impression he wasn't listening, but just a little movement on his part so that Anna loosened up enough to respond, less exposed than under his direct stare.

'That's something I wanted to mention. I was given some sleeping pills for a few weeks by my previous GP in Brighton, when it all started happening. That was a while ago.' Anna started counting on her fingers and

Doctor Jacobs watched. She grimaced as she said it: she knew it wasn't going to sound good. 'That was fifteen years ago when I was thirteen.'

If this was bad news, he didn't show it. His expression didn't change. He wheeled his chair over to position himself directly in front of her and asked her to turn her head to one side so that he could take her temperature. He slid the reader quickly into her ear.

'Have you had any periods of time since then when you have noticed the nightmares recede for a while? Or has it been a fairly constant problem?'

'Pretty constant.'

He Velcroed the blood pressure armband tightly around her upper arm and inflated it until Anna could feel her pulse beating against the constricting material, a regular pulsing thud.

'Good.' That was all he said about that. 'Did anything happen around the time you started having nightmares, anything that could have contributed to you feeling unsettled?'

Anna knew these questions were drifting dangerously close to the barbed territory of a therapist's conversational arsenal. She was about to be sent to a counsellor, she could tell.

'My parents separated. When I was younger I believed it was my fault.' She looked out of the window for a second before turning back to face him. 'I found out about my mum's affair, and I was the one who told my dad.'

'Ah.' A little noise, that was all, an exhale with a slight sound to it, but no judgement.

'I don't think that any more of course. I'm close to both of them. If that *was* the reason I started sleeping so badly, I'm not sure why it would still be affecting me, now that I'm over it.'

'I think you know what I'm going to say.' He spread his palms wide in an apology. 'It would be irresponsible of me to prescribe you sleeping pills for something that would really benefit from a more causal approach. I don't think it would do you any favours to deal wholly with the symptoms in a situation like this, instead of thinking about a reason for it all.'

'Can't you give me some sleeping pills for now? Just so I can have a break from the nightmares?'

'They are quite vivid, then. Troubling?'

'I feel like I'm going mad.' She wished she hadn't said that.

'Is there anything in your waking life that's bothering you? Anything at all? Or is it simply confined to your sleep patterns?'

There. There it was. He had stumbled upon the kernel, the little seed that had sprouted her insanity: she had started to carry things back and forth between her dreams and the real world. She was dreaming about Jack, she was seeing him, and she was struggling to keep the two threads separate. Her honesty had run out.

'Why do you ask?'

'I don't think it's necessarily relevant to you, but there are certain groups of people – schizophrenics for example – who commonly have extremely vivid dream recall, who find their dreams especially troubling and distracting in their day-to-day lives. At times, for these people, it can be very difficult to distinguish between dreams and reality, and that in itself can be tiring and upsetting. I am not for one minute suggesting that you are schizophrenic. But, if you are not getting enough sleep, well that alone can make you feel fragile, less *in control of things*. If this is the case, I would concede that perhaps helping you get a few good nights' restful sleep with a light sedative would be beneficial, as long as you also allow me to refer you for some guidance with the emotional side of this issue too. What do you think?'

Anna thought she wished he weren't such a good doctor. She had been hoping for a younger, less authoritative, prescription-happy pill pusher who wanted her out as fast as possible so the next patient could come in. Instead, she was face to face with somebody who was succeeding in making her acutely aware that this was something she needed to sort out, and soon. It would have been easier if she *had* been laughed out of the room, a doctor amused that she had come to him with her silly night-time neuroses. Being taken this seriously was a validation, a stamp on her own private suggestion to herself that something was wrong with her.

'What are the other groups of people?'

'Excuse me?'

'You mentioned certain groups of people who have sleep disturbances, vivid dreams. Schizophrenics, and what other groups?'

'Many. People with drug and alcohol problems, addicts, recovering addicts, people suffering from psychosis. Post-traumatic stress disorder, that's a common precursor to severe and recurring nightmares. Your parents' divorce is unlikely to be a violent or psychologically shocking-enough event for something like this, unless there is anything else you can think of from around the time this started? A particular trauma? Are you certain nothing else happened?'

Anna insisted that there was nothing. She wondered how Truss's murderer subjects slept at night, the details of their crimes safely erased, discarded by their own minds. If an experience was too terrible even to be written into your own memory, surely it couldn't keep you up at night?

He gestured towards the prescription paper as she folded it up and tucked it inside her purse. 'There is every chance that those won't really help, I'm afraid.'

'What do you mean?'

'You said yourself that you don't have any trouble in getting to sleep. It doesn't sound as though you are suffering from insomnia. The sedatives may well affect your dream sleep, but I'd say it is entirely possible that whatever is causing you to wake up in the middle of the night will continue to do so.'

Anna left feeling disappointed, with a prescription for a short course of sleeping pills, and a referral letter to take to a local NHS-run counselling service connected to the surgery. She knew she wouldn't go. There were elements to the whole thing that would make her seem wild and unsound if she had to say them out loud, and not sharing them would make any counselling session pointless.

Anna also suspected that, as Doctor Jacobs had said, the sedatives wouldn't work. No tranquiliser could numb her to that chest-grabbing claustrophobic panic, immunise her against the shock of seeing people's bodies break into pieces inside the walls of her own head. The appointment had begun with such hope, uplifted by Doctor Jacobs' calm capability, but this was too complex. As soon as Anna looked at it in any real detail it became a dense and infinite tangle of black weeds that she could not find a path through, an infection spreading darkly without end or cure.

# CHAPTER ELEVEN

Anna arrived late at the gallery after her appointment, and spent the rest of the morning catching up with work: head down, eyes barely blinking in front of the computer screen. The atmosphere in the office was tense. Occasionally a remark flew like a lit flare, sparks erupting from whoever it landed nearest. Most of the team was overworked, racing to get too many things ready for the same date. The exhibition launch loomed on their calendar, a thick red line drawn around the date – Red Friday, Poppy named it. Anna had too much noise going on in her head already; there wasn't room for everybody else's stress as well. It crowded her, made her eyes hurt.

She took her laptop and a bunch of notes and went and sat downstairs in the café. She often worked there when the air in the office turned thick and busy. It reminded her of all the studious summers of revision while she was at school, and then at university, deliberately seeking out the busiest place in town to read. She had always been able to find a deeper groove of concentration among the sounds of coffee grinders and tinkling china than surrounded by the oppressive silence of the library. Here, the laughter and conversations around the café tables sunk into the background much more easily than the urgently ringing telephones upstairs.

Her morning appointment with Doctor Jacobs lurked, sidling in and out from between her emails and research, every now and then swooping alarmingly into crisp focus. Before she noticed what she was doing, Anna was out of her emails and into her Internet browser. It was too tempting. She couldn't sit there and work when there was a huge quantity of potential knowledge right in front of her, online, that could help lessen this suffocating paranoia. At the touch of a few carefully placed fingertips, her laptop screen might at least trick her, convincingly, into thinking she was getting some of her questions answered, her panicked superstitions silenced. She slid round on the bench so that her back was tucked against the corner wall, the laptop screen facing away from prying eyes.

She spoke silent warning words to herself as

she searched for articles. Anna knew that even the most far-fetched theories would find an ardent core of supporters online, receive solid back-up from the niche fringe groups that gathered facelessly over the Internet. She needed to find an authoritative position on why we dream, on how our sleep patterns affect our personality from somebody with adequate qualifications. If she collated all the different theories, ideas and experiments that were out there, if she read as much as she possibly could in the next few hours, she may be able to get a balanced view of it all. She needed enough information to be able to make up her own mind as to whether there was any hope left, now that even prescription sedatives were supposedly not enough to knock it out of her.

She pored over the hundreds of journals and papers that were listed with a variety of titles under the topic of 'Insomnia-Induced Psychosis'. There was a common theme throughout, each investigation revealing just how little sleep deprivation it took before an otherwise healthy brain began to exhibit signs of mental illness. There were cases where people reportedly displayed symptoms similar to that of schizophrenia after just twenty-four hours without sleep. Anna had rarely spent a night entirely without sleep, but she couldn't remember the last time she had enjoyed a full uninterrupted seven hours. Could the disruption to her sleep patterns be having the same effect as insomnia? If she added up the time she had spent awake when she should have been fast asleep, it would surely amount to sleep deprivation. Perhaps her recent feelings of madness were simply that. Maybe she wasn't totally broken, just yet.

Anna knew that sleep deprivation had been her mum's reason for only having one child: she couldn't handle any more years of sleepless nights. Mum said it changed her personality and made her doubt herself, that she became scared of her own fraying anger when she threw things at Dad, screamed at the baby, and once slammed the front door so hard that the wood had split in its frame. Could it be genetic? Was Anna especially susceptible to the effects of reduced sleep? It was odd to think that a significant factor in the shape of us, the outline of a personality, might be down to how many hours we spent in sleep each night.

As Anna continued to read, the tentative reassurance began to disintegrate. The sense that she may be close to finding answers or advice receded into the distance. There were hundreds of different and opposing theories. Anna understood that this was how science worked, an accumulation of tests and experiments that eventually corroborated a theory, filling in the blanks until a phenomenon made sense. But on this particular subject, there were too many gaps and spaces, too many disparate ideas, and vast swathes of the sleep process left bizarrely untouched. Even the scientists themselves referred to their studies as speculation.

Anna navigated through the explanations, patches of evidence crowding in from wildly different directions. Dreams were everything from Freud's conviction that at night our heads were filled with manifestations of our deepest desires and anxieties, to Jung's insistence that dreams were messages to the dreamer, that recurring nightmares demanded attention, evidence of an emotional problem that needed resolving. More recently scientists had questioned both these notions, deciding that dreams were simply the brain's response to external sensory stimuli, the temperature in a room or a sound from outside, rather than the mystical meanderings of the subconscious. Others connected them to our pasts, suggesting that dreams were the constantly turning cogs of long-term memory, present even while we were awake but more vivid when they became isolated thoughts during sleep. Then there was the most extreme suspicion, the Simulation Hypothesis, in which our entire reality was a controlled digital universe we were all unaware of, dreaming and waking both parts of the same artificial computer programme. The most commonly held explanation was that dreams were probably a random by-product of REM sleep. How could science be content with the word 'random'? Her skin prickled as though an electrical current was charging her entire body. The reality thudded like a dead silence in Anna's ears: nobody really knew why we had dreams.

As her thoughts peeled away from the straight line of sanity, Anna searched for an online test for madness, each word appearing letter by letter on the screen as though typed by someone else's hand. On the very first page of results she found something relatively official: *A 17-Question Schizophrenia Test and Early Psychosis Indicator*. 'Early psychosis' wouldn't be too terrible, a smaller, less threatening version of a full-blown mental illness. It sounded reversible, embryonic, a pregnancy that could be aborted. Whatever was happening to her mind could still be undone. She clicked the link to the test page, holding on tightly to her mum's assurance that the mad did not worry that they were mad. She repeated it to herself like a mantra in her head that would keep her safe, while the page loaded. *The mad do not worry that they are mad.*

Anna expected the questions to focus on

imagined voices and split personalities, on believing that you were being guided or instructed by an authority invisible and inaccessible to everyone else, scenarios firmly at the polar end of 'crazy'. She wanted her fear to be blown away by seeing just how bizarre and tenuous some people's clumsy-fisted clutch on reality was.

There was a little of that, but she was shocked at how much of the questionnaire discussed dreams and visions, asked about invented psychological connections, and the belief that you possessed a unique and transcendent brain function. Last Saturday, outside the nightclub, she had stood next to Jack and allowed her mind to indulge in a crazed comparison between their strange affinity and John Wyndham's science-fiction classic, *The Chrysalids*. She had likened her preoccupation with Jack to pure fictional legend, to a book about invisible telepathic mutations of the brain in the aftermath of a nuclear fallout on an imagined future version of planet Earth. For a few seconds, Anna put her head in her hands.

*I sometimes have trouble distinguishing whether something I experience or perceive may be real or may only be part of my imagination or my dreams.*

She read the question so many times that in

the end none of the words made sense any more, and she had to close her eyes to think it over instead. 'Sometimes have trouble' was vague, but 'experience' and 'perceive' were surely two completely different things? No, she had to admit she had not experienced any concrete, unequivocal proof that she and Jack were linked in any way, but she had *perceived* something. She had sensed the presence of a higher purpose to their meeting, through his eyes in her dreams, the way he had breathed smoke out into the night like a whisper sliding from between his lips, the way he had looked at her as if they had meant something to each other for a long time.

That moment had a place in her mind now, at the end of a slideshow collection of images, each one capturing a moment where Jack's gaze had met hers. Anna watched through them at night, dancing from that moment outside the pub, to their more recent early-hours pavement encounter, waiting to place his face in a memory. So yes, she was 'having trouble', but that didn't mean she had crossed the line from functioning human to babbling idiot. She hovered the arrow over the 'yes' box, hesitating long enough to lose her nerve, and read on down through the next few questions instead.

*I think other people can sometimes read my mind, or I can read other people's minds.*

Anna swallowed. That was so hard to assess for certain. Had she amplified what was simply a rapport, an intuitive connection with somebody, dialling up the volume until it sounded like magic to her ears?

*I think I may be able to predict what will happen in the future.*

This, she felt sure, was a sensation contained entirely within her dreams. She never carried the same sense of premonition or prophecy out into the waking world. But perhaps the way it suffused her dreams, the lucid control she had over things while she was asleep, was an indication that she was struggling with the rest of her life. Was it enough to brand her unhinged, that everybody in her dreams was a puppet on a string for her grand urges, her desire to save or be saved?

*I believe that someone may be planning to cause me harm, or may be about to cause me harm in the near future.*

She hadn't thought of that one, which probably should have been a good thing, but instead made her twitch and look around the room, her eyes skittish and restless. Exhaustion was making her paranoid.

Anna scrolled back up to the top of the questions. There were too many answers that she was unsure of, not enough definite 'no's and one or two troubling 'yes' answers. In the end she didn't respond to any of them. She had visions of a flashing red alarm going off somewhere in a psychiatrist's office if she filed a dangerous set of responses, mental health professionals tracing the entry to her laptop and putting her away for a very long time in a bright white box out of harm's way.

She had dreamt of Jack, but she had also met him: he did exist in the real world. Maybe she wasn't having trouble separating the two, it was just that he was there in both. If there was a connection they hadn't yet placed, an easy, simple answer to his pondering whether they had met before, then hardly any of these questions would concern her. Once she had worked that out, she could answer the test properly, clicking a straight line of 'no' all the way to the bottom of the page, and never worrying about it again.

The nightmares would still be a problem, and she still suspected she had black holes growing in her brain after dark, but she wouldn't feel so compelled to hand herself in to a psychiatric hospital. She could return her focus to finding a way to sleep soundly in her new bed. After all this, that sounded like a small problem to fix.

# CHAPTER TWELVE

Anna left work. She didn't go back up to the office, just walked out of the building with her laptop under her arm and her notes hastily crammed into her bag. She craved peace like it was medicine, her feet sidestepping lamp-posts, turning corners and peeling in hurried arcs around parked bicycles. She was in a rush to be inside, away from everything, to be alone.

At home she separated her work notes from the hurried biro scribblings of dream research, her crawling black handwriting rushed and unfamiliar. She stapled them and stuffed them in the top drawer of her desk, unsure why or when she would need to consult their inconclusive ramblings again.

She could never share her bed with a man. The thought hit her more and more frequently now, like a thump to the centre of her chest as she climbed under the covers. She peered back through the years of urgent affairs, the ragged harsh-breathed intimacy of casual sex when the distance between her and whoever was inside her was so wide and substantial she could almost choke on it. She couldn't get to know a man here, not properly, tangled in sweat-soaked cotton sheets in the worst corner of her life. She was in a relationship with herself, an abusive series of domestic hauntings rising from a soiled cellar of her personality that she didn't recognise, attached to her somewhere unseen.

Anna opened her eyes and looked around. Everything was shimmering, daring her to work out what had changed. She hadn't even realised that she had fallen asleep. Was that something she usually noticed? She stared intently. It was like playing a cheap comic book game of spot the difference. They were the sort of puzzles found on the games pages of her childhood magazines, in between the readers' letters and the embarrassing stories, the kind of thing you found printed on the paper placemats at family restaurants, meant to keep the kids entertained while they waited for their food to arrive. Chicken, chips and baked beans. Anna hated baked beans. And she hated spot the difference. She was as bad at it back then as she was tonight, watching her own bedroom with eyes wide in concentration, trying to remember what colour her door handle usually was, whether the desk was always at that slight angle.

She realised what had happened with a quick 'pop', like a bubble bursting, the way the world suddenly reintroduced itself to you when you came down from a high, everything clear and definite as a grey day. Anna was watching her own sleeping form lying in the centre of the wide double mattress. The bedroom was the inside of her own head. The two big bright skylight windows that slanted up to the sky were her eyes. The roof and walls around her were her skull, and her body, coiled around her duvet with her eyes tightly shut, was her mind.

On the back wall where the door should have been, there was a large keyhole, a black space cut neatly into the white plaster and nearly as tall as the door had been. Anna strained to hear what was happening on the other side of it. There was some movement, voices, and then three men in white robes emerged, stepping carefully over the threshold, making sure not to trip over their long bright skirts. They moved quietly, with appropriate respect, for they were in another person's inner world. Anna knew they were gods from the way they were dressed and the manner in which they held themselves.

The first to enter held a large golden key in his hand, glowing gently in the darkness. It was big enough to be very heavy, but he carried it without effort. The second god had a pair of shining metal scissors, short, sharp blades that were elegantly curved at their outer edges. The scissors made a cruel slicing sound as the air whistled over and around them, but the god's expression did not seem threatening. The third carried a neatly wound loop of finely spun metallic thread, hung over his shoulder and gripped at his front between his hands. He placed his coiled burden at the foot of Anna's bed, as though in offering, and she saw her legs twitch under the covers, moving a few inches to one side to accommodate it.

At first, the gods looked around her room, studying the artworks that leant against the walls with appreciative concentration. One of them pointed to the most recent painting that Anna had started, the pair of eyes from her nightmare, staring back at their voyeur with a stark and fearful agony. The gods started murmuring, stroking their beards and nodding their heads, leisurely holiday visitors to an art gallery who had alighted upon a work that pleased and stimulated them all. After a few minutes, they fell back into calm silence. They each pulled up a chair at the bedside of Anna's sleeping mind. Their presence created a strange ethereal halo of light around their shoulders as they gazed down, attentive and loving, dedicated attendants at a friend's bedside in hospital.

The first god seemed to be the leader. He had arrived through the keyhole before the others; he had initiated their little tour of the room, and he had pointed out the eyes to his companions. Now he pulled a Polaroid photograph out from inside the folds of his robe. He caught the others' eyes and gave them a meaningful look as he pushed it deftly into Anna's mouth. She watched herself struggle to swallow the photo, sticking between her sleepy lips, and tried to make out the image on its glossy surface. The gods were feeding her dreams, slotting them into her body like coins into a vending machine. Could it be one of Joe Denning's photographs that they wanted her to digest?

Anna was floating, lucid, along the surface of a dream as if over water. She heard one of the gods speaking and her ears pricked up at the name 'Jack', but she couldn't make out the rest of their hushed conversation. The others nodded sagely. They jumped up swiftly, moving faster than they had done so far. They threw their skirts over their shoulders so that they could climb out through the keyhole nimbly, at speed. They carried their talisman cargo with them, and the first god paused for a second in the corridor outside to turn his golden key in the lock. The room went very dark.

Anna crossed the floor. Everything was still and silent. She gripped the window sill, standing on tiptoes to stare through the backs of her skylight window eyes, out onto the street below. The world outside was a desert, a single dry path crossing the featureless landscape. The lumpy tarmac road ran straight as a staff towards the horizon, disappearing over arid red rock scrubland. She heard dusty footsteps and saw Jack, tired and alone, weaving a limping path down the road towards her. He stopped, and staggered for a few paces with his back to her. Anna could already hear a car's engine roaring from far away, the noise echoing around the vast valley they were trapped in. Jack turned to face her, raising his hand to shield his eyes from the desert glare and frowning questioningly up at her in her tower. *What? What's wrong?*

It was difficult to breathe through the sheer dread of the car accident she knew was about to take place in front of her. Jack lowered his hand, his eyes squinting, beads of sweat climbing down his forehead. The car was almost on top of him. He could hear it. Why wasn't he turning around?

'Turn around!' Anna shouted, but then she realised that wasn't the right thing to yell. She should have just told him to run, to get out of the way. She started to will the car over to the other side of the road, begging it to find a route around Jack instead of through him.

At first she hoped she had thought it all through; there wasn't anything for the car to smash into like there often was. There were no traffic lights, no buildings, just clear barren acres of nothing. But then she saw the look of horror twitching in Jack's eyes as he followed the speeding vehicle past him; it missed his arm by centimetres and continued on towards Anna. She was in the middle of the road, too, of course she was. How had she not worked that out? Jack's face gaped, his jaw going slack, his eyes rolling as the car careered into her. His stare turned into the half-finished painting on her wall and Anna was inhaling car fumes, slipping down her throat like tar around the corners of the dream Polaroid that was still jammed between her teeth.

Anna woke up choking on her long hair. She had plaited it before bed, the braid now stuck in her mouth like a rope, lodged at the back of her throat. She swung herself up onto her hands and knees and coughed it out, retching as the bristles scratched her back teeth. She cried, hot tears stinging her eyeballs and springing out in big fat droplets that patterned the sheet beneath her in messy wet polka dots.

The moonlight made the crystals on her eyelashes shift and sparkle, like a kaleidoscope, when she blinked, dizzy and shaking, collapsing back on the bed beneath her.

The air still shivered in the wake of those powerful charismatic men who had sat in her room wearing their glowing white robes, and hijacked her mind. Their presence remained, and it made all sorts of thoughts possible that shouldn't have been. Was somebody tampering with her mind as she slept, giving her night terrors that she did not want? It couldn't be normal to have such intense nightmares over and over, and over and over. She tried to close her eyes, to lengthen her breaths, in and out, but each time she did she could feel the shadows of the three gods cast across her skin as though they sat watching her, forcing photographs between her lips.

# CHAPTER THIRTEEN

It was midsummer, the weekend of the summer solstice. Anna welcomed the closing of the gallery doors on Friday evening with a sense of hard-fought triumph; she had survived her second week in London. There was going to be a street party on her road tomorrow afternoon, a communal celebration to mark the watershed moment from when daylight would begin trickling away, lost droplets of sunlight every day now until Christmas. Anna wasn't looking forward to December in the city, to cold toes packed tight and numb inside hard winter boots, crossing black-iced roads at rush hour, emerging from her nightmares to see her breath hanging as a frightened smoky vapour in front of her face.

She read the event flyer that was pinned to the lamp-post outside their house on her way inside. The road was well known for street parties, but Anna couldn't quite picture the atmosphere of a rural village fête working here, tombola stands and raffle ticket confetti flying around the tarmac between rows of crumbling student lets, party flats, council estates, and older long-time Hackney residents. She had visions of a row of small trestle tables covered in cheap gingham cloth, groaning under the weight of Victoria sponge cakes and jugs of watery home-made lemonade.

When she stuck her head out of the living room window on Saturday morning, though, it was to find lines of shiny colourful metallic bunting strung between the lamp-posts. Each triangle caught the light and swayed, rainbow-coloured shards of metal in the breeze. Food stalls were setting up all the way down the pavement, the road already closed to traffic. Inside a gazebo on the estate next door, somebody was testing a sound system, boxes stacked full of vinyl piled up in the car park. Every few moments the harsh electronic static of amplifiers and leads being connected disturbed the quiet morning with a sudden buzz. There was laughter from inside the tent, the noise of someone being shushed each time they accidentally plugged things in while they were switched on.

By afternoon it was too loud to relax

inside, and too hot to close the windows. Anna headed out into the fray with Holly and Libby, milling elbow to elbow with the crowds beneath hazy clouds of yellow sunshine. People flooded the street, flowed in from the side roads, carrying streamers, balloons and loud speakers.

She kept seeing Jack even though he wasn't there. Her eyes magnetically tracked any dark-haired man who wandered past, following him along the pavement until a turn of the head, or some other small detail, convinced her that it was somebody else. And so it felt overdue, rather than surprising, when at last she spotted him, walking along with friends, holding a can of beer and laughing so hard that his eyes had almost disappeared inside his smile. He raised a hand to shield his face, an echo of the movement he had made when he was trapped out in the arid wasteland of her last nightmare, moments before she died, or woke up, or both.

Jack saw Anna and stopped, breaking away from his companions and crossing the road towards her, shaking her free from the memory of that dream until she could detect the combination of shampoo, scent, and soap, that she knew must be his smell. Thankfully this time the girls had enough tact to busy themselves being indecisive at the drinks stall behind her, and Anna found herself standing alone beside him once again. Thoughts, dreams and imaginings were replaced with flesh, blood and breath. Her eyes traced the curve of his jaw, the neatness of his earlobe, and the line an inch or so behind it where his dark hair began. Her cheeks felt hot. She needed him to speak first.

'Anna. I was sort of expecting to see you here today. Whereabouts have you moved to then?'

She craned her neck over the sea of heads stretching down the street, but it was too far and the people were too jumbled in front of everything for her to see her front door clearly. She pointed in the right direction.

'A place a few doors that way.'

Jack followed the line of her finger towards the other end of the street. 'I live up there.' He nodded in the other direction. He looked, for a second, as though she had answered his question from the other night, solving the mystery of their recognition. But then he sighed and turned back to her, confused. 'I really think I've met you before. Where did you use to live?'

'Brighton.'

Anna liked his direct questioning. After

the many fictional narratives her mind had provided for the two of them this past week, a face-to-face meeting might have been awkward, revealed a complete lack of meaning to one another, a reminder that they were strangers. But Jack felt as familiar here now as he did each time he appeared in one of her dreams.

She had seen her famous teenage crush in the flesh when she was twelve, some shiny pop singer she had fallen in love with who was barely older than her. He was having dinner with his family in the same restaurant as Anna and her parents. After an hour sitting at their table with Anna so senseless from excitement that she was unable to eat or speak, her dad had made her go over and say 'hello'. She could still remember that terrible jarring sensation, trying to line the face in front of her up against the one plastered across screens and posters and magazine covers, and finding it not quite fitting. The illusion that she knew him, that he knew her, that she mattered to him in some way purely by dint of having thought and talked about him for hours each day, was shattered when she stood in front of his polite but blank expression, forced to face her fanaticism as a fabrication.

But Jack smiled warmly, as if he knew

where they had gone together in her head, widening his eyes at her mention of Brighton.

'What?' she asked, when he didn't say anything. 'Did you go to Sussex University too?'

'No, Goldsmiths. How long did you live in Brighton for? Were you just there while you were studying?'

Anna hated answering that question. It made her sound so stay-at-home, so unadventurous. She shook her head. 'I grew up there; I was actually born there too. I've lived there my whole life, until this month.'

Jack smiled, and tilted his head to one side at her, taking this in. She wanted him to reach out and touch her face, or else to look away. Something about him just staring at her like that was too much.

'Mystery memory solved then?' He spoke slowly. His words had a question mark as though he still wasn't quite sure, as though he needed her to agree with his suggestion.

'You're from Brighton too?'

'I am.' He frowned. 'But I haven't lived there for fifteen years.'

Natasha's birthday party.

'Do you know someone from Brighton called Natasha Grove?'

He didn't. Anna clutched at half-formed

thoughts and dreamy details, false memories, nightmares and then, almost by accident, remembered all the shadowed places she had imagined putting Jack's hands. If Anna liked someone, if there was a connection or an attraction there, she usually knew from her easy free-flowing speech, the fact she felt relaxed in their company, happy and calm in their presence. This was different. Jack did draw her in; he made her want to stand closer to him, to watch his mouth while he spoke to her, and he mirrored her desire to unwind the complicated knot of some shared past. But he also made her feel exposed and self-conscious, jittery and over-alert. She spoke in short clipped sentences when she talked to him, unsettled and shy. Having a conversation was tiring, like learning how to speak all over again.

'We must be faces from the past then. We probably go even further back than I thought.' His voice was definite; the riddle had been unravelled. 'If you remember exactly where from, let me know. It's been bothering me.' His eyes lingered, fiery green in air that was filled with sunrays.

Jack's friends crossed over the road behind him to catch up, ducking and weaving through the moving hordes, a hand up in apology when one of them trod on somebody's foot. They introduced themselves and Holly and Libby ambled over to join the circle. It made the group too large to hold court comfortably in the centre of the crowd. Anna almost lost her balance from all the people pushing against them, trying to get past. Reluctantly, they parted ways. Jack gave her a quick kiss on the cheek and said into her ear, out of earshot from the others chattering noisily around them, 'We're having a few drinks at our flat when everything finishes out here. I would ask if I could have your number, but we seem to keep finding each other anyway, don't we? I'm sure I'll see you again.' He looked mischievous.

The midsummer sun dipped slowly, reluctantly, a hot pink drop of oil sinking through thick liquid. The crowd thinned, the road covered instead by the long dancing shadows of the few who were left, smiling at the gentle spots of rain that appeared for a few brief minutes before dry evening warmth prevailed. The girls ambled slowly towards home from the far end of the street, Holly ducking into a shop to buy another round of drinks on the way back. Libby and Anna stood on the pavement, waiting. She nudged Anna, pointing up to the first floor of a house nearby where a big French window was wide open over the street, a party inside getting into full swing.

'We made that mistake a couple of years ago. It was a nightmare. I had to take the morning off work on the Monday because we were still cleaning up.'

Holly joined them and they crossed the street, walking past the music, riotous whooping laughter, and the rhythmic sound of high heels dancing across wooden floors.

Anna walked straight into Jack. He had his head down, fishing in his pocket for keys, a clinking carrier bag of bottles cutting into the skin of his other hand.

'There you are,' he beamed. 'What did I tell you?'

He made it sound like he was joking, as though they hadn't really been looking out for each other all afternoon, even though Anna had thought of little else since he had kissed her cheek a few hours before.

'This is our flat. Why don't you all come up for a drink?'

That was how Anna, along with her new flatmates, ended up in Jack's flat, surrounded by his friends, a large crowd he had accumulated through his graphic design and illustration work living in London for years. A few less well-acquainted guests were causing most of the noise, taking full advantage of the open house atmosphere to continue their own more raucous festivities in the front room where the music was playing. Jack lived there with three friends. Anna had seen them in various configurations of ones and twos each time their paths had crossed.

The main areas of the house were scrappy and impersonal, neutral blank magnolia walls and bare wooden floors, but Anna poked her head around a bedroom door upstairs on the way back from the bathroom and knew instantly that it was Jack's. It was so similar to her own room, with half-finished artworks and doodles leaning against the wall and strewn across the desk. Only his work was mostly in monochrome, intricate black and white illustrations and designs, instead of her own colourful oil paintings. Jack made her jump when he appeared behind her, laughing at her fright, shaking his head in apology. He took her hand and steered her downstairs into the kitchen to introduce her to people.

'You were born on Clifton Terrace? Really?' Anna was tucked up on a window seat in one of the bedrooms. Jack's housemate Trystan had bravely allowed his own private space to become party overspill territory. 'Don't you think it's weird that we lived

135

almost next door to each other for years, and now I've moved a few hundred yards away from you again, in a completely different city?'

'I think the emigration route from Brighton to London is a fairly established one.'

'You know what I mean.'

Jack was sitting opposite her at the other side of the window. His legs were crossed, his toes grazing hers.

'It's coincidence, and don't people say that life is more strange without coincidences? With an infinite possibility of scenarios, it's natural that sometimes there are uncanny connections.' He nudged her foot. 'So why did you decide to move to London?'

Anna sighed, flattening her back against the wall behind her. Why *had* she moved to London? She asked herself the same question, silently, every time she woke up from another of her increasingly frequent and increasingly traumatic episodes.

'So many reasons.'

'Bad ones?'

'Not exactly.' She looked at him, braving herself to share too much. If only Holly were in the room with them instead of jumping up and down to music next door. Holly had done her a favour by telling all on that first night in London; the girls didn't know how much the nightmares upset Anna, but at least they knew about them. At least she didn't have to worry that she should find an excuse for the fact that last week she had sleepwalked into Sophie's room and asked her who invented paper. It was just a fact that had become accepted, even in the short time she had been there; Anna was a crazy sleeper. Jack was waiting for her to carry on talking.

'It was the right time. I got offered a great job here in London at the Whitechapel Gallery. My best friend, who I've lived with for years, already worked here; she spent most of her life on the train getting to the office and back. I shouldn't have stayed in Brighton for so many years.'

'How old are you?'

'Twenty-eight.'

'Why did you stay so long?'

'I loved it – I still do love it. It wasn't something I did against my better judgement, or forced myself to do. I enjoyed being close to my parents.' Jack smiled. 'They split up when I was younger. I worried about them a bit, wanted to be near them to make sure they were OK.'

'Do you not think they're happier now?'

'I guess they must be, but neither of them

has a new partner, no new relationship. I know children probably always think this when they're younger, but I still do; they were perfect together, as far as I remember at least. I didn't like the fact that they were both alone, so I probably stayed near home for longer than I should have.'

'You can't necessarily be perfect together forever. Maybe they like being alone. Are you alone?'

'Are you asking me if I'm single?'

Jack's eyes sparkled, but instead of replying he asked, 'Did they tell you why they broke up?'

'There was the obvious reason, the unfaithfulness; that's never a lucky charm. But my mum said the oddest thing when I asked her why. I told her what I just said to you, that they had always seemed so perfect for each other.'

'What did she say?'

'She said, "We were too similar, too close. We talked our love into exhaustion, and then it was just gone."'

'That's sad.' Jack unfastened the handle on the window beside him, clipping it on and off as the breeze blew in, gently cooling their skin. He laughed to himself, quickly and quietly.

'What's funny?'

'It's not funny. It's just the opposite of my dad's grand proclamations about romance and love. When I was about fourteen, this girl at school really fancied me.'

'I can't think why.' It was an easy admission that she wanted him, lightly disguised, sarcastic. Anna watched him take it in. He was grinning, nodding at what it meant.

'Well, exactly. Her name was Rosie. She told me she loved me, wrote me letters and left them in my desk in the form classroom, that sort of thing. I remember my dad saying she was very verbose for somebody who claimed to be infatuated. He said true love should be like a silent spell, unspoken and unwritten, that if you talked it through too much it would disappear, be undone.'

'That's quite a beautiful thing to impart to a fourteen-year-old.'

'Not really. He only said it because it was Valentine's Day, Mum was standing next to him, and he hadn't got her anything.'

She snorted. 'Did it work, the romance of few words? Are they still together?'

'We'll never know. They're not around any more.'

It was obvious what he meant. There was no other thing it could mean. Still, Anna hovered, unsure how to continue.

'You mean, they're not alive?' She wanted to have got it wrong, to have missed an obvious joke, something that would make him shake his head and explain.

'No, they're not alive.'

'I'm so sorry.'

'I never know what to say when someone says that.'

'What should I say?'

'Say what you want.'

'How old were you? What happened?'

Jack leant forward over his crossed legs towards her, peeling her hands away from where they gripped her knees. He threaded his fingers through hers.

'It was a long time ago. We'll talk about it another time. I'm not being cagey,' he squeezed her hand, 'but it's not great party chat, trust me.'

As it drifted past midnight, the large busy groups sharing loud conversations at high speed, the breaking glasses, slamming doors and thumping music, all began to settle down. Trystan turned the volume down. People relaxed, chatting in corners, kicking their shoes off and sitting down on the stairs or standing in tight-knit circles in the kitchen. A few were huddled under a makeshift blanket of jackets and coats on the sofa, smoking through the open window.

Anna and Jack had warmed into a gentle silence, her eyes starting to close where she sat. 'You look cold. Just say if you want to go home.' She shook her head and he smiled. 'Do you want to go up to bed?'

He reached down to pull her up to standing, wrapping an arm around her as they crossed the room. Holly was in the hall putting her shoes on, waiting for Libby to finish saying goodbye to somebody. She squeezed Anna's hand when they passed one another, clear that she wasn't going to be joining them on the walk home. They exchanged goodbye kisses in the narrow stairwell, before Anna and Jack climbed up the stairs away from everything, through the door and into his bedroom.

All evening it had been difficult to relax with him completely. He made her too aware of her own body, of how she was sitting, the way her limbs were arranged. An over-sensitive sensation prickled across her skin when he looked at her. By the time they got upstairs, all that tension had worn her out so that her nerves were quiet at last. Or maybe she was deliberately shutting them down because she wanted them to leave her be, to feel like herself again finally, to soften against his chest where they stood together in the middle of his room. She tried not to think about what might come for her in sleep if she lay down beside Jack, or to decide whether this odd sense of familiarity was special or sinister. It took such effort to block the nightmare out she had to close her eyes, screw them up tight, and shake her head ever so slightly in the darkness.

Jack's hands were on her hips, hot through her dress, but then he stepped backwards away from her, clicked the bedside light on, and went over to his wardrobe against the far wall. He rustled through a shelf at the top and handed Anna a white T-shirt, apologising that it was old, but assuring her it was completely clean. He stepped out of his jeans while she got changed, unzipping her dress and shaking it down to the ground, wriggling out of it. She saw him glance over at her, trying to be polite and not stare. It was too obvious; of course they didn't have to sleep together, not tonight, through a hazy mix of approaching sleep and the edginess she couldn't shake. They had only just met properly. And she didn't want to be blind when they did that for the first time, for it to happen around her while she tuned out, distracted by how anxious her attraction to him had made her feel. It was better like this, to watch him wanting her while she pulled his old white T-shirt over her sleepy head and climbed under the duvet. It was lovely. She lay down, warm, her heart swelling like it was breathing for her.

Jack had stripped down to his boxers before she saw his scar, a livid red bumpy line all the way from his right hip to the tip of his left collarbone, at his shoulder. He looked like he had been cut open and stitched up again, except it wasn't neat enough to be medical. When he held her across his chest in bed, she ran her finger across it, slowly, unable to stop an audible gasp escaping her as she followed it to its tapered point by his hip bone. She could feel him holding his breath while she explored it. He stroked her hair and when she spoke there were tears at the back of her throat.

'What's it from? Is it something bad?'

He shushed her. 'Yes, it's bad, but I'm fine. I'll tell you everything another time. I survived.'

# PART 2

# CHAPTER FOURTEEN

It was already bright and sunny when Anna woke up for the first time the next morning. She wasn't used to that. The backs of her eyelids glowed neon orange. For a second it looked like an illusion, the fiery afterglow of a violent explosion from her nightmare burnt onto the inside of her eyes. When she opened them the room would be dark and lonely, as it always was. Where was she?

'Morning.' Jack spoke as she flickered awake. Her first night in his bed and she hadn't shouted the house down. She sank further into the soft sheets, joyful at the discovery.

'Morning,' she replied, her voice thick with sleep. No sounds of life rustled from the other rooms.

If she reached out, stretched her hand towards him under the covers, she would feel that smooth bump of the deep red line that crossed his body, cutting him in two. She felt up to her left shoulder, to the small square of

147

patterned skin that was still there from when she had poured boiling water onto herself as a toddler. It happened when she had only just learnt to walk. Her parents weren't yet used to finding her stumbling alone around rooms she was never usually able to get into. She had reached up to investigate the patterned china mug perching on the edge of the wooden table above her and knocked it over, searing white-hot pain spreading across her body as its steaming contents flooded down over the baby softness of her chest. Her polyester pyjama top had melted into the skin on her shoulder, leaving an angry patch of it shiny and wrinkled, like plastic, when her dad ripped her clothes off and dowsed her in cold water. She saw Jack's scar, livid and red on his stomach as he jumped out of bed and pulled a T-shirt on.

Jack made coffee downstairs. Anna perched on the side of his bed and looked around for her clothes. There was a framed photograph sitting on top of the bookcase of Jack at about ten years old, standing in between his parents. Anna knew exactly where it had been taken, down on the Brighton promenade, almost to the inch, from the position of the main pier in the distance. They were standing in front of the heavy iron railings, the geometric design thickly covered in peeling light-green paint. There was a blur of pebbled shingle on the shore below them all, the sea stretching out behind. It felt illicit, to steal a glimpse of a bright, happy day in Jack's past, without him there to watch her doing it.

Her mum had had to spend a week in hospital when Anna was about the same age as Jack looked in the photograph. She had been born with a faulty heart valve that stopped working properly when she was only thirty-eight. She needed an operation to have it repaired or replaced. Anna had heard her panicked clipped words on the phone to her sister the night before she went into hospital.

'I don't understand how something can be *minimally invasive*. Either they're going to operate on my heart or they're not.'

Oblivious to the danger, and too young to appreciate the potential for tragedy, Anna only saw a series of inconvenient disruptions to her day. She didn't understand why she had to go to Mrs White's house before school. When her dad explained that he needed to be at the hospital to see Mum into theatre, Anna wondered why they couldn't just change the time of the operation. She sulked all morning, remaining rigidly unimpressed when Mrs White gave her Coco Pops for breakfast and let her put Take That on in the car. 'Fake food' and pop music were not usually allowed at home; it should have all been delightfully exciting.

She didn't see her dad in school that day at all. He wasn't waiting for her in the Art department when she finished, or at the gates. Instead, Mrs White drove her to meet both her parents at the hospital, where Anna was shocked by how pale her mum's face was, and how fiercely she hugged Anna from her bed. The anaesthetic had made her feel very ill. Anna thought she behaved better on the ward than she had done in the morning before school, sitting quietly on the funny smelling blue chair beside the curtains and hiding how upset she was when she found out her mum wasn't coming home for nearly a week. But her dad stalked around the house when they got back, his eyebrows slanted in scary diagonals on his face, the way they went when he was about to shout at her. He sighed a lot, and slammed the cupboard doors shut too hard while he cooked dinner.

They ate in silence. Anna lifted each trembling forkful of broccoli to her mouth, too frightened by her dad's mood to remind him that it was the only vegetable she didn't like. Big fat tears slid down her cheeks. Why was everything so different? She didn't say anything, hoping he wouldn't notice. Her mum's white arms had scared her, resting on the clinical blue hospital blanket with needles coming out of her hands, liquid pumping steadily into her veins from the bubbling gelatinous bag that hung above her head. Chewing slowly on her vegetables, Anna felt guilt settling inside her like the slow intravenous drip drip drip from that bag, ashamed that she hadn't realised how ill her mum was. If Anna could wake up to that day again, she decided she would behave differently; she would laugh at Mrs White's jokes, and be more patient about the fact Dad couldn't drive her to school.

But when her dad saw her crying, he jumped up and ran round to her seat. He wrapped his arms around her and rocked her back and forth until she realised, horrified, that he was crying too, great big heaving man sobs she had never heard before. His hysterics only made hers worse, and they held each other and wailed in the kitchen until he stopped and shook his head at the two of them, crouching there together.

'You've been so brave. I know today's not been much fun. Mum's going to be fine though; we're very lucky. She'll be back home and cooking us both dinner again in no time.' That made them both laugh; Elizabeth's skills in the kitchen were a family joke, on account of her not having any.

'Oh dear, really?' Anna asked, pleased when it made him cheer up a bit.

She was relieved she wasn't going to be told

off, and pleased that her mum would soon be able to take off that sad bleached-out patterned hospital gown and come home, but why had it taken her so long to realise how serious the situation was? Her mum had spent the whole day lying unconscious on an operating table, her life in the hands of people who knew nothing about her except her blood pressure, body temperature and pulse.

She hadn't been as much of a selfish brat that day as she thought; she had just never entertained the thought that her mum might die, that she even could. It hadn't registered as a possibility. Jack was about the same age in the photo as she had been back then. His happiness was crushing, innocent and ignorant of what was ahead.

It was always easier to let your imagination run away with you when you were that age, to indulge in terrifying and improbable scenarios, than it was to fear something as ordinary as an unsuccessful operation. Anna spent hours panicking that her parents' bodies had been taken over by aliens or criminals. She would make up wildly sensational horror stories while her dad did something entirely ordinary, like leave her in the car for two minutes as he ran into the shop to buy milk. When he jumped back in the driver's seat, Anna would be convinced he was somebody else, an evil monster using her dad's body to trick her into believing it was her father. She would work herself up into a frenzy, utterly convinced that he wasn't who he claimed to be, setting him a series of secret test questions that he had to answer to prove he was still her dad: 'What is the name of my second favourite teddy bear? Not my favourite, my *second* favourite?'

It never occurred to her that a sophisticated shape-shifting alien criminal would probably be able to get hold of this information too. And those fears were second only to the bad dreams where her parents left her, abandoning her somewhere to go off to the other side of the world, leaving Anna to wake up shivering and crying, fearing that nobody was there to look after her.

That was her solid ten-year-old list of possible future disasters, all of them exaggerated supernatural nonsense. She had no grim, real-world possibility where someone simply fell ill, where her mum died of complications during heart surgery. How long had it taken Jack to accept that his parents were never coming back?

'Coffee?' Jack pulled the door open with his foot, a mug in each hand.

'Sorry.' Anna dropped the photograph like it had scalded her, but his face didn't falter.

'It's there to be looked at. It's fine.'

She stared back at the two identical copies of the same smile. 'You—'

'—Look so like my Dad. I know. I still do; let me show you a picture of him when he was my age.' He pulled out an album from the drawer beside his bed, individually laminated photo-sized pages packed inside a cumbersome spine, like a book of carpet swatches. It had been open, as though he was always halfway through it, a book he read at bedtime every night. There was his dad, leather jacket and 1970s flares, a darkly handsome glance from under an artfully dishevelled haircut that was meant to look as though he didn't care much for style or fashion.

'See, still uncanny.'

'The fashion, too,' she grinned at him, teasing. 'It's nice that you look so like him.'

'It's nice that it's so obvious he's a part of me, but it's eerie for the rest of the family. I show up and they think they've been visited by a ghost.' He lay down on the bed. Anna settled next to him, propping herself up on the pillows.

'Do you think we could have gone to the same school, before you left Brighton? Where did you go when you moved?'

'I came here to London straight away, lived with my aunt for a few years further south while I did A-levels, and went to university down there. And it's unlikely we were at school together; I was at Brighton College for Boys. I must have been a couple of years ahead of you. You said you were twenty-eight?'

'I did. So, what's it like over the hill?'

Jack nudged her indignantly so that she had to hold her coffee cup out over the carpet to stop it from spilling onto the bed covers. 'I'm still on my way to the top, but the view's meant to be better from up there anyway. What school did you go to?'

'Lewes Old Grammar.' She frowned at yet another dead end. 'My dad taught art there.' She blew on her coffee. 'Maybe we just walked past each other so many times when we were young that we've stored each other's faces in our memory.'

'Maybe.' Jack smiled. 'Maybe we'll never know.' He kissed her on the mouth, not hidden and half-seen in the middle of the dark night, but open and honest, wide awake in front of the rising sun.

* * *

Her dad's van was parked up outside the flat when she walked home, the engine still running. She knew the number plate from years of school pick-ups, trips into town and long drives down to their holiday cottage in Devon. As she got closer, the driver's door swung open and he stepped out onto the pavement, lean and weather-beaten as always. His skin was darkened from the hours he spent outside walking, gardening, or painting on the coast – 'my pensioner's perma-tan', he called it. He walked round the back of the van to open the doors and spotted her, his keen blue eyes smiling as Anna broke into a skipping half-run.

'What perfect timing,' he shouted down the street, spreading his arms out wide to hug her. Perhaps it was spending the night next to someone who was so burdened by the hollowed-out shape left by his lost parents, but Anna felt overwhelmed with gratitude for the healthy beating, loving heart of her father. She grabbed him round the waist and squeezed him so hard that he had to step backwards a couple of paces to stay balanced.

'What are you doing here? How did you know I'd be in?'

'Why wouldn't you be in? It's a Sunday. I thought people relaxed at home on Sundays.'

'That was me coming home now. You're very lucky.'

He spread his hands. 'That's me: lucky. Don't you live with about fifty other women?'

'Four, Dad.'

'Well, one of them would have been in.'

She shook her head. It was typical of him to embark on an impulsive journey that he'd pleasantly decided might be quite a nice thing to do, but not to make any plans to ensure it would work out. He refused to buy a mobile phone. He absolutely refused to buy a satnav and, sure enough, when Anna peered through the driver's window, she could see reams of paper with directions printed on them, an out-of-date ring-bound *A to Z of London*, and a few scribbled notes about one-way systems. She raised her eyebrows at him.

'I got a little lost.'

The funny thing was, she knew he wouldn't have been put out if nobody had been at home. He would have just driven back to Brighton again, maybe gone to the park first, or stopped off on the way home if he found somewhere pretty to sit and read his book. When they eventually caught up on the telephone, he would say something like, 'I saw the outside of your house the other day, your feminist commune. It looks lovely; great kerb appeal.' And that would be that. She wondered how they had ever let him loose in the classroom.

'Why don't you see what's in the van?' He sidestepped towards the back, pulling at the door handles with a flourish. 'Go on, stand there while I open it up.'

She peered inside the darkness. The whole thing smelt of fresh wood, paint and varnish. There was one large canvas leaning against the side in polythene, tethered down with ropes to stop it from flying around on the journey.

'I can't see. It's wrapped up.'

He jumped up inside the van and pushed it towards her so she could help him lower it onto the road. 'You're always asking me to make another *Circles* for you.' He looked excited, his teeth and eyes shining at her from the shadows. 'I've finally done it, as promised. It was supposed to be a house-warming gift. Sorry it's a bit late; the bloody paint took an age to dry.' They pulled the canvas out of the back of the van together. 'I hope your walls are high enough.'

It was big, bigger than the first one. It was beautiful. Anna looked down and saw a summer sunset, diffused through the layers of clear plastic wrapping around it but visible. It was like the sky at the most beautiful time of day, burnt oranges and pinks rising to bright white yellow and sinking down into deep red, that crisp black circle lying across the soft wash of colour behind. They put it up in her room; it was almost the full height of the back wall. He hung the rest of her paintings for her, the canvases that were still propped up around the edges of the carpet, shrugging off Anna's excuse that she hadn't had a second to do it since moving in.

'It's just nice to know I'm still useful for something. That's going to be wonderful. It's quite chilling.' He pointed at her painting in-progress, the only thing she was working on at the moment: the nightmare eyes.

Anna showed him round the house. He peered through the garden window when they got into the kitchen – 'this is the bit where you make me a cup of tea' – and Anna filled a tray with two mugs of tea and a plate of fresh fruit.

'Go and sit in the sun. I'll follow you out.' He was already halfway to the door.

'I've been meaning to ask you something.' They were side by side on the garden bench, eyes closed like Mediterranean lizards in the heat. 'Why did you decide to call it *Circles* when there's only one circle?'

'Because it's not just about that circle.' He chewed on a grape, thoughtfully. '*Circles* wasn't the original title for that piece anyway, not the one that I chose initially.'

'What did you want it to be called?'

'*The Circles We Draw*. Elizabeth made me change it.'

Anna twitched whenever he called her mum by her first name; it always took her a second to work out who he was talking about.

'She thought it was too pretentious, which I didn't agree with. Still don't. But she pointed out that it constricts the interpretation, and even the intention, to just one instead of many. Now that I concede she was absolutely right

159

about. *Circles* is much truer, more open.'

'Why do you need it to be open?'

'It's about so many different things.'

'I thought circles were meant to symbolise eternity – the never-ending shape.'

'They do. It's a never-beginning shape as well, though, and supposedly one of man's first symbols – one of the first that held significance. That's why it features so often as a magical shape, a protective circle.'

'Like a fairy ring?'

'Or Stonehenge.'

'Or the Dharma Wheel.'

He swirled his tea. 'Or a clock.'

'So why did you want to call it *The Circles We Draw*?'

'A circle implies a centre. Each person constructs their own universe within a bigger world. We all draw our own horizons, mark out a circle around us, make ourselves the centre. But it's all just an illusion, because of the circles we draw.'

'Mum was right, that is pretentious.'

'It's very easy to discount a good idea with that word.'

'I remember you once calling it—'

'—*A knee jerk response to the deeper subjects in life by pitifully small thinkers*. Not one of mine, an old friend from art school. Now he *was* pretentious.'

160

'Not all clocks are circles though.' Anna flashed her digital Casio at him.

'That,' he pointed, 'is a watch. And the circular clock is the most interesting circle of them all.'

'Why?'

'It hints at another way of seeing time, more natural than our rigid linear sequence of past then present then future.'

'Funny, I was watching something the other day about a tribe somewhere – Papua New Guinea I think – where they believe time flows uphill.'

His eyes twinkled. 'Fascinating, isn't it? Some cultures believe the tenses develop simultaneously, present in the middle, past below us, future above us: you can move between the three of them at any one time.'

'That's creepy.'

'Is it? I think it's magical. Creepier, if that's the right word, to be the tribe that has no concept of time whatsoever, no verb tenses, nothing. Or perhaps they are liberated in ways we can never know.'

'So why is a clock a circle?'

He shrugged. 'Maybe time is a circle and we're all sitting at a certain point on a huge repeated cycle, rather than an ever-progressing line. It makes sense in a way. We go round in circles from one to sixty, seconds and minutes.

We go from day to night, from spring to summer, to autumn to winter and back to spring again, all the planets spinning ceaselessly in space. Our whole life is arranged in cycles. Perhaps birth, life, death and rebirth all fit into that too.'

'You sound like you believe in reincarnation.'

'That's the beauty of being a flighty and non-committal painter; I don't have to believe in anything. I think about all this a lot, but I certainly wouldn't dedicate myself to one interpretation.'

It was true. Long before Anna was born, he had lived in an ashram in India for twelve weeks. He observed dawn purging rituals by drinking pints of salt water, passing thin ropes through his nostrils, and spending hours in seated meditation on the banks of the Ganges. Years later, he had camped with the Druids in a scruffy mud-covered tent down on the Cornish coast for the month of the summer solstice; they still had Reverend Druid John Morley to stay for the weekend every now and then. More recently, he had painted a series of bold colourful interiors while spending a school summer holiday living with a group of French squatters in a huge crumbling château in the countryside outside Yvelines, near Versailles – 'I'm only immersing myself in situations of relative luxury from now on. I'm far too old to sleep on the hard ground.' He didn't hold on to the attitudes or outlooks, though they must have shaped him in some way. They were adventures, born of curiosity and a constant craving for new stimulation, rather than the desire to discover one truth, or adopt a single belief system.

'If you had to believe in something, though, one way of seeing the world, what would it be?'

He turned his hand through the air, his wrist circling around in the sun. Anna saw Jack's hand making the same motion, when they had first spoke, his fingers travelling in a moving circle through the night.

'Just that, whatever will come around, comes around – is coming around. Something like that.'

Anna looked over at him, shiftily. 'You know, I've met somebody up here.'

'Already? Fast mover.'

'It's more confusing than that: I remember him from somewhere, and he says he remembers me.' She frowned. 'Or maybe that's not quite it. There's a definite sense of familiarity though, as if we have seen each other before, or already know each other. What you're saying about time being more fluid or flexible makes me think, maybe we

163

could have met before in the cycle?'

He shook his head. 'What you're talking about sounds like something else: attraction. I'm serious.' She had started laughing, embarrassed. 'Love – or lust – can feel like that. It's nature's beautiful way of creating the illusion of fate, the *this is meant to be* sensation, because we humans are so chronically averse to randomness.'

'We are, aren't we?'

'When I first met your mum, I saw her name written down somewhere, on a letter I think, while I was staying at her flat. *Elizabeth Rose Golding.* I knew I had already met her, already known her or was meant to. The name was so familiar, so *right*.' He chuckled in gentle mocking of his younger self.

Anna looked at him sideways, his sunlit profile tilted back and up to the sky, the hairs on his arms shining silver. 'You've got paint on your T-shirt as always.'

He stuck his chin down to look at a messy splodge of blue up near his shoulder. 'But, at least ninety-seven per cent of my T-shirt doesn't have paint on it. Which is quite an achievement.' He gave her a squinted grin and his skin sprang back into its happy crow's feet, smile lines that it travelled to often.

'You're not meant to be with anyone, are you, Dad?'

'Certainly not – not at the moment anyway,

but who knows what might happen. *You*, I think, are meant to see this man again, if that is where you were coming back from when you so merrily skipped towards me earlier.'

Anna blushed. 'Why?'

'Because you looked like you'd been painted by the sun. I've never seen you so lit up.' He squeezed her shoulder. 'Be careful, but above all, be brave.'

# CHAPTER FIFTEEN

Jack clinked his coffee cup against Anna's, in commemoration of their achievement. 'At last, we meet up on purpose.' He waved his mobile phone at her. 'It almost felt old-fashioned, texting you.'

'Shall we go back to how we were doing it before then?'

Jack looked around them furtively, protecting their secret from unwelcome eavesdroppers. 'What, magic?'

'We could give it a go.'

He needed to drop some prints off at a shop near the Whitechapel Gallery, and had texted Anna to see if she had time for a coffee that week. Her nerves did a shivery backflip when his name appeared on her screen, shining and illuminated, and she replied immediately, spending the next few minutes eyeing her phone as though it were an unpinned hand grenade. She was a teenager again, briefly, navigating the treacherous landscape of text messaging, remembering the way she used to clutch her plastic Nokia between sweaty palms and wait for a reply. There was no danger now of finding her nine-message-capacity inbox already full and unable to download new texts, of having to delete things and wait for everything to reload; the technology had advanced, but the helpless anxiety was almost identical.

'Seriously though, I can't just have you in here as "Anna". What's your surname?'

'Caldwell.'

She didn't have to ask his. Jack's full email address came up when he texted her, and so Anna had already stopped hoping for what might possibly be the final glimmer of recognition. She had fingered her way across the shiny surfaces of every single photograph in that box of family photos, waiting for a forgotten face to trigger a memory of his name. She had written it down on paper and typed it out on her computer screen, just to look at it, closing her eyes and trying to summon up the same sense of fated familiarity that her dad had experienced when he first discovered her mum's full name. She had come up with nothing. Reluctantly, she admitted that she definitely didn't know the name 'Bridger'.

But when she gave him hers, Jack clapped his hands. 'I've got a painting here in the London flat that I brought up from my parents' old house.

They bought it at one of those Sussex Guild art fairs. It's got Daniel Caldwell written on the back of it. Are you related? Didn't you say your dad was an art teacher?'

Anna smiled at Jack's memory of their first proper conversation, perched on his window sill in the early morning.

'That's my dad! It's up in your flat here?' He nodded. 'I didn't notice it at the weekend. He came over actually, on Sunday afternoon after I left yours. I wish I'd known.' She smiled as she said it, imagining her dad's reaction to this news. *What terrible taste, really, I take it all back: never see him again.*

'You wouldn't have seen it past all the people on Saturday – it's in the hall above the stairs and it's really big and black. It would have just looked like a massive shadow.'

'I know the one you mean. He did loads of those, just painting in black for weeks. They remind me a bit of Rothko.'

'That's sort of why I took it with me. I dream of having a Rothko on the wall, but there are no possible futures to my life where I am able to afford one. Oh God, is that really rude?'

'No, no, it's a solid marketing strategy: economical art for the frugal Colour Field fan. I'll suggest it to him.' Anna laughed.

'There's something tortured about covering a canvas in so much black, I always thought. I don't know what it's called, do you?'

'It's called *Kaamos*. It's funny that you think it's emotionally dark. It's not actually an abstract: it's Kilpisjärvi at night, the darkest part of the winter on the north-westernmost tip of Finland, in Lapland.'

'What's Kaamos?'

'Polar night. The squares, all those straight edges of black that you can make out are the edges of the town buildings. You can see a few stars too, if you look closely. You can in most of his black paintings anyway.'

'The tiny splashes of white paint near the top?'

'Exactly. It's a skyline.'

'Were you there with him?'

'We went there for Christmas when I was about thirteen.'

Anna could remember her dad painting it. He didn't do any art while they were out there, and she worried that he wasn't enjoying the trip. He usually went alone on these sorts of things. She panicked that perhaps having her and her mum there with him was blocking his work. But when they got home he bought a stack of huge canvases and settled down in his studio. He bought bottles and bottles of black paint: Ivory Black, Chromatic Black, Mars Black, Black Spinel, Blue Black, Lamp Black, Perylene Black, and Black Pitch. He mixed them with each other. He tried drying them with a hairdryer to find a different colour, tried leaving them out in the winter air, pegging the samples to the washing line like an experimental clothing collection hung out to dry. 'Black is the new black,' he would repeat when he got tired, rubbing his eyes and covering his face with the paint. She wasn't sure if he had sold all of the pieces, or if there were still more Kaamos skylines sitting in his attic.

She shook her head at Jack. 'I can't believe you've got one of my dad's paintings hanging on your wall.'

'I bet my parents knew what it was of. It's probably why they bought it. We went to Tromsø in Norway one Christmas for a holiday, to find the Northern Lights.'

'I'd love to see them.'

'Well, we didn't: it was too cloudy. It was a really dark couple of weeks. Probably not as black as Lapland, but the sun didn't rise properly the entire time we were there. I remember it feeling really strange, full of foreboding, like there was this horrible black death shroud over everything.'

Anna's eyes flickered when he said that. She had occasionally wondered whether that short spell of darkness in Finland had permanently damaged the delicate cogs of her body clock. The nightmares had started not long after. Her sleep had been disrupted. Born in Brighton, was her body even equipped to maintain its natural rhythms in an environment where day never came? If she had seriously thought it was a possible explanation for everything that had followed, she might have raised it as a question at her doctor's appointment. But now, talking about that holiday again and hearing somebody else admit that the constant darkness had affected them, the suspicion started circling again, demanding to be considered.

'When we took off out of Finland, got away and up above the clouds into the sunshine, I almost cried with joy at the light.'

Jack was nodding, understanding exactly what she meant. It was like a grown-up version of an early conversation with her first boyfriend. The first time she had met Luke, they had been reassured and unnerved by the beautiful catalogue of similarities that linked their thirteen-year-old lives. They had both broken their coccyx, they both hated cats, they both thought Nirvana was overrated – they were destined to be together. Clearly that hadn't worked out. She couldn't believe she was sitting here in her late twenties comparing Jack Bridger to Luke Jamieson from her Year 9 form group. Holly maintained it was a common but ridiculous mistake, to try and take lessons or warnings from your previous relationships or encounters – 'It's counter-productive. Just remember: every single relationship you've ever had up to the one you're having now – if you're having one – hasn't worked out, so it's pointless thinking about them. Unless you're still with all of them, which would be stressful and extremely time-consuming.'

Anna tapped Jack's arm. 'Let's see the book you bought. I love that shop.'

He had been paying for something in the gallery shop when she came down to meet him, and pulled out a plain blue book with bold lettering across the front of it. 'It's Descartes. I was looking for it at home last week to read for an illustration I'm working on, and I couldn't find it. Pure luck I spotted it in the shop.'

Anna held it, looking at the cover and trying to work out whether she had heard of it. '*Cogito ergo sum*. Or is that from something else?'

'I think that's Descartes, but I'm not sure it's in this. It's a meditation on the proof of God's existence, but the beginning is all about trusting our own experiences, or not. How dreams can completely erode our sense of what's real and what isn't.'

'How do we know when we are dreaming and when we are waking?'

Jack nodded, solemnly. 'Keanu Reeves asked the very same question.'

Anna went back to the bookshop after Jack left, and bought her own copy. She took it out onto the flat roof below her bedroom at the back of the house when she got home, sitting crookedly on one of the old half-perished garden chairs with a cup of tea balancing on a coaster on her knee. The evening air was still hot. She was facing west, the setting sun trailing its fingers over and across the lip of the roof and down onto a corner of the garden below. She read until it was too dark outside to see, her eyes growing tight and tired in the shadows.

She understood the anxiety written across these pages; so many of her own fractured and fragmented thoughts were brought together in that one long stream of doubt. Her dreams exposed fallibility in things that should have felt real and concrete, made her mind mistrust her senses, constantly pitted her intellect against her imagination as she compared her visions with some preconceived idea about what was possible. What if she was wrong, and there were dimensions to reality that she hadn't even uncovered yet? Jack might be sitting up the road just a few houses away reading the same thing. What illustration was he working on that he needed to study and consider the tricks our minds play on us while we sleep?

Anna kept journals when she was a girl as though it was her religion. Every evening she devoted an hour to sitting at her bedroom desk – an old wooden classroom one with a hinged lid that her dad had stripped of its compass-carved graffiti and painted purple – faithfully recording the events and emotions of the day just past. Occasionally she missed a day, and it preyed on her mind with the guilt of a sinner who had forgotten to confess. It never felt the same to write things retrospectively, a few days or even weeks later when thoughts had had a chance to settle, had been analysed and assessed. The mistakes she made when she wrote with furious immediacy, desperate to transfer what was inside onto paper, were often helpful to read later. They revealed problems she didn't realise were troubling her. The strange and incorrect ways she interpreted the actions of her friends and family taught her things about herself.

If she wrote down her dreams now, recorded the visions and the fears they evoked immediately upon waking, she might be able to read through it all in a few weeks' time and spot something important and unexpected. Her own hidden corners were not necessarily areas of herself that she wanted to look into deeply but carrying on as she was, and not doing anything to try and work it out, didn't feel like an option.

She would write a nightly download of all the places she had gone, and the things she had seen in sleep. Maybe she would start spotting things, make discoveries, gain mastery over the hallucinations. That speeding car was an obvious similarity, but there were so many other smaller connections, mirrors between the dreams, too many to keep in her head at once. A dream diary could help her keep track of the tangents and the permutations. And then there was the major change; the introduction of Jack into almost every single nightmare. That development made working this out all the more urgent.

She climbed back over the window sill and up to her room to look for a blank notebook in her desk drawer that she could use. There was a message from Jack on her phone, asking if she was home from work yet, if she wanted to come over. A wave of heat passed strongly across her face. Would it be too much, to see him twice in one day, the third time that week? But his question had turned the corners of her mouth up into a smile. She rested her hand on her stomach to calm the butterflies, and packed an overnight bag, silently intoning her dad's advice to be brave. He couldn't possibly know how much steely courage it would take to lie down next to Jack again, to risk it all disintegrating in a mortifying crumble of unexplained paranoia in the early hours when she was chased from dreams of disaster. It would be too much to dare to hope for, a second silent sleep beside him.

# CHAPTER SIXTEEN

Walking up the stairs behind Jack in the beautiful shadow of *Kaamos* was like coming home. They hovered in front of it for a few moments on the way up, standing side by side, their eyes finding the stars, the tops of buildings, the black night. Anna imagined she could see right through the layers of paint to her dad's pencil markings underneath. He had pinned his scribbled sketches of Kilpisjärvi on to the side of the canvas, and frowned at them while he decided whether to represent the configuration of those small wooden outhouses faithfully, or take artistic license for the sake of the composition.

'When did you go to Norway?'

'I'd just turned fifteen, so ... Christmas '99.'

Anna smiled: of course, these coincidences would stop surprising her soon. 'That's the same year we went to Finland.'

Jack's house evidently kept later hours than hers, which had already been quiet and dark when she slipped downstairs and through the front door. Here, everybody was still up, conversations in full flow. The low tones of a serious discussion emanated from the front room, and two women joined them in the kitchen as Jack was pouring Anna a glass of wine. She recognised their faces from Saturday's party, the girlfriends of two of Jack's housemates.

'Anna, this is Hayley and Eva.'

'Come and join us next door for a bit.'

Jack read Anna's mind. 'I'd love to but we're both shattered. It's been a long week.'

'It's only Wednesday.'

'Exactly.'

Anna just wanted to be with Jack, alone, to sit in his bedroom and look at his drawings, to nose through his commercial graphic-design projects, to see the typography he did in his spare time. There were scattered splashes of paint on the polished wood of his drawing table, hardened multi-colour droplets. His bigger designs, the ones framed over his bed, were almost entirely rendered in crisp black and white, often with one single bright accent of shining red or electric blue – They were imaginative, unusual compositions, done to commission on a strange variety of topics from retro logo designs for shower gel and a pet shelter rebrand, to the poster design for a children's literature event.

Jack showed her the fonts he had been working on, stashed in the top drawer of a filing cabinet that only just fitted between his bedside table and the wall, its frame squeaking each time he pulled a drawer open. For each typeface, he had cut out large versions of every letter on squares of paper, putting one ring through the corner of them all, so that you could flick from front to back through the entire lower case, then upper case alphabet, and onto the numbers. He had created comic-book characters of his friends, their profile images pinned to the wall above his desk. They were drawn holding strong triumphant stances, surrounded by weapons or talismans, symbols of their most important character traits. Underneath these, Jack had captured them moving nimbly as a group through the frames of a comic strip, having adventures, exhibiting violence, heroism and true love all within one thirty-inch strip of card.

'Those are just doodles,' he gestured to his home-made cast of superheroes. 'This is the work I actually get paid for.'

His illustration work was darker, more

intricate and elegant. Great swirling walls of lines swallowed the images at their edges, and turned each scene into something more abstract. Everything was half-drawing, half-design. One of his bookshelves was filled with publications that he had done all the design work for: the illustration; the layouts; and the typeface. They were mostly self-published or small-label anthologies by poets and essayists, the sort of works that were celebrated anywhere people were hungry to discover something they hadn't yet been told about. The effect of such intensity etched across every page, and of Jack's painstaking attention to detail and beauty, turned them all into precious collectables.

'What illustration did you buy that book for earlier?'

He twitched. Had he changed his mind, no longer thinking it was a good idea to give Anna free reign to look through everything? He closed the book she was exploring over her hands, gently but unmistakably retreating from his own show and tell.

'I haven't started it yet. Maybe I'll show you when it's done, if you like.' He didn't sound like he wanted to.

'That's OK, you don't have to.' She had said something wrong, but she wasn't sure what. It was nearly midnight. Perhaps they were both just tired.

On her way to the kitchen to wash up the empty wine glasses like a good house guest, Anna froze; she had heard her name in a sentence. Somebody had said, 'Anna seems nice.' There was less noise from the living room. Hayley and Eva were the only two still up, chit-chatting in confidence now that the boys had headed up to bed. Anna slid silently over the tiles on her socks, back towards the door. She kept the wine glasses in her hand so that she would have an action to be getting on with instantly if she were discovered. True, she had barely met them both, but 'seems nice' implied they were leaving room to be proven wrong. And why was the other hesitating, rather than replying, agreeing?

'What?' The first voice spoke again. It sounded like one of them had pulled a face.

'I'm just not getting my hopes up again. I never understand why he doesn't give anyone a bit more of a chance. Besides, he's only just met her.'

Anna was right up against the door to the main room now, hovering in the protective darkness of the landing, frowning at the long silence that followed this strange remark. When a reply came, it was spoken in hushed conspiratorial tones, a secret being shared, lines of discretion being crossed on tiptoes.

'Chris says Jack hates sharing a bed with anyone.' That voice must be Hayley then. Chris's girlfriend was sharing a conversation with Eva that she shouldn't be, a conversation that Chris should never have had with her, something Jack probably regretted discussing in the first place.

'What do you mean? Is it a sex thing?'

'He says Jack has nightmares.'

'Why would that stop him from getting a girlfriend?'

'I think they're really bad ones. Apparently he prefers to sleep alone.'

Eva sighed like she didn't understand. 'We'll have to see what happens then.'

'Exactly, but like you say, I'm not getting my hopes up again. I really liked Jasmine.'

'Me too.'

Anna felt an uncontrollable green fist of jealousy curl inside her chest. She wanted to know exactly who Jasmine was, what she looked like, the colour of her eyes, where she lived, whether Jack had loved her, or had even thought he loved her for a brief mistaken moment before deciding he was wrong. It was the first normal sign that strong feelings were brewing. The strange recognition, the connections and the dreams, they all just made her feel crazy; this regular stomach-clenching envy was refreshing.

She sped across the room to the sink when she heard them turning the door handle, but they didn't come anywhere near the kitchen, just padded upstairs to bed. Did Hayley know how long Jack had been having nightmares for? Had they started when he was plunged into a world without sunrise, resetting his clocks with twenty-four hours of darkness, the same way her body could have been recalibrated by the Lapland Kaamos? Had something scientific, rather than mystical, happened to the two of them? She looked at the painting again on her way back up to bed. It would be too strange if they had been standing there looking at her dad's depiction of the environment that had damaged them both.

Anna lay quietly beside Jack in the dark, listening to the ins and outs of his breathing, the little pauses in between. She had her brand new dream diary stashed in her bag beside the bed, its virgin pages ready and waiting for her to fill them with whatever came for her in sleep. If she had an instant activity to direct her fear towards when she woke up it might focus her, stop her from panicking and trapping Jack in the tangled bed sheets beside her as she thrashed around like a frightened bird. Did she want that to happen or didn't she, now that she knew his nights weren't peaceful either? What had Chris meant when he told Hayley that the nightmares were really bad? She very much doubted Jack had ever thrown himself down the stairs, smashed a window, or woken up paralysed and unable to breathe.

Anna watched the ceiling. Her lips had held on to Jack's kisses from earlier that day after coffee, and from this evening before she had gone downstairs to put their wine glasses in the sink. She looked across at him and saw him looking back, open eyes glinting at her from the other side of the bed. It was too exciting to relax, lying next to him like this. She was close enough to feel the heat from his body.

'I'm not sleepy any more,' she whispered. His hand found her under the sheets, crawling across the mattress until his fingers slid around and through her own. The room was quiet. The darkness erased everything. They were entirely alone in a wide blank space that Jack reached across, holding his arms out to Anna and gathering her close, putting his mouth against hers.

Anna wasn't expecting it to feel so easy, after the quick excitable way her heart beat just talking to him, but it was, her body melting comfortably to Jack's own bare skin.

She didn't have to ask him to do anything differently, to move his hand slightly, to hold her softer or tighter, to alter the pressure. Jack sensed what she wanted from him, knew how much to give, understood how much or how little she needed. It was a surprise that this was the first time they had done this, the first time he had held her there, kissed her there, that they had never been here before. She had to remind herself that she didn't really know him yet.

It was too natural to feel brave or courageous. It was softer than that, a sigh in the air around them, a letting go. They weren't forcing anything; they were simply moving with the current, allowing water to flow. There were moments when it was too intense. A strange rising tide of panic threatened to stop Anna's breath from filling her lungs as she looked up at Jack in the middle of it all and realised that she was looking into the same wide eyes that had somehow found their way into her nightmares. But then Jack held her tighter, and being overwhelmed became wonderful again.

Afterwards, he took hold of both her hands and guided them through the darkness to touch his face, the corners of his mouth.

'I'm smiling, just in case you couldn't tell.'

It was so deliciously simple to fall asleep that tears of frustration pricked the corners of her eyes when she woke up again a couple of hours later, terror raging hotly through her body like a fever, her heart beating so hard she worried it was making the bed move. She could have cried with disappointment. Car-crash debris littered the atmosphere in Jack's room, fragments of scorched car tyres, an explosive cloud of burnt petrol, reminding her that no bed was safe if it had her head resting on the pillow. She wanted to reach across and check that Jack's scar was still healed in that long knitted red line, instead of gaping wide open and leaking blood as she had just dreamt.

She lifted the notebook and pen from her bag and tiptoed out, trying to keep her ragged breathing as soft as she could without hurting her chest. She took it down to the kitchen. It would be the most natural place to be discovered in the dead of night, sitting alone with the lights on. She would hear anybody who came down the stairs with enough time to hide the book, pretend she was getting a glass of water.

Anna held her breath in her mouth, her heart thudding heavily in her chest as she put pen to paper for the first time, writing the date and the time, the image of Jack jumping out of the way of the car. He had fallen and landed on his back, his scar beginning to bleed again, peeling open to reveal a red sea filling his chest. Anna had knelt down beside him on the road and – she realised now – started looking around for that wound-up ball of golden thread that one of the gods had brought into her room. She hated it when her dreams connected like that, as though some ongoing disaster was developing in the spaces between each nightmare, a low hum in the background of every day. She hadn't been able to sew him up, and it was the look he had given her, lying on the ground in her arms and accepting that there was no hope left, that had woken her up. He had known that he was about to die. She hadn't been able to take it for a second longer, forcing her eyes open, forcing herself up and out of bed.

It was private and quiet down in the cool whiteness of the kitchen, but when she went back upstairs Jack was wide awake.

'I was just getting a glass of water,' she said and immediately panicked; she couldn't remember if she had run the tap while she had been down there, if Jack would have been able to hear it from upstairs anyway, or if it even mattered. Part of her wanted him to know she was lying, to press her for the truth so that she would have a way to draw it out of him, too, that he had nightmares. She lay back down beside him and rested her head on his chest. Her fingers travelled back to the line of his scar. Jack stroked her hair.

'It's from an accident when I was younger, the accident where Mum and Dad died.'

Anna stayed still and silent, wrapped up in a little ball against his side. She instructed her hand to carry on moving, to keep squeezing Jack's side, so he couldn't tell that she had stiffened slightly in expectation, so there wouldn't be too much pressure on him to share anything.

'They died there and then. I was in hospital for a long time, but I survived eventually.' He sighed. 'I didn't even know they had gone for the first few days. I was mostly unconscious. I just remember waking up a few times and wondering why they were never there at my bedside, when bits of my brain bobbed up for air.'

Anna didn't know how to reply to this, so she just said, 'I'm so glad you survived.' – because she was.

'When I found out I was going to live, I was terrified. I didn't want to be alive without them.'

'Do you think the same now?'

'No, but ... I wouldn't have noticed if I

had died. I was so out of it, I wouldn't have minded, or even known. It would have been so easy; they could have let me slip away to be with them.'

'I never imagined death being so simple.'

'I'm sure it's not, most of the time, but it would have been for me then. It will probably never be that simple again. I deserved it; I thought it was my fault they died, my decisions that put them in danger.'

She kissed his chest. 'You know that can't be true.'

'It is true. I just don't hate myself for it any more, most of the time. I even like the scar. It's easier to have something there, to remind me of it all, not that I'd forget. It stops me from worrying that one day people are going to start thinking I'm fine.'

'It will never be fine.'

He kissed the top of her head. 'So, now you know.'

Anna held on to him without saying anything else, without asking any of the questions she wanted to. What was the accident, and how could it possibly have been Jack's fault? Had they been attacked? Was that line what a clumsily healed knife wound looked like after fifteen years? How could anybody survive after being opened up so completely, their entire anatomy exposed to the open air?

She lay back with her eyes open and tried to remember whether Jack had been awake when she had opened the door. Had he been pulled through the exhausting rigour of a nightmare at the exact moment she had, or had she woken him when she climbed back into bed? She had dreamt about his scar, and then he had started telling her about it. Maybe these coincidences went so far and deep that they were lying side by side and dreaming of the same thing, warped mirrors of each other's lives.

She jumped when Jack spoke. She thought he had slipped away to sleep.

'Did you have a nightmare earlier? Is that why you went downstairs?'

'Yes.' Her voice sounded small in the darkness.

'I have them too sometimes.'

She squeezed his hand. 'Have you had them for a long time?'

'Fifteen years.'

'Me too.'

'Ever since my parents died.'

So, what was her excuse?

# CHAPTER SEVENTEEN

Anna caught sight of her reflection sliding along the sides of the glass city buildings beside her, as they walked down towards the Southbank. She watched the mirror image of her hand smoothing the silk of her green dress over her thighs against the gusts of wind that rippled past them. She looked smart, wearing a dress usually reserved for exhibition openings, black court shoes, and earrings that sparkled beneath her long hair. Jack's aunt was playing clarinet at the Royal Festival Hall, a rare London performance for her Cornish symphony orchestra. He had invited Anna to join him.

'Didn't you say Jack went to live with her when his parents died?' Holly had asked with interest, sitting on Anna's bed, still in her pyjamas on a Saturday afternoon, watching Anna get ready.

'For a few years, yes. Down in Cornwall.'

'So, is this him introducing you to the family?'

Anna had shaken her head, brushing off the significance of the invitation, until she met Jack on the corner of their street to walk to the train station and he held her hand and said, 'Thanks so much for coming. I know it's really soon for you to meet her, but they hardly ever play up here.' Anna really was nervous then, her stomach wriggling inside itself as they sat down at a bar on the river and ordered drinks, waiting for Marion to arrive.

'Why did you move down to Cornwall? Why not stay in Brighton with your other relatives?' Anna asked.

'I wanted to get out of there, go somewhere new. Marion was named in my parents' will. We were all really close to her, although she lived far away. I think Dad knew that she'd be amazing at looking after me. But it was about logistics too, even though that sounds dreadful; everybody else in the family already had their own children to look after.' He sighed. 'I remember the judge asking me if I agreed it would be the best thing. I had all these great memories of our Cornish summer holidays. I could picture the beach lifeguards, hanging round the harbour on a Friday night and surfing in their free time, and I thought ...' He hesitated. 'I thought it might be easier to completely change my life, to start a new one, rather than staying at home, trying to get over

191

everything in the place where it happened.'

Anna understood that feeling. Dipping in and out of somewhere, the way she used to on family trips to the south of France, she often caught herself assuming that a life spent running a tiny local patisserie in the Dordogne must surely be simpler, more beautiful, than the many-layered complexities of life back home. When you only saw a place in the calm golden light of summer holiday relaxation, you missed the detail, the personal stresses and strains that were the same the world over, no matter who you were or where you lived.

'And *was* it easier?' Anna thought of her own reasons for moving, how Jack had asked her if they were 'bad ones' when they had first talked about things that night at the party, by Trystan's bedroom window.

'Much easier. But probably still not the right thing to do.' He looked at her. 'I didn't have to go through some of the things I'd been dreading, arriving at school suddenly an orphan, getting stopped in the street for months afterwards by people to be awkwardly showered with condolences, or going into town with friends on a Saturday knowing that I couldn't just go home and have dinner with my mum and dad. It was like being on a really weird holiday. But I don't think I properly grieved for them until I came to London and had to look after myself. Marion had kind of incubated me from it all.'

'Maybe that's good, that you were a bit older when you finally dealt with it.'

'Maybe. That beachy future I'd imagined was never really for me anyway. I'm not sure if you've noticed – you probably haven't – but I'm not six foot two with an athletic, bronzed physique, intricate floral tattoos across my torso, and wavy shoulder-length sun-bleached hair.'

'Well, now that you mention it ...'

Jack reached out and twisted the bottom of Anna's hair around his fingers. He did that sometimes, when they were chatting. Anna would feel a sudden tugging at her head and look down to see him winding his hands through the bottom of her hair, near her waist. It made her want to close her eyes for a second.

'I thought I might be a bit of a third wheel.' Jack's aunt Marion arrived between them, smiling from one to the other as Anna jumped up, blushing, to say 'hello' and pull another chair over to their table.

Marion was tired after three hours of rehearsals, and Anna's own awkwardness disappeared as soon as she saw that it was Marion who was nervous, her hands fidgeting slightly as she apologised for the awkward time they were having to meet, in between her afternoon practice and the evening performance.

'Five p.m.'s a bit of a dead-zone, I'm sorry.' She gestured to the empty bar. 'But I have to eat at least two and a half hours before I play. Nobody wants white wine and ...' she glanced at the menu, '... chicken and leek risotto, flying out the end of one of the clarinets in the middle of a concert.'

'How did it go?' Jack asked her, calling a waiter over to take their orders.

'OK, I think.' She turned to Anna. 'We're performing with a London choir. You don't usually rehearse with them until the day itself, that's quite common. Sometimes the combination's magic, sometimes it's a bit more of a jigsaw puzzle. It went well, but we're being conducted by our musical director, and he's definitely an orchestral conductor rather than choral. They took most of the rehearsal to get used to him, to be honest.'

Jack put his hand on Marion's shoulder. 'Are you worried about it? Don't be.'

'I'm just concerned that I don't have enough embarrassing stories about you to really do this dinner justice.' She smiled at Anna, 'This is the bit that I've always looked forward to, as Jack's guardian, making him squirm in front of his girlfriend.' Anna wasn't sure that that's what she was, not yet at least. But the word gave her a funny teenage thrill. Did that mean

194

Jack had never introduced his previous girlfriends? He was thirty. Was that something to be flattered by, or worried about? She caught Jack's eye and he squeezed her hand.

'I don't think I've ever done anything that embarrassing, have I?' Jack asked.

'Oh please,' she scoffed. Jack looked nonplussed. 'You turfed me out of the house for your sixteenth birthday party and had to have a friend call me back a couple of hours later to look after you because you had apparently "mistaken a glass of vodka for water".'

They shared a bottle of wine over dinner, Marion insisting she would be fine as long as she had just one glass and a black coffee after the meal, before she left them with the bill and some cash, to go and get warmed up.

'Sorry it's been so brief.' She kissed Anna on the cheek. 'But it's wonderful to meet you. They'll no doubt whisk us all away when it finishes to share some congratulation, or commiseration, drinks with the rest of the gang. If I don't see you after, I hope you like it.'

Anna and Jack enjoyed a few moments sat in silence, their fingers laced together under the table, watching crowds of people pass back and forth on the other side of the glass, in front of the grey waters of the Thames, before they headed inside the concert hall to take their seats.

'It's just one piece? *A Sea Symphony*?' she asked, leafing through the programme amongst the bustle and conversation of the settling audience.

'Just that, yes. It's over an hour long though.'

'Have you heard it before?' They were murmuring now, their faces half-hidden behind their concert programme while people sat down around them, and the huge hall grew quiet.

He nodded. 'They perform it almost every year. When I lived at Marion's she used to practise for hours every day. I started to recognise all these little snatches of the clarinet part, tiny melodies I listen out for now, that I'd never notice if I didn't know they were there. It took a few years before I felt as though I really knew it well though. I still spot new moments each time I listen to it.'

'Wish me luck now then.' She scanned the Walt Whitman poem that Vaughan Williams had set the *Sea Symphony* to. It was a very long poem.

The performance began and for a few minutes Anna concentrated hard, trying to focus on everything she could hear, to think about how it sounded and who was playing what. She scanned the stage for Marion's shiny auburn hair, and watched how she held her clarinet, her elbows pointing out elegantly, her head bobbing slightly each time she played. After a while though, she stopped trying to understand the music, or work out where they were within the structure of the piece, and just let it wash over her like water. The sound of the orchestra swelled and subsided, ebbing and flowing in waves, time stretching and bending in between the notes. Anna didn't fidget, but occasionally her mind wandered outside of the piece, turning it into a soundtrack for her thoughts.

It was nine-thirty when they emerged, but the sky still held some light as they crossed Hungerford Bridge and headed to a bar by Charing Cross. The atmosphere was rowdy, half the crowd gearing up to test their charms with the infamously difficult door staff at Heaven, 'the world's most famous gay nightclub', just down the road.

'Fancy it?' Anna raised her eyebrow at Jack, nodding towards a group advancing towards the door. They were all wearing normal clothes apart from one, a stag perhaps, who had dressed up as Tina Turner, quite successfully, Anna thought.

There was a very definite moment, when their taxi reached Dalston Junction, where the evening should have started to wind down. It was like watching a film and sensing that you were enjoying a measured, poignant denouement, only to see some secondary storyline getting tied up messily in the next scene, grumbling and limping along for another ten minutes until the credits eventually rolled. Jack leant forward to speak to the driver, asking him to let them out earlier than planned, suggesting to Anna that they have another drink on the way back. Anna obliged, surprised by the change of plan, but happy to stay out, surrounded by buzz, activity and laughter. She saw Jack's expression a bit later, though, on the corner of their road, when he offered to buy a final round at the pub on the corner, and realised she was watching him perform a series of diversionary tactics similar to those she often used when she didn't want to climb into bed and risk another nightmare. Anna wondered, sitting on his sofa watching Jack plug his computer in, scrolling through his music collection for something to put on, were they both afraid of going to sleep?

# CHAPTER EIGHTEEN

'Do you mind if we stay at yours tonight? There'll be loads of people at mine; Trystan's having a bit of a party.'

Anna and Jack were standing on the corner of their road, at the junction where they would turn right to go to Jack's house and left for Anna's. She hesitated at his suggestion, panicking. She hadn't expected them to go back to hers; she didn't want him to see what she had been up to. She tried to turn her dawdling into something less conspicuous, a decision over whether or not she had any milk in the fridge; she might need to go and get some now on the way back. It would give her time to work out what to do.

*Automatism* had opened with a well-attended Private View, an evening of artists' talks put on for gallery members, and the official launch to the public. It was Friday evening, and Jack had come to look around the exhibition at the end of the public opening. The past two weeks had been fraught getting it all ready, Anna's whole body slackening in relief when the doors finally opened for the first time and everything got under way. They hadn't seen each other for nearly ten days while she'd been working, and she loved him for taking his time over the exhibition, for reading through things slowly and carefully, and for going straight back inside when he got to the end, to have another look at Denning's photographs.

'So that's what's been stealing all your time. It's brilliant, but I can't imagine it's helped your nightmares much,' he had said on the walk home. He squeezed her shoulder as they headed north through bustling clusters of pavement drinkers and late-night shoppers. 'You've done an incredible job.'

Was that what their nightmares were going to become then? A trivial little couple's foible that they'd refer to flippantly every now and then, teasing each other for the affliction they shared? She hoped not.

She tensed as they left the shop and turned left at the corner. She had run out of time to come up with a good excuse for them not to stay at hers. Over the past week she had taken her dream diary to a new level, transferring thoughts and moments that seemed important, from inside her private notebook out onto her bedroom wall in a huge scrawling chart. She had needed a more visual method of investigation, something larger and easier to follow. She wasn't getting anywhere by reading through the pages of her cramped handwriting, thirty nights' paranoia all crammed into one tiny A5 block. It had been a busy day, and casting her mind back to the early morning when she had stretched and yawned her way out of bed, scrabbled her things together for work and left in a hurry, Anna couldn't remember whether she had covered the diagram up or not.

She had chosen the biggest wall in her room, the one that stretched all the way along the back end of the house, *Circles* hanging at one end. Leaning next to her dad's present was the pair of haunting eyes, finally finished. Waking up in the middle of the night it was often too much, to go from one ghostly stare to another, seeing the same thing gazing impassively back at her from across her own bedroom. She was relieved when the paint dried and she could finally turn it round and lean it against the wall. She only had to look at the back of it now, its innocuous blank canvas stretched over a pale wooden frame.

She bought wallpaper liner paper from the hardware shop in Dalston and unfurled the long thick grainy rolls over the wall. She lifted *Circles* down carefully, almost toppling under the weight of it, and stacked it to one side so that she could stick the paper across the whole space with gooey blobs of Blu Tack. She bought a thick black marker pen and started writing. She was unsure what shape or structure would work best, what would be more likely to reveal a pattern, so she put the car crash with those staring eyes at the centre of everything and then drew lines shooting out and back from that point to other elements of her dreams, charting the ways in which she always found herself back at the centre of it all. It reminded her of a murder investigation, a complex evidence chart on a police detective's crime wall, with its smaller line drawings and numbered lists of things she thought might be significant.

In the day, she kept it hidden, making a hole in the liner paper for her picture hooks so that she could rehang *Circles* over the top of it, keeping most of the ramblings out of sight. If she propped the eyes up along the wall next to it, facing away from her, the whole thing was almost invisible apart from the spidery ends and beginnings of a few letters around the edges of the canvases, if you knew what you were looking for. Each morning when Anna woke up, she slid the paintings along in front of the door so nobody could burst in, and transferred her notes from the book she kept beside her bed, onto the main chart. She felt like she was getting somewhere at last.

All week she had added to it, but in the last few days, something had begun to change. At first, she had made notes on the three bearded gods in their robes, the things they had done and said, how Jack was always standing alone in the middle of an empty road, how she always got involved even though she shouldn't. She had included questions beside everything, often jumping up from where she was working at her computer in the evenings to add another one that had just come to her.

*Why do I feel as though we are in danger in the dreams? Have we met before?*

As the nights passed, and the surrounding details of each dream remained relentlessly random and unconnected, Anna began to include facts from the daytime, things that were happening in the real world, like the fact they had both started having nightmares fifteen years ago. She remembered what Jack had said at his party, that coincidences were the most natural thing in the world, but it seemed too perfect that she had met somebody she recognised who had been going through precisely the same thing as her, for the same length of time. She couldn't let it go. Jack said his dreams began when his parents died, but Anna had never lost anybody she was close to. That couldn't be the link; she was looking in the wrong place.

It wasn't just the dreams she should be considering, it was her entire relationship with Jack. Fifteen years ago, just before they had both stopped sleeping properly, Anna and Jack had each spent Christmas in the dark shadows of twenty-four-hour polar night. While Anna had been curled into a ball of nausea on the hotel bed in Lapland, her body confused and jumbled by the absence of sunrise, Jack had been suffering the same confusion two hours north in Tromsø. As soon as she shifted her focus to the Kaamos, everything else fell into place: Jack had her dad's painting on the wall; she had met him properly for the first time on Midsummer's Eve. They needed to reverse the damage, take themselves north of the Arctic Circle together and sit in the midnight sun, let a full twenty-four hours of unbroken sunlight rain down on their skin and cure them. That was why they had found each other; that was why she had started dreaming about him when they met. Her body was trying to tell her something: together, they could make each other better.

She needed to tell Jack her theory, but she didn't want him to see the rest of her dream wall with its graphic details of death and injury, all the deaths her sleeping mind had conjured, the car crash that repeatedly threatened to smash Jack's body into a million broken pieces and the way she had been obsessed for days with whether they had met before. As they climbed the stairs to her room, she prayed with closed eyes, crossed fingers, and held breath that her mania was completely covered up behind the paintings.

Jack was in front of her on the way upstairs. He pushed the door open and went inside without a gasp, without a scream or a wobble, and, when she followed him in, everything was safely tucked away. The chart on the wall was hidden, and the painting of the staring eyes was turned to face the wall. Jack didn't ask what was on the other side of that canvas, if he even thought there was anything there. From the back it looked unpainted. Still, Anna's heart flew into her mouth every time he looked in its direction or went to stand over on that side of the room.

Part of her was glad when they both

opened their eyes in the middle of the night, a stunned gasp from each of them, as if they were both in pain. It was a final reminder that this needed to be fixed, strengthening her resolve, making the conversation easier to start. Jack choked next to her. She stroked the soft palm of his hand.

'It's OK, you're awake now. I'm here.'

He made a little moaning sound and rolled onto his side towards her, pushing the breath out of him.

'How much longer is it going to go on like this?'

Anna swallowed. It was better to say it now. The room was too dark for her to see the expression on Jack's face when he decided she was insane.

'I've been thinking,' she whispered. 'I've got a plan.'

'What do you mean you've got a plan? A plan for what?'

'A way to take away our nightmares.'

He propped himself up on his elbow. She could hear his breath slightly closer to her face, could tell he was looking down at her pillow, to where he knew her eyes must be.

'Go on.'

'I know we don't completely agree on whether this is all fate or coincidence, but whichever one it is, don't you think it's odd that we've both had nightmares for fifteen years, that we recognise each other? Maybe there is a reason why we've met.'

'I don't think there has to be a "why", but I'm glad we have.' He stroked her hair.

'You have my dad's painting of Lapland on your wall. That's exactly when I stopped sleeping properly, when we got home from our Christmas holiday. It sounds like it was the same for you, that it happened around the same time.'

'No, I stopped sleeping properly about two weeks after we got back, when my parents died.'

Anna's mouth gaped open. This was the only part of the perfect delicate shape of her theory that had had the potential to fall through: she had started having nightmares two weeks after they got home from Lapland. She had planned to skim over the imperfection of that detail. Now it was right at the top of their strange, mirrored list.

'What date was that?'

'20th January 2000.'

'It was a Thursday. That's the date my parents decided to get divorced. That's exactly the time I had my first really awful nightmare.'

'So what are you saying? What does that prove?'

207

'I think that our bodies got messed up by the polar night, that it caused us to stop sleeping, to have nightmares, to wake up at odd times and to feel tired all the time. It knocked our rhythms off. The fact that we both started having them two weeks later,' she was improvising now, 'maybe that's how long the problem took to reveal itself. We both experienced some kind of trauma afterwards and maybe it set everything off. I'm not claiming divorce and death are equal in any way, but I think that twenty-four-hour darkness broke something in us, something that started to develop when bad things happened.'

Jack sighed, disappointed. 'I'm not sure that's the most rational explanation.'

'I know, but none of this is rational, is it? Our nightmares, all the similarities we share, even the fact that that date is significant for both of us. It's all a big riddle. I'm trying to work it out.'

'How though? How does the *darkness is our kryptonite* theory work?'

'It's not completely illogical. The human body's made up of something like forty per cent stardust; we're all built from the same stuff that the rest of the universe is made of. It makes sense that we would get pushed and pulled by the same forces, affected by precisely where we are positioned on the planet, where our body is sitting in the solar system. We're linked in some way, I just know it. We're mirroring each other at every step.'

She sat up and crossed her legs, reaching down to hold Jack's hands where they rested on his stomach. She turned his wrists in excitable circles above him until he gave in and laughed at her enthusiasm.

'So what plan do you have?'

'We met on Midsummer's Eve, the day before the summer solstice.'

'We met two weeks before that, when I caught you spying on me outside the pub.'

'You know what I mean. We met properly on the weekend of the summer solstice.'

'OK, whatever you say.'

'I think we can reverse this. I think we need to move fast while the days are still long, go north of the Arctic Circle, together. We need to sit in the midnight sun, to spend at least twenty-four hours somewhere it never sets.'

He reached up and touched her face. 'I love that you are this focussed on trying to help me, to help us. Nobody – *nobody* – has ever tried to fix this before.'

'So you'll do it? There's a place called Svalbard in Norway that has twenty-four-hour daylight for another couple of weeks. It's a two-hour flight from where you were in Tromsø, but I think it should be somewhere neither of us has ever been before, since it didn't happen to us in the same place.'

'Sure. Why not?' He shook his head in disbelief at what he was signing up to, and put a hand around the back of her neck, pulling her down to kiss him. 'It will be an adventure at the very least. Let's do it.'

'You can't just do it because it's an adventure. You have to have faith in it.'

'I have faith in the possibility that we might, in some mad and unsound way, ignite a placebo effect that will make us both come home and sleep like babies. Don't ever underestimate the power of the placebo.'

Anna bounced up and down on the bed, willing him to agree with her.

'You have to believe it will work! Say you believe it will work.'

'I believe it will work.'

# CHAPTER NINETEEN

Norway was incredible. They landed at Tromsø and boarded a smaller plane, flying further north for hours until Anna looked down and saw Longyearbyen's thin grey runway perched on a flat spit of land in the middle of a wide grey sheet of water. Snow-capped mountains stood in a horseshoe around the airport. It looked like an optical illusion, the plane too big and the runway too small and short. She closed her eyes when the wheels of the plane touched down and felt Jack's fingers fluttering inside her hand. They were at the northernmost settlement in the world. They had arrived.

She had expected weather complications, for there to be wind and rain, sleet or snow, but everything was eerily calm and still. There was no breeze, no raindrops in the air and barely any clouds, just peachy summer sun shining through the cold, making the snow crystals sparkle on the summits. The shock of the temperature was exhilarating after the staleness of the humid city summer. Anna pulled her fur coat further up under her nose, warming her face so her breath became a big white cloud when she puffed it out in front of her like smoke.

They stayed at the Svalbard Hotel, in a dark wood-panelled room with huge pictures of polar bears on the walls. Everything was made from thick planks of spruce, fresh honey-coloured timber that looked as though it had only just been sliced and sanded. They laughed at the lime green blankets on the bed, the tiny sachets of tea and coffee sitting on the side, and at how far away from home they were. Jack sat outside on the terrace for a few minutes, bundled up in his coat and scarf, before coming in to unpack, rubbing his hands together furiously to warm them up.

'What do we do now then?' He asked Anna, appointing her the leader of the expedition.

'We just let it do its thing, wait for our body clocks to get totally fucked up, sit out there in the midnight sun and heal ourselves.' She frowned. 'I think.'

'You think?' He grabbed her. 'You *think?*' Anna dropped back onto the felt green blankets beneath him, wrapping her legs around his back, squeezing him so hard that he couldn't breathe. Jack stopped tickling her and started kissing her face instead. 'Where did you come from ...' he kissed her cheeks, her eyelids, her forehead, her lips, '… with your crazy Arctic mission?'

She put her finger over his mouth, closing her eyes. 'It's going to work.'

'Are you tuning into the silent voices of the mountains?'

'Shut up. I can feel it.'

It would be the reverse of the last time she came north of the Arctic Circle. Then, she had sat in thick ski gear around a huge campfire with her parents out in the still winter air, while a guide toasted char fish for them over the flames. It had been too black to see anything in either direction through the darkness, apart from the little glowing windows of their lodge a few hundred feet away. Anna had looked up through the fire to where the sparks licked the black sky. Above that there were only ice-white stars, thrown far and wide across the night in a messy scattered handful. Now, it was nearly midnight and nothing sparkled above them. It was all daylight blue, with soft stripes of blurred pink air drifting behind the snowy peaks.

They went out for a walk, through the little clusters of low-lying houses. The buildings must have been strong structures capable of withstanding fierce winters where they would be buried beneath deep snow in minus temperatures, but they all looked like little kit models, arranged in a small untidy sprawl at the edge of the mountains. The miles of untouched land that stretched out around them made everything feel unfinished, as though someone had decided to try to build a town out here and then thought better of it. It was late and everywhere was quiet. They trod the cold ground back to their hotel with their arms around each other, made tea in the small plastic kettle by the cupboard, and dozed with the blinds half-drawn for a few hours.

'Did you have any nightmares?' It was the clock that told her day had arrived; everything outside still hovered beneath the same mild northern sun.

Jack groaned, stretching tired arms overhead and frowning at her.

'I didn't sleep. Did you sleep?'

'I don't think so.'

'How do we tell if it's working or not?'

She was too tired to work out whether he was humouring her.

'It won't be, yet. I don't think we'll know until we get home.'

'Oh. Right. Makes sense.' Jack nodded, then burst out laughing. Anna elbowed him gently in the ribs.

She was surprised by how busy it was downstairs in the breakfast room. When they arrived the night before, it had felt as though they were the only people here, the only people in Longyearbyen. Now, couples, families and groups of friends were emerging from bedrooms, rubbing sleep-filled faces and pouring themselves coffee. A weary young dad in the corner was trying to stop his sons from throwing cereal at one another. Through the window, everywhere was still deserted. It was the temperature, just a few degrees above zero, keeping people inside, making the streets look abandoned.

They got zipped and buttoned into their warm clothes and went off to visit the Svalbard Museum, exploring big rooms full of wooden walkways that took them on an indoor journey between taxidermic polar bears and seals, seabirds, walruses and reindeer. They bought lunch and ate it standing up outside, wandering along the edge of the water, shocked when a gigantic cruise ship sailed silently past.

When Jack finished eating, Anna watched him hold his fingers up like a photo frame in front of his face, sectioning off parts of the landscape, turning the mountains, the water and the sky into smaller rectangular designs. How was it that after only a few weeks, she could no longer imagine, or even remember, how things had felt without him? What would she be doing now, if she weren't with Jack? All the other options seemed to lack shine. Even her own past needed polishing; everything had been tired and dull until the moment she first saw him.

They spent the afternoon sitting out on their

cold terrace, ducking back inside to make each other hot drinks when their teeth started chattering. Anna painted, and Jack drew. Every now and then she had to put down her sketchbook and stand up, star-jumping wildly to get the blood flowing. She found colours for the sky, but the soft clouds were harder to recreate. They were so faint that in the end she dipped scrunched up handfuls of tissue in watered down white paint and dabbed them over the blue, like a mist in the atmosphere.

Jack's hunched-up position over his drawing paper looked painful and awkward, and Anna couldn't see what he was working on until he stepped back through the glass doors to make a coffee. He had drawn Arctic Anna, a fur-clad super heroine holding a polar dagger made of icicles. She had horn-rimmed snow goggles on with jewels set in the corner of the frames, a luscious full mouth and long flowing hair full of snowflakes.

'She doesn't look like she'll stay warm for long in that fur bikini thing,' she said when Jack came back out and handed her a hot drink.

'It's a sealskin utility suit with reindeer trim. And that's one of her super powers.'

'Staying warm in a cold climate?'

He nodded.

'I could do with that now. What are her other super powers?'

'This on her wrist is a Solar Dial. It's like a sundial, but for controlling the sun's movements instead of reading them; she makes the sun rise and set.'

'Is there a need for that in the superhero community?'

'Yes, a dire need. She can also make the snow fall from her fingertips.'

'Can I keep it when it's finished?'

'Of course.' He looked at her colour wash. 'If I can have your Midnight Sun.'

At the front desk the concierge recommended a local restaurant, but when they arrived at the door and read the five-course tasting menu of Arctic fish, whale carpaccio, reindeer, seal and grilled whale meat, Anna baulked and looked at Jack with a grimace.

'I'm really sorry, I don't think I can eat that. It seems pretty extreme to come here for two days and make a dent in as many species of wildlife as possible.'

They went down the road to the next place that was open and picked their way through a big sharing bowl of underwhelming vegetable-fried rice. Anna tried to make up for a disappointing last supper in Svalbard by buying Jack a few too many drinks at the Karlsberger Pub on their way home, getting him drunk enough that he started doing impressions of Arctic Anna. He sprung his fingers open in an abracadabra motion over her drink, trying to turn her vodka into snow, and waved his arms at the windows outside to make nightfall.

'The sun doesn't seem to be setting,' Anna pointed out.

'I don't think it works when she's pissed.'

'I think we need to go to bed.'

Jack nodded, hiccupping most of the way home and leaning so heavily on Anna's shoulder that she collapsed, puffed and worn out, onto the bed with her shoes on as soon as they got through the door. Even then they didn't sleep, not properly. They dipped below the surface, jerking each other awake with little movements, soft whimpers of tiredness and comfort as they wrapped themselves up again in the blankets.

The light outside was too hopeful. Fingers of bright anticipation crawling their way around the sides of the blinds so that they were held in the atmosphere of crisp expectation, a never-breaking dawn. After a few hours Anna got up again, put her boots and coat on, and took a mug of hot water out to the terrace. It was beautiful. The land felt like it was waiting for something. No darkness fell to rub out the marks of the day before, wipe the sky clean before a new morning. Without wind, everything was static. Sitting in the cold by herself, in the silent endless daylight, it was easy to believe in magic.

Jack groaned at her when she came inside.

'My head hurts.'

'Well, Monday morning feels the same over here as it does back home then.'

He rolled over and beckoned her to him, holding her hand where she stood, next to the bed. He looked up at her.

'This has been amazing. I don't want to leave.'

Anna knelt beside him, saying the only words that could find their way to her lips, even though they didn't go half way to expressing what she felt.

'Do you think we were meant to meet?'

She could see immediately in his smile, the flat happy openness of his expression, that he heard her question only as romance, nothing fated or paranoid behind the words, even though he had flown with her to the top of the globe to put things right.

'Of course. Of course we were meant to meet, Arctic Anna.'

# CHAPTER TWENTY

'Do you like spicy food?' Jack asked from the doorway. Anna nodded, sorting through her suitcase on the living-room floor while he went back into the kitchen to cook. They were back in London. Everything was towering and concrete, swarming with people and covered in smoke. Norway felt like a dream. Anna hadn't had a proper sleep since they woke up at dawn to get to the airport on Saturday and now it was Monday night. She had only been able to take one day off work. It had been a ridiculous thing to attempt, flying all the way up to Svalbard for two nights, but now she considered it a lucky escape from a more extended period of sleeplessness. Or maybe they would have both got used to it. Outside the window the sun was setting, and for the first time in years Anna was relieved and grateful that night was about to fall.

The smell from Jack's cooking hit her nose, the hot fragrant sourness of lime juice, soy and lemongrass, ginger, coriander and chilli. It took her back to Thailand, where she and Holly had travelled years ago. They slept in colourful hammocks suspended from the precarious ceilings of their wooden beach hut, and when Anna screamed herself awake in the dark middle hours, she could rock herself back to sleep again like a baby beside the surging ceaseless rhythm of the sea.

She met Leon one evening while she was reading on the beach, immediately writing him off as rootless and immature when he approached her and started talking about the sunset, the importance of travel, of discovering strange cultures and crossing new frontiers. It was his standard method of seduction, it transpired, indulged in only because of how embarrassingly successful it was, rather than how faithfully it represented his personality. He laughed when he clocked her look of utter boredom and disdain, her evident wish to return to her book. He relaxed, becoming instantly funnier and more interesting, telling her all about his greetings card and stationery business back in Europe. He explained how he worked from out here for a few months of the year, convinced it was the only thing that stopped him from becoming a stressed-out businessman in a terrible suit, with a boring blue tie and high blood pressure.

'Plus, I can grow my hair long, and have conference calls in my swimming shorts.'

'Is that what you've got in there? I thought you were just pleased to see me.'

By the end of the week, Anna decided she would stay on Ko Samui with Leon, while Holly caught a boat up to meet some old friends on Ko Pha Ngan, went on to Ko Tao with them, and then came back to collect Anna ten days later before they returned to the mainland. Even now, when the holiday came up in conversation, Anna would start talking about their island-hopping journey up the Gulf of Thailand and have to be reminded by Holly that she only went to one island.

Those ten days on Ko Samui were a painful and upsetting collision of the blissful rootlessness of a holiday romance, and the reality of her debilitating neuroses. It was a far cry from the paradise that she had imagined when she had waved Holly off down at the port. Anna's nightmares were even worse to be around back then, louder and more out of control whenever she woke up. She hadn't yet learnt the skill of jerking awake and silently holding it all inside, letting the screams reverberate around her ribcage and down her spine, instead of out into the room around her.

Leon never said anything, but it was impossible to maintain the wonderfully simple

222

two-dimensional views of one another that they each wanted to indulge in, a necessity for a brief, futureless and passionate affair. She didn't want to learn anything about him, and she didn't want him to discover any dark hidden fears in her. Quickly, over that first week, Anna watched until he was unable to see her as a breezy, light-hearted English rose with long legs and dark hair, as her anxiety pushed its way to the surface. She grew into something else, something less simple, and less intoxicating: a woman with issues who couldn't sleep at night and cried alone to herself on the porch looking out to sea.

Leon, too, shrank back into her initial impression of him. His business wasn't successful; his dad threw obscene amounts of money into the bottomless pit of Leon's disorganised half-mast ambition while he drank piña coladas on the beach at sunset and waved around non-committal plans to fly back and 'face the music'. By the time Holly returned, they were just waiting out the days, Anna resigning herself to a life spent making bad choices or sleeping alone if she couldn't shake the nightmares.

That was the last person she had had anything close to feelings for, four years ago this winter. Even those weren't real feelings, just pleasant misconceptions that had evaporated swiftly in the wake of getting to know each other. She had lived the lifespan of a dysfunctional marriage together with Leon in that fortnight, from seduction to honeymoon to stagnation, just one of many affairs that the nightmare had interrupted, twisted from fun to failure.

On the last night, after everything had fallen apart for the final time, she had stood out on the rickety wooden jetty that ran along the side of the rocks, down at one end of the island, and made a promise to herself that she would beat this haunting, sort herself out and learn how to sleep without being afraid of what the world had in store for her. So much time had passed since then. Now, for the first time, she was trying to work it all out. Slowly, she would learn enough about it that she was able to make it stop.

That night, Anna closed her eyes with apprehension when she settled down next to Jack in bed. It would be the conclusion to their experiment, restful proof that their long journey north had successfully exorcised the demon.

She went back to Longyearbyen in her sleep. Not dressed for the cold this time, she shivered and shook in a pale blue dress out on the water's edge. She could see ice in her eyelashes, and frozen onto the ends of her hair. Her bare feet ached. Jack stood beside her in a mechanic's boiler suit, black with heavy poppers down the centre. He had steel toe-capped boots on. They left big heavy dents in the frosty grass as he walked around her, peering this way and that. She tried to move but she couldn't. She wasn't even able to redirect her gaze to where he walked, circling her as though she were a statue. He had the name of a company sewed in delicate gold thread onto the top pocket of his overalls: *Matrix Laboratories. They sound official*, she thought.

Jack pulled a screwdriver out of his pocket and unscrewed a panel in the side of her head. Then he walked round to the other side and unscrewed another one. The wind whistled through her skull. He gazed directly into her brain, tightening things, turning things this way and that, slipping loose chains back onto tiny cogs and pulling his hands out with oil all over his fingers, wiping them on himself.

At first he seemed just to want to have fun with her. He moved his finger inside her brain and she felt her eyes swivel in one direction. He took his finger out and they sprang back to neutral. He laughed, unkindly. Then he opened a metal flap deep inside the frontal lobe portion of her brain, just behind and above her eyes. It sounded rusty, squeaking, almost knocking her off balance when he wrenched it open. He

225

pushed a small cassette tape into it and snapped it shut. There was a piece of paper tucked into his back pocket that he unfurled, unfolding it and reading the list of conversational openers written in a neat list, like a script. He tried them all out on her, checking that her automatically programmed responses were correct.

It was wonderful. It was as if they understood one another perfectly, knew what the other person was about to say, how they were going to react, what they would find funny and what they would think fascinating. It took the cold out of Anna's icy bones, making her feel warm where she stood underdressed in the chilled air by the lake. It felt like bliss, but how bittersweet. She had no idea that their love was all programmed, that her mind was controlled by Jack. She was devastated. She tried to cry, but it hurt. No tears appeared. She strained at her facial muscles, pulling water through the backs of her eyelids. Eventually Jack noticed. He sighed aggressively and pressed a button on her hand, allowing one single teardrop to fall from each eye and land on the ground beneath her.

'Thank you,' she tried to say, but nothing came out.

He was growing bored of her. He slotted a photograph in behind her eyes, and all at once her surroundings changed. She was standing out in the middle of the airport runway. Jack was still beside her, holding the sort of handset that usually operates a children's remote-control car, a comically long antenna in between two big joystick levers. There was a plane landing in front of them. It hit the runway smoothly, gliding across the ground without even touching it, coming straight for the two of them where they stood, exposed in the middle of the tarmac. Jack was too busy playing around with the controller to notice they were about to get wiped out, making Anna's arms lift up and down in a clumsy dance.

As her left arm sprung up in front of her face, Anna took advantage of the momentum it created to swing her mechanical body around on the spot and swipe at Jack, trying to push him out of danger. The airport, the runway and the plane all disappeared with a pop, and she was standing back beside the lake with Jack directly in front of her, ripping things out of her head and staring her down with a look of total indifference. She was just a machine. He didn't even know she had a soul.

'So you see,' he growled, putting his face unnecessarily close to hers, 'I control *you*. Not the other way around.'

She woke up. Jack was sound asleep. Anna

had no idea what was real and what wasn't. She had seen a different side to him, a side that she shouldn't have seen. At that moment, surrounded by the threat of it all, she didn't care that it had revealed itself to her in a dream. It was still valid. She shouted, but Jack didn't wake up. That was strange in itself; why was he sleeping so deeply, so comfortably?

'Pretending you're asleep is just more suspicious,' she whispered, knowing it made her sound crazy. Jack didn't stir. She held the back of her hand in front of his mouth to check that he was breathing.

Anna crept out and into the living room, fishing her dream diary out of her open suitcase on the floor. She had had no need to write in it the entire time they were in Norway. Why on earth Jack had let her take them there, if her stardust sunlight theory really had been a complete invention?

*Something is not right.* She started writing. *There has not been one dream since I first saw Jack when he has not been at the centre of my nightmare—*

'—Can't you sleep?'

Anna jumped so high that she lifted off the sofa. Trystan had come back home from working late in his studio. His concerned expression shifted, almost imperceptibly, to something more suspicious when he saw her staring back hollow-eyed and shocked, like she had been caught red-handed. He peered at the book she had in her hand, trying to see if she was reading something she shouldn't be.

'No, can't seem to.'

It was all she could manage. She tried to smile to make the exchange more casual, to show that she had simply not expected someone to be watching her, but she could see in Trystan's expression that her alarm hadn't gone unnoticed. Her face burned as he walked up the stairs to bed. She knew how she had looked, jumping up as if he had given her an electric shock: she had looked guilty.

# CHAPTER TWENTY-ONE

Trystan let her in on Friday evening. Jack had been held up in a meeting in Stoke Newington. He only let Anna know when she was already at his front door, so she rang the bell anyway in case someone was at home. She set her bag down in his bedroom. It looked different: the wardrobe had been pushed away from the wall and into the room, revealing a large cupboard that was usually hidden behind it, the door slightly open. Anna could see sketchbooks stacked inside, a few paintings and drawings propped up above them, mostly sketches on card or canvas, but when she peered further in she saw some more elaborate finished pieces down the other side. Some of them looked like they'd been sitting in there for months, forgotten, their edges slightly battered, the corners softened and folded over. As she went to pull herself back out into the room, to go and sit downstairs, a wide frightened stare caught her eye from somewhere, and she scanned back over everything to see where it had come from. It was the closest illustration to her, down by her feet. Crisp and fresh, recently finished, it was sitting by the door on an A3 piece of white card. She picked it up and sat on the bed with it cradled in her lap, a black pen and ink abstract design-like illustration, all dark and swirling like a lot of Jack's work.

There was a pair of eyes at the centre of it all, staring horrified from among a sea of lines that looked like waves, the flowing curling whorls of a rough sea. They circled into perfect tight little spheres where they collided, and stretched out again fluidly around the frightened stare at their centre: it was the dream illustration he had been working on. Stylistically it was completely different from Anna's impressionistic daubs of oil, but the subject matter was identical. Even the feeling it evoked in her matched the way her skin went cold when she saw her own vision watching her from the canvas across the room. She turned the illustration over, to look at the title Jack had given it, *My Nightmare.* The date he had pencilled beside it was from just a week ago.

She was stunned, frozen. However nonsensical her dream narratives were, they had always felt deeply personal, born of her own unique struggles, impossible for another mind to replicate. Jack hadn't been tussling with separate issues from his own life. He had been running away from the very same eyes that chased her.

How different would things be today, if Jack had seen her painting of her own nightmare when she first did it, weeks ago? She put her hand to her chest, spots collecting at the edges of her vision. Her heart echoed in her ribcage and up her neck.

Downstairs, the front door opened and Anna heard Trystan shouting down to Jack through the open door of his bedroom.

'Anna's here. I just let her in.'

Did she imagine that urgency in the way Jack slammed the door and ran up the stairs, his feet pounding along the landing, knowing he had left the cupboard exposed, that his secret treasure trove had been plundered? She could tell from how fast he was moving that she didn't have time to run over to the cupboard, slide the drawing back to the right place and sit back on the bed without looking flushed, suspicious. It was going to happen, he was going to know she had seen it. Would she tell him the truth, that she saw the same eyes? The door flew open. She tried to arrange her face in an expression of calm.

Jack's eyes flickered between her face and the drawing she was holding, taking in the fact that she had read everything written on the back.

'I didn't mean to look in there, sorry.' She gestured to the open cupboard door. 'I just saw all the drawings and got a bit carried away.'

Jack sat down. He lifted it out of her hands and put it down on the bed, out of sight.

'Anna I'm sorry, I know how much you wanted it to work.'

She was still dizzy from the fact that their visions were one and the same, caught up in the shivery possibilities of what that might mean, what it spelled out for them. She couldn't work out what he was apologising for at first. For a stomach-dropping moment, she thought he was talking about the two of them being together. Then Jack squeezed her hand.

'I wanted to believe in your magic sun too.'

'Norway? Svalbard? It didn't work for you either?'

'What do you mean "either"?'

Anna's face crumpled. 'It didn't work for me.'

He put his arm round her, rocking her back and forth. 'What a pair.' He held her tighter. 'Since I met you, it has got a lot better. That's something.'

'You don't have to say that.'

He looked put out. 'I know I don't.'

Jack put *My Nightmare* back in the cupboard, and together they repositioned the wardrobe. Was she meant to discover this? Was it connected to that terrible Arctic dream where she was a mechanical toy and Jack was her operator? She blushed at her own thoughts. The Kaamos theory had felt so right, but been completely wrong, meaningless. She was an idiot. She shook her head at her own mistake.

After her parents split up, she preferred staying at her dad's. It wasn't necessarily that she was closer to him than she was to her mum, but that he was sympathetic to her new and unexplained fear of climbing the stairs alone to bed each night and settling down to sleep. Her mum just told her she was being stupid, or ignored her and went to bed, too tired to deal with the irrationality of it all. So Anna and her dad developed a routine, a ritual that they shared. He pointed at the clock half an hour before Anna's bedtime, and they would sit up at the breakfast bar in his new kitchen and drink hot chocolate and talk for a bit until she was calm. She could smell it now, the milk warming on the stove, putting teaspoons of chocolate powder into the pan and stirring it with a wooden spoon until it was all the same even colour.

Sometimes it did take that half hour. Other times they were down there for ages, talking things through until midnight. He never got impatient. He knew she'd get there in the end. But he let her tell him what she was frightened of, that she was having bad dreams, that she missed hearing the murmuring voices of her parents playing along like a lullaby on the other side of the wall, keeping her safe. He never laughed at anything she said.

That night Anna had a false awakening. She

234

dreamt she had woken up in Jack's bed where she had been sleeping, her head crystal clear, the light bulb shining brightly even though it was night. She could hear somebody whispering around her. It was coming from the bedroom walls or the cupboard behind the wardrobe. She twisted round in a circle, trying to find out where the voice was. The wardrobe was still pushed into the middle of the room. Hadn't they put it back? Jack was sitting alone in his storage cupboard talking to his illustration. He was trying to be quiet; he didn't know she could hear every word.

'No, we didn't blow it: she doesn't suspect a thing. We've completely fooled her. She thinks I don't know anything about the nightmares, and she certainly doesn't know it's us, so let's just keep doing it.'

There was silence while he listened to something, pressing his ear up against the drawing. He nodded.

'We have complete power of her mind, of course we do. She's dancing about like a broken puppet on a string. I'm never going to tell her why she recognises me.'

He caught her looking at him, glaring out at her from the shadows, and said 'hello' with false brightness, his expression fixed in an unnatural smile. 'Anna! Did you hear any of that?'

'Any of what?' She tried to mirror his breeziness. 'No, why?'

'Good. No reason. Come with me.'

That was when she realised she must be asleep: it wasn't the violent madness of Jack's words, it was the fact he was instantly completely satisfied with her answer. Of course she had heard everything; she was wide awake, all the lights were on, and Jack was whispering to a drawing just a few feet from where she sat.

So she followed him downstairs, curious, cold and exposed in her grey knickers and her little white vest. Her skin glowed pale and frightened in the square chunks of moonlight they crossed to get downstairs to the front door.

Jack pushed her out onto the street, his fingers hurting her arm where he gripped her too hard. She squeaked in pain but that only made him laugh, closing his fingers around her even tighter. The road was rough and wet beneath her bare feet where they stood, side by side, in the middle of the road over the white dashed line that should separate the lines of traffic. Except there was no traffic, nothing apart from one speeding car with her parents sitting in the front. They were arguing with each other in the low-voiced irritable way they used to do before they separated. They weren't looking at the road. Jack sighed aggressively.

'They're shouting at each other again.' He stared morosely, a smirk of boredom creeping across his face. 'My God. Can't they at least be happy that they're alive?'

'Are you playing a game with me?' Anna shouted above the noise of the wind. Her hair was damp with summer rain and her teeth were chattering. 'Are you making me see these things? Do you know what's going on in my head? Why are you doing this?'

'I've been *doing this* to you for fifteen fucking years, Anna. The least you could do is work out what I'm trying to tell you. You're so fucking slow.'

The car wasn't slowing down or changing course. Even in the face of this new cold blank anger that she didn't recognise, she didn't want him to die.

'Get out of the road, Jack.'

'Leave it,' he commanded fiercely, holding his hand out to stop her from getting any closer. But she couldn't watch it smash them both to pieces. She hesitated. The rain fell harder. She launched herself on him, pushing his body out of the car's path. Jack stumbled backwards and fell against the side of the house, his feet scrabbling over the pavement to stay upright. He turned to stare at her with craziness locked in his wild eyes. The car slammed into her from the side and she was thrown bolt upright and awake in bed. She had heard her bones crack.

She was still screaming; she couldn't stop.

'Why are you doing this to me?'

Jack's hands were around her face. He was kneeling up in bed beside her, stroking her neck, moving his hands down to hold her hands, rubbing her palms with his fingers and trying to make her look at him. It was the first time she had seen him look this frightened.

'You're awake now. You're with me.'

Anna burst into tears, shaking her head and collapsing into his chest in a reflex of relief, of having somebody there to hold her when she escaped her dark place. As her head cleared though, and she felt his arms around her, everything became unnatural and uncomfortable. She had been bent and manipulated by Stockholm syndrome, she was diving straight into the arms of her oppressor, holding the man who had been her torturer, just minutes before, close to her half-naked body. She looked at Jack, still lost in the possibility that he had made all that happen, had made her do that, that he had been awake and watching her writhe around on the bed, waiting for her to wake up so he could pretend to comfort her. The car always avoided him, but lately it had begun to crash into her instead. Why was that?

'You're OK now. I promise you're awake.'

'I'm not – I'm not OK.'

'Yes, you are. You're fine.'

'You don't understand. I think I'm going crazy.'

# CHAPTER TWENTY-TWO

They were throwing a house party. Libby had been made a director of the small jewellery design business she worked for, in the same month that she was turning twenty-nine. The girls reckoned that the promotion bolstered what would otherwise be a non-significant birthday year, and meant they had reason to celebrate. They put out a boldly open invitation: best friends, close friends, university friends and other friends; colleagues, neighbours, Jack and his flatmates. The house was overrun. People coming from further afield started arriving on Friday evening and, by Saturday, most of the bedroom carpets were invisible beneath rows of sleeping bags and fold-out beds. The kitchen surfaces were a multi-coloured glass sea of bottles, their own party stock embellished with generous gifts from each new guest who showed up.

Anna prepared food on the kitchen table,

watching through the window as Holly, Libby and Fran set out chairs in the garden. In the living room upstairs, Sophie was trying unsuccessfully to connect her laptop to a more powerful set of speakers they'd borrowed from a friend. Loud music blared intermittently from the open window as she worked out which lead went where. On the grass outside, the girls turned Sophie's technical incompetence into a game of musical statues, freezing wherever they were each time the music went off.

'When's your birthday then?' Jack sat on the last remaining free patch of space on the kitchen worktop, blowing up balloons.

'January 28th.'

'What will you do for it?'

'It's five months away! I don't know. It's not a good time of year.' Jack nodded. 'Holly and I have a bit of a birthday tradition. We both take the morning off work on each other's birthdays and make the birthday girl breakfast. Holly does pancakes, red fruit, maple syrup. If it's hers I usually do potato cakes, smoked salmon and scrambled eggs. We have champagne, too.'

Birthday breakfasts were one of the best things that Holly had introduced Anna to and, more recently, as she began to wish the numbers were going down rather than up, made each year older a little more enjoyable. As an only child Anna realised it was expected that she must have been spoilt somehow, that she would have been pampered and indulged while she was growing up. She thought the opposite was true, that she had been forced to mature and get on with things quickly because there were no other children around for her to be a stupid kid with. Birthdays were low key in her household, usually with a family day out rather than a party, and a cake if she was lucky. Nothing much changed when her parents separated; they were both intent on not making up for anything with presents. Anna wasn't sure she would have minded the compensation.

Holly, on the other hand, was one of five, and making a fuss of each child on their birthday had been her parents' way of reminding every one of them how important and special they were. Holly insisted it made the rest of the year easier to bear, when their requests were repeatedly drowned out, their toys broken during one of the other ones' tantrums, their trips cancelled because the youngest ones had chickenpox.

Holly told her, 'For about a week before my birthday I couldn't sleep, I was so excited. It's like an egomaniac's Christmas.'

'Champagne for breakfast?' Jack laughed. 'Is it acceptable to be pissed when you show up at work?'

'On your birthday? It's remiss not to be. What are you doing?'

'I'm putting your birthday into my calendar. I'm dreadful at remembering things like that.' He waved his phone at her. 'I've set a reminder. We'll do something fun.'

Anna's lips twitched into a smile. 'Don't worry. I won't let you forget.'

She tried to let it fly over her head, the assumption that they would be celebrating her birthday together in five months' time, and concentrated on chopping beetroot for the salad.

She had to take a deep breath when things got under way, to deal with the loud music, the crowds of people stomping up and down her stairs, people talking to her about the others that lived there and Anna having to explain she was one of them. Every five minutes she got introduced to somebody new, forgot their name instantly, even while they were giving it to her, and spent the rest of the conversation panicking that she was going to need to remember it later on. She had forgotten that it was impossible to pace yourself when the party was at your own house. You began drinking when the first guests showed up and ended up accidentally, automatically, topping your own glass up every time you took a new arrival down to the kitchen to pour them a drink.

The first party she and Holly ever threw together was a brilliant disaster. New tenants in their first student let, they committed themselves to becoming known providers of hedonism and debauchery across the university, not only sending out invitations to the entire faculty of Arts & Humanities, but also putting flyers up through the town centre. It was an unbelievably terrible decision. The house was so busy that real hands-and-feet climbing skills were required to scale the bannisters, dangling above people's heads by your fingers to get upstairs. Anna was too slow in taping dust sheets over all the carpets, and made a half-hearted attempt to rectify this glaring error after a couple of hours of muddy boots and spilt drinks, by dropping loose sheets of newspaper down that were promptly trodden to brown mulch into the fabric.

The next morning was a stressed haze of aggressive and over-zealous domesticity, rubbing concentrated Vanish into the floors and hoovering energetically, only to suck what scrappy threadbare chunks of carpet still remained up into the vacuum cleaner. They had to pay for the carpets to be replaced in every single room, a cost that plumbed the depths of their already dwindling student loans. Anna moaned while she took photographs of the damage for the landlord.

'I'd much rather be the kind of middleweight maverick who does something funny, but essentially harmless, like putting washing-up liquid in the dishwasher. You get a story to tell your friends but you don't have to declare bankruptcy.'

'We've done it all the wrong way round. I have no stories. I remember nothing. We are idiots.'

Holly shouted when she saw the bill: 'Can he not just have them all ripped up and leave the wooden floor? That would look much nicer anyway.'

Anna jabbed a finger at their landlord's email on her computer screen.

'Look at the choice he's given us.'

It was replacing the carpets, or paying to have them ripped up and then to sand, polish and varnish the exposed wooden floors. The latter would have seen them out on the street and living below the breadline before the second term was even over.

There were remarkably few accidents or

spillages at Libby's party. Somebody burnt themselves, standing chatting on the patio and not realising they were holding their cigarette the wrong way round, the lit end melting a burning hole in their thumb. And there was an almighty crash as one of the old chairs on the flat roof collapsed underneath someone.

Holly pointed out, 'Those chairs are tiny: they didn't have far to fall, and I *did* tape a sign to the back of them all saying "Health Hazard".'

As it got later, Anna became increasingly confused. She'd had too much to drink, but nothing was making her feel better. She was too tired to be happy, to enjoy herself. She kept thinking *one more drink, just one more. I'll have this one and then I'll get into the swing of things*, but it didn't work. It started making her angry, fixating with pointless intensity on everything that was worrying her, going over and over the weird moments between her and Jack last week and getting irritated that they hadn't talked anything through properly. Why hadn't she told him that they had the same nightmare? Didn't she trust him? The worst thing about her nightmares now, was how Jack was unkind and aggressive, evil and manipulative in all of them. She had woken up and screamed louder than she ever had before, stared into his eyes and not even seen him, just looked right through him and carried on shouting. Why had they gone straight back to sleep afterwards, and not mentioned it since?

Maybe he was happy with the way things were, pleased that after fifteen years he had met someone who was as fucked up as he was. Maybe she should be pleased too. She'd never find anyone else who'd put up with it, that was for sure. It was too depressing, to be destined for somebody just because you both had the same glaring unresolvable issue with your life. Anna didn't want a shared disaster. She wanted somebody who could pull her out of it.

All day she had been trying to undo that terrible invention of hers, the Jack that was violent and unfeeling, who hijacked her mind and forced her to live a half-life where he controlled her dreams. But now, her thoughts slack and heavy and dull with alcohol, that didn't seem so preposterous. She watched him, next to her in the garden, telling jokes to her friends, making them like him.

She ignored the warning fog of drink, the fuzzing in her fingers and in her lips, and launched herself on him. Not physically, not in the awful, painful way that he had wrenched her down the stairs in her dream, but verbally, laying into him in front of the confused guests, shouting her accusations loudly to his face in the middle of the garden.

'Sometimes I think you're putting things in my head.'

'What would I be putting in your head? What are you talking about?'

He was whispering, trying to keep it private. He looked concerned rather than indignant. It only fuelled her suspicions.

'Have you any idea how many times I have let myself take a hit for you? Every. Fucking. Night. Don't pretend you don't know what I mean.'

'I don't know what you mean.'

'Now you're manipulating me. You're trying to make me think I'm going crazy.'

'You're the one who keeps saying you're crazy. I'm sorry that Norway didn't work, I really am. But we'll be OK.'

'Fuck Norway,' she spat.

'You need to stop talking like this, now.'

'Why is this happening to both of us?'

She cried and Jack held her by the wrists. It was like some dreadful soap opera choreographed by a rubbish, cheap director who didn't know how to make emotion look real.

The whole night was a complete broken disaster. Even while Anna was talking, oblivious to eyes of other people revelling in their domestic showdown, blind to Jack's embarrassed expression as she repeatedly raised her voice at him and he responded with soft words and tried to calm her down, she knew she was talking nonsense. She needed to say every single stupid thought she had become obsessed by, to spit them out onto the floor so they would die a painful public death, and then she'd realise that they didn't sound like the truth. She needed to accuse Jack of the worst thing she thought him capable of, and see no recognition of the charge reflected in his eyes.

She was going to lose him, at some point. When he had said that they would do something together on her birthday next year, she had smiled, but she had also thought what a ridiculous shame it was that that was patently untrue: the nightmare would mess everything up long before then. And now she was helping it, just like she had helped make sure her parents' hovering distance accelerated into decline and divorce. She knew her behaviour was wrong, and yet she couldn't shake the feeling that meeting Jack had set something terrible in motion.

In the end she wore herself out and came

to a stunned halt, her voice hoarse. Her heart beat with every sickeningly slow second that followed, waiting for Jack to bow his head, turn away and leave, to wash his hands of her. But he didn't. He held her by the shoulders and looked her in the eye. They were talking too quietly now for anyone else to hear. People lost interest as soon as it became obvious that the warring couple were about to make up, going back to their drinks and conversations.

'This is happening to me too, you know, and it isn't my fault.'

'I know.' Did she?

He shook her shoulders slightly.

'Anna – you have no idea. This sounds terrible, but when I found out you didn't sleep well, even when you had that awful nightmare last week, I was glad. I admit it.' She looked at him. 'You must know how alienating it is, to be a wreck after midnight? It's like one of those nursery rhyme curses.' He put on a voice: '*You don't know who I am when the sun sets.*'

She laughed at his creepy troll impression in spite of her mood.

'I thought you of all people would understand. We can help each other; we can look after each other. I sleep better with you most of the time anyway. It doesn't mean anything spooky, that we have bad dreams. I should have made that clearer, before we went to see the Midnight Sun.' He looked at her, biting his lip. 'I didn't realise that you really thought that was going to work.'

'I don't know if I did.'

'All this, it really is just another reason why it's so amazing we found each other.'

'One of many.'

'Exactly.'

She hung her head. How had she built such mountains out of something that sounded rational when he explained it like that? She whispered that she was sorry, and she kept saying it again as he kissed her.

'Sorry. I'm so sorry'.

# CHAPTER TWENTY-THREE

None of the girls batted an eyelid during or after Anna's outburst at the birthday party. As far as they were concerned, she was in a blossoming relationship with somebody she was head over heels for, she had got far too drunk, briefly forgotten where she was and embarrassed herself at a party. It was hardly an uncommon chain of events.

'You misplaced your marbles, that's all. You found them again almost instantly,' Holly insisted. Anna was just grateful none of Jack's friends had seen what had gone on.

'It's self-sabotage,' Libby said. 'It happens all the time. You finally realise you might be in the right relationship, the one you've always dreamt about, and you have a wobble and try and make everything fall to pieces in advance so you don't have to keep worrying that it's going to shatter spectacularly further down the line.'

They were, however, extremely impressed

with how Jack had handled the situation and kept saying things like 'he's a keeper' whenever Anna hung up the phone to him, or waved him off from the front door.

She spent hours in her room, creeping between the dream-web diagram on her wall, her notebook, and the drawer stuffed full of the notes she had scribbled down a few weeks ago. She went back over the list of indicator questions that somebody somewhere had decided would determine whether or not she had the germinating seed roots of psychosis burrowed into her bones, or worse, that they were almost full-grown, that she had a whole green garden blooming inside her.

She stood by the door and surveyed the bedroom. If she stumbled across this, a stranger or a house-guest looking for another bathroom, and had to see it all with no explanation, no excuses, and no apology, she would back slowly and carefully out of the room and leave. She wouldn't want to meet whoever lived here, obsessed with their own dreams of death, injury and manslaughter. She had to push her hallucinations firmly into the background, to stop seeing every day as an interlude to be struggled through in between each darkly significant night. She needed to start living in the waking world.

Anna took the Descartes book to a charity

shop on Kingsland Road, along with a couple of other psychology books she had recently bought but not yet opened. The volunteer cashier congratulated her for bringing in paperbacks in good condition, 'you haven't even cracked the spine on these,' assuming they were study books from a degree course she must have taken. She borrowed Libby's shredder, claiming she had finally seen the light on personal security and needed to shred her bank statements, and destroyed everything she had ever written about dreams, car crashes and her imagined connection to Jack. She ripped each page out of her dream notebook and put them in there too, until all her paranoid imaginings were reduced to a bag of curling paper spaghetti that she chucked in the big industrial bin outside.

She gave her painting of those eyes, intense and frightening, to her mum who loved having anything by Anna up in the house, even something that would instil fear in the hearts of visitors. Anna was tired of having to hide it every time Jack came over, spending every minute he was at their house on edge in case he discovered it, breathing a sigh of relief each time he walked out the door and she was safe again until the next time.

'It's lovely, darling, I've put it in the cloakroom, out of the way a bit.'

'No one goes in there!'

'I sometimes go out without a jacket, or with the wrong shoes on, just to avoid looking at it.'

'You don't have to keep it, honestly, Mum. Throw it away. Give it to Dad. Put it in storage.'

'I'm joking. It's in the hall upstairs.'

Ripping down her dream diagram was a bigger job. The Blu Tack had hardened, fused to the wall, threatening to pull big chunks of the paint off when she tried to remove the sheets of wallpaper liner. The room needed repainting anyway, so she spoke to the landlord and offered to do it herself if she could find a colour he liked. That way she could patch up the damage without him seeing it. She chose a few paint samples and sent the options over. For now, it was all safely covered behind *Circles* and a tall bookcase that Anna had bought, giving herself the project of filling up the shelves over the next few months. When he told her which paint he wanted, Anna would go and buy enough of it that she could splash it all over the diagram and let that dry first, before she pulled the wallpaper liner down. If anyone came in she would just say she was testing out the colour on a large surface area, and it would cover all her marker pen writing so that nobody would know what she was throwing away. Then she would redecorate properly, paint the wall underneath.

She half-wished she could keep the chart, show it to Poppy, maybe even the artist Joe Denning, and see what they thought of it as a piece of dark detective work into her innermost mind. But whenever she read it properly she knew she couldn't do that, not when she was with Jack, when they were growing closer every day. It was too plainly written. There was no ambiguity to the sentence 'Jack and I must have met before, and it has something to do with death'.

As she purged her life of all her own evidence, she started to focus on one final experiment she needed to do, something that would put this whole superstitious messiness out of her mind: she wanted to watch herself asleep, to film herself at night so that she could play it back and see herself lying there in bed alone, having the nightmare, and waking up from it. She would realise once and for all that she wasn't in any danger, that there were no holy sorcerers putting Polaroids into her mouth, no malevolent forces at play; it really was all inside her head. She was just somebody having a bad dream, on her own, safe in her room.

Jack was away for the weekend with Mark and Trystan, eating tapas and drinking Rioja in Barcelona, sunning himself in thirty-three-degree heat. Holly was on a work trip, so Anna borrowed a Go Pro camera from her room. She would have time to wipe the card in the morning and replace it before she got back. Holly had been making films for so long, she had accumulated quite a bit of kit over the years. Anna remembered the fixed-position cameras Holly had used to create a time-lapse clip of Anna's team setting up their opening exhibition at White Walls. Holly had stuck the Go Pros in a few rooms and pressed record; the cameras carried on filming for hours.

Anna worked out how to operate it, and where to position it in her room. A quick search online told her that she would have about three hours of recording time if she were lucky. She usually fell asleep at around eleven or half eleven, and if she had the nightmare it was often around two in the morning when she woke up. It might just work. She would have to sleep with more light in the room than usual, but she was so tired she was sure that wouldn't stop her drifting off.

Anna fixed the Go Pro to the corner of her wardrobe with gaffer tape, angling it down so that it would be watching her while she slept. She was looking for the opposite proof to what was commonly sought through the lens in ghost films, where the inanimate mechanics of a camera revealed paranormal activity the

257

human eyes could not discern. She wanted this footage to show her the small and underwhelming reality of her nocturnal haunting, the insignificance of those bedtime fears that she had nurtured so sensitively that they had grown into something cancerous and incurable.

For the first time in her life Anna was pleased when she walked away from the children's play park that she had been standing in, searching the ground for a lost golden necklace, and saw Jack standing in the middle of the road. She was dreaming. She could hear the primary-coloured roundabout in the park behind her grinding its way to a rusty squeaking halt. The swings stopped swinging. The butterfly chorus of children's laughter fluttered into silence.

There was a screech of brakes before she saw the car, swinging wildly out to the side, almost flying up onto two wheels as it took a corner. Jack wasn't moving. It looked like his feet were stuck to the ground. His eyes were closed slightly and he was nodding his head. He had headphones in. He was standing in the middle of the road listening to music. She started concentrating on the car, focusing on redirecting it with her mind.

At first she didn't feel fear. This was what always happened, and tonight she was welcoming it, a lucid-dreaming scientist on a mission. But then he ripped the headphones out of his ears and turned to look at her and his eyes were so awful, so full of pain and suffering that Anna knew he had just lost his parents, orphaned and alone in a world that would never really give him the space or time he needed to recover, that would push him to grow up and look after himself. He looked at her like it was her fault. Anna recoiled from his stare, screwing her eyes up as the car lost control of its hastily re-plotted trajectory to avoid Jack, and crumpled into the black iron railings that surrounded the park.

The Go Pro was looking down on her when Anna opened her eyes, taped at an angle to the top of her wardrobe. She lay still, coaxing her frantically beating heart back to a normal speed, waiting for the paralysis to dissolve from her limbs and lungs so she could take a breath. It was only one-thirty. Instead of the usual hopelessness that followed her realisation of just how many hours were left until dawn, the slight pit-of-the-stomach nausea from waking up at the wrong time, she felt excited. The red light on the side of the camera was blinking; it was still recording.

Anna unstuck it, stopped the camera and took the card out, inserting it directly into the reader on the side of her laptop, knees bunched up around her in bed as she leant over the screen. She didn't get back to sleep for the rest of the night, she just downloaded the single long clip and watched it intently on repeat, four times until the morning. Every time she pressed play her heart was in her mouth, waiting for the thing she had missed, some kind of alien flickering in the corner of the frame, a face at the window, an unexplainable physical change in her own body. There was nothing. She had slept almost completely still, even peacefully, for two hours, lying with her arm above her head and one foot slightly outside the duvet. The only thing Anna noticed was a low moan from her mouth as she dragged her arm down and across her chest before she woke up, her eyes opening and blinking at the light from the floor lamp she had had to leave on.

She yawned as the sun rose outside, the muscles in her head tight from watching the footage instead of resting. Once she had accepted that she had seen and heard everything the recording had to offer, everything that had actually happened in the real waking world, Anna realised how much she had expected to make a discovery. It was the last hurdle, the final obstacle she had built before her own self-imposed finish line of the investigation. She hadn't anticipated sliding over it without a hitch or a fall. It was an anticlimax.

She spent Saturday listless and horizontal on the sofa after an almost completely sleepless night, watching films by herself in the front room without fully engaging in any of them. It had made her miss Jack more, her heart softening towards what was growing between them. Perhaps there really wasn't anything rotten there, waiting to tiptoe blackly on to centre stage and put an end to some macabre performance. If he were there beside her now, she would enjoy being next to him, not worrying that disaster was just over the horizon. They texted back and forth for a few minutes until he told her he was going to meet the others downstairs for dinner, and Anna finally fell asleep, her chest rising and falling slowly under clasped hands in the flickering light of the screen.

# CHAPTER TWENTY-FOUR

Anna wandered around the exhibition. It was easy to forget or grow blind to art you'd been looking at every day, when it was up on display around you for months at a time. She'd noticed it happening with *Circles* at home, had even started getting up in the mornings and being close to fully dressed before she remembered it was there and looked at it again, seeing its beauty.

She was taking Joe Denning for lunch, a professional engagement, but one she undertook gladly, to thank him for his involvement and to congratulate him for his part in bringing a difficult show to life. He was darkly bearded and handsomely dishevelled when he joined Anna at a deli café at the top of Brick Lane, twenty minutes after they arranged to meet. Alexei had told Anna to take him somewhere nice, to push the boat out, but when Anna suggested either Les Trois Garçons, or the five-course tasting menu at The Clove Club, Joe had said he couldn't stand that sort of thing and couldn't they just have a coffee and a chat.

'Sorry I'm late. I'm a mess.'

'Don't worry at all, and you're not a mess.'

'There's no need to be kind,' he scoffed, gesturing to himself. 'I look like a child's drawing of an artist.'

He didn't order any food and Anna self-consciously tucked into her quiche and salad, assuming he wanted to keep it short. They were still there over an hour later.

'Why did you stop taking the photographs? The first time I spoke to you, over the phone, you said it had been an enlightening experience; didn't you want to carry on doing it?'

'Hell no. I can't think of anything worse than being enlightened. Stay well away from enlightenment, whatever you do.'

'I suppose I see what you mean.'

Of course she did. After the grim torture she'd suffered over the past few months as a result of turning her gaze inward, to herself, she would go so far as to say that she wholeheartedly agreed.

'It was pretty much the darkest most difficult year of my life. It took me to a very fragile place.' He caught her eye. 'Am I being dramatic?'

Anna shrugged. 'You can be dramatic.'

'All I have to show for it are a few photographs, but the process of living as much in your dreams at night as you do in your life during the day, utterly destroyed me.'

'I remember you saying, that day in your studio, that we all have a second mind.'

'Yes, we do. And I'm not sure we're meant to get to know it. As soon as I started remembering everything, I spotted all these links between what I was feeling or doing that day and what my mind had gone and turned it into at night. I think we're meant to stay ignorant of those processes.'

'But you didn't necessarily have nightmares?'

'The content wasn't scary. It wasn't like I was watching a horror show every night or anything. But I was waking myself up all the time, and it made things feel … darker. Dreams that didn't contain anything terrifying, just kind of felt wrong. I was being jerked awake by my alarm all the time, coming back to reality halfway through something that my brain needed to see through. My thoughts got stuck there, in the things I'd been seeing. Most days I felt like I was haunted.' He shivered. 'Horrible.'

'So you think if you'd seen the dreams through to the end they wouldn't have troubled you?'

'Precisely. There's a cycle, when we sleep, that I now know shouldn't be interrupted. We should go through all the stages of sleep, allow all of our crazy, psychopathic, violent, sexual urges to develop and die, and then slip back into nothing, erasing the memory of our own madness, so that when we wake up we are blissfully unaware of the layer of depravity, paranoia, and nonsense that lies at the bottom of our thoughts.'

'I thought that having screwed-up nightmares just meant you were sorting through your issues. That it was a helpful process.'

'Sure, but you're not meant to be conscious while it's going on. That's the whole point of dreaming. It's happening behind the scenes. Your mind is sorting through things every night while you're asleep, but you don't want to wake up while that's in full flow, to carry all that shit with you into your daily life. It's like bursting into the back office of your memory to find a weird twisted version of yourself, hunched over a filing cabinet head-deep in your private archives, pulling out records of things that happened to you when you were six or something. Think about it: I bet you can remember a few times when you've woken up in the middle of an odd dream, and it's affected you all day, made you feel like you don't like someone, or that you're scared of something totally bizarre. Imagine that happening every day.'

Anna raised her eyebrows. 'It's just one interpretation though, surely, that dreams are a kind of self-reflexive therapy?'

'I guess, but it's quite common advice – if you read enough about it – for people who suffer from recurring nightmares to be told that they should teach themselves how to see the whole experience through – if you can learn to engage that part of your brain while you're in there of course. You're meant to confront whatever is weirding you out in the dream. *Ask the monster what it wants.* It helps you realise there's nothing there after all. Helps you get over it.'

'And that's the officially recommended way of curing a night terror?'

'All I know is, deliberately remembering my dreams every night did not work for me. I might unwittingly be sharing my bed – and my head – with a fucking lunatic, but I certainly don't want to know about it.'

Anna pushed the rest of her lunch around her plate, unable to fit it around the hard knot of worry forming in her stomach. She knew he was partly right, that people did mostly remember the nightmares they woke up from, the dreams where they were jerked awake mid-flow, as she did herself every night. She'd heard people say that everybody dreams every single night, at least two or three times, but most of us don't remember any of it because the visions are safely contained, cushioned between a layer of restful blackness on either side. Anna was deliberately, lucidly, pulling herself awake, running from the most distressing things she saw in her dreams. Was that what was making this all so traumatising? She was bringing things back into the world with her each morning from a dark secret place, preventing herself from deleting the damage by completing the arc, never working through it all to the very end.

Who knew what might happen if she allowed herself to remain asleep? She would have to force it; it would never happen naturally. The need for air and sanity at the very worst moment of it all was so strong that waking up was like a reflex. She pondered the outcomes, surely infinite and variable. She might discover that the whole dream was just an elaborate joke, that nobody really died, they were all acting in a film. She might even be able to engineer it that way, if she really was mentally in control of everything as it played out.

Over the next few days Anna started going to sleep with a sense of curiosity in her mind, instead of the vice-like grip of dread in her chest. It was the next development in her journey back to the land of the living. She had quelled the obsessed and superstitious part of her with that video footage. It was still saved on her computer for her to watch through, when she felt things begin to disintegrate after a particularly rough night. Now she needed to see the nightmare through and face up to whatever it wanted her to face up to, slipping back into the dreamless sleep that was waiting on the other side of it all, gently forgetting what she had seen as soft waves of nothing rolled over her head.

And that's when it retreated, shy of being

found out; Anna didn't have a single dream for the next four nights. She couldn't understand it. Instead, she drank in sleep like she had found clear cold water after days in the desert. At ten o'clock each night she dropped down into blank space and woke up with her alarm the next morning at seven-thirty. It was the longest run of good sleep she could remember. For the first couple of nights she even missed the nightmares, forsaken by an unwanted companion. Jack watched, amused each morning, as Anna rolled over to hit 'snooze', moving her body for the first time in hours.

'You slept well,' he remarked, gracious enough not to let a hint of jealousy creep into his face as he massaged the tired skin under his eyes and padded off to the bathroom to splash icy water on his face. Maybe it had been as simple as going to bed a little earlier. Maybe she had cured herself.

But on the fourth night, back in her own bed and alone, it came for her, and she opened herself up to the colours around her, like opening her eyes underwater. It had been waiting to speak to her, waiting to get her by herself. It gave little preamble, few elaborate nonsensical events or bizarre and untrue experiences to sidetrack her somewhere surreal before a narrative got under way. It dropped her directly into a memory, to the tail-end of the most dramatic,

268

distressing moment she could remember, vividly, from her childhood. It was soon after she had discovered that her mum was having an affair. With the self-righteous zeal of youth and a burning sense that she personally had been betrayed, she had told her dad everything with no idea of what consequences would rain down on their heads.

She hadn't thought about that day for years, had done everything within her power not to. Sometimes it stayed silent and never surfaced. Other times it felt like forcing the door closed on a room that was overflowing with water or filling with fire. It was difficult to forget, but now she realised it was going to be far harder to let herself remember, faithfully, without distortion.

Ever since Anna saw her mum basking in the happiness of a new love with a man who wasn't her dad, she had looked for signs. At home, she tested them, deliberately sitting on the armchair instead of in between them on the sofa, so that they had no choice but to sit together. When they were on the way somewhere she walked behind instead of up front like she usually would, chattering this way and that to one or both of them. Now, she waited a few paces back for them to link arms or hold hands like they used to and felt a 'ha' of satisfaction followed by a great swell of sadness when they didn't.

That night in her dream she went back to the

time and place when she had ruined it all, standing in the hallway at home after an argument with her mum. She couldn't remember exactly what it had been about, but they fell out a lot then. Anna had stopped trusting her mum now she knew that she wasn't faithful. She didn't recognise her; she didn't look like her mum any more. So Anna told her dad what was going on right there and then in the hall. She told them both that she knew her mum was in love with somebody else.

'I've seen her with a man, at his house on the way back from town, in a special dress. She was laughing.' She turned to her mum, disgusted. 'You were sitting on his lap.'

Instead of the hell-raising row she had expected, had even clenched her fists for, there was silence. Fury and rage would have been easier to cope with than the half-smiles her parents gave each other, her dad hurt and shocked but also, infuriatingly, amused at the unhappy state they had both found themselves in. Eventually he spoke.

'You were laughing?'

Her mum's eyes flickered from the grim acceptance of her cuckolded husband to her young daughter. She put her hand on Anna's head and stroked her hair before she looked back at him.

'I was,' she whispered.

Her dad put his head in his hands but stayed standing up, rubbing his face with his fingers and sighing. He exhaled with a groan. 'We've kept this going on for a while, haven't we?'

'We tried.' That was all her mum said.

For a while afterwards, when they were still attending mutual friends' parties and dinners together, Daniel and Elizabeth would recount the tale of 'how he asked', a romantic divorce story that involved Daniel getting down on one knee in the hallway and asking if Elizabeth would grant him the honour of divorcing him. She had burst out laughing and he had said, relieved, 'at least I can – on occasion – still make you giggle,' and tears had crept into her eyes.

Now, as an adult, Anna could see the dark comedy in it, could understand why people enjoyed hearing it at the time. It was so much easier to react to than the usual morose template, a family torn apart by infidelity, a dreamy long life together cut short by one terrible transgression. At the time though, it was painful and inappropriate. Her parents might have half-realised that their relationship had fragmented into something even more apathetic than animosity over the course of her childhood, but she hadn't. Where was the crying, the frustration, the betrayal? Why were they laughing and agreeing to split up, trying to make Anna feel as though she was a part of

271

the whole sorry conversation?

'Wouldn't you like it if we were both happy again? Even if it means we don't all live here together?'

She didn't understand. They were happy now.

Anna couldn't believe it. Her stupid short-sighted actions had precipitated the breakdown of her whole family. She had wanted some kind of tearful embrace, for her dad to realise that they needed to fix things, urgently, and for them to all cling on to one another and stick together. Other people's parents got divorced, not hers. Divorce, separation, broken families, were for people like Kerry at school who had brothers and sisters from three different fathers and a snappy pink track-suited Rottweiler of a mum with a drink problem. Or else it was a glamorous, Bohemian decision, like the twins Jessica and Anthony, whose parents were too *artistic* to remain together 'in the traditional sense' and now lived in houses next door to one another, their mum with her long-term girlfriend and their dad with his band. That was a utopian divorce, pioneering a trend for familial counter-culture. Hers was just sad and unfortunate, two people who had fallen out of love and an only child who was now going to be even lonelier at home than she already was.

As Anna forced herself to settle into being back there, to remembering this in all its ugliness, the swift curtains of dread started folding down around the memory and she knew that an accident was waiting just around the corner. She kept her dream eyes open, making herself watch their conversation from start to finish and then beyond, as she left the house and stepped out through the front garden and up the road, unable to stay in the same room as her parents and their bizarre twisted cheerfulness at the prospect of ending their marriage. But where had she gone? Why couldn't she recall the rest of that evening? She had been soaking, wet through to her cold shivering skin when she got back to the house. Her mum had screeched at her like a banshee, crying and asking her why she had been out so long in the winter rain, shouting that they had thought she had run away or got lost.

*Good*, Anna had thought. *So you are worried about how I'm taking all of this. You should be.*

'We thought you'd been run over.' Her mum wept, hugging her.

Run over.

Rain.

Anna followed the dream wave. She was crouched in the middle of the road just above her house. It wound its way up and out of Brighton, over the South Downs to the picturesque red-brick villages and hamlets beyond. It was after rush hour, just before nightfall, and everywhere was quiet. How had she never gone through this before? She had never allowed herself to remember how she had slipped down that grass verge, the tread of her shoes wet and worn smooth by the rain and the gravel. She had fallen onto the tarmac by accident, trying to push herself up on her arms and get out of the road.

That twisted dread, the need to wake up, to stop looking at all, it wasn't fear of a nightmare: it was fear of a memory. She was living her life in abject terror of being reminded of a horror she had fought to keep silent, almost as though it had been forgotten. Except it hadn't. It was written in her bones. It had been dormant, and now it was waking up.

Anna was trying to get to her feet, tiny stones sticking into the soft skin of her forearms as she pushed herself up and away from the surface of the road. A car was coming towards her. The light was on inside. Maybe they'd been map reading, or looking for something. It illuminated Jack's dad in the driving seat, squinting against the dazzle of the bulb they had forgotten to turn off. Jack was in the passenger seat next to him. His mum was in the back, leaning through the gap in between the front seats so she could have a conversation with the two of them. Anna recognised them both from Jack's photograph.

His mum had no seat belt on, but Jack did, and all of a sudden his scar made sense. A laceration from hip to collarbone from the force of a seat belt wrenching into his body, cutting him open as it was saving his life. She had been there. She shook her head at how slow she had been, how reluctantly the cogs in her mind must have been turning over the past few weeks for it to have taken her so long to get to this point. She forced herself to stick with it, holding herself back down like she was pushing her thirteen-year-old self back onto the wet ground. Her eyes met Jack's and locked onto his stare, the same stare she saw almost every night in her sleep, the eyes of somebody who has seen their future, who knows that something awful is about to happen and cannot do anything to stop it.

Jack saw her crouching in the road, but the car was too close. All he had time to do was scream. He screamed at his dad to look up, to stop bending his head down to listen to something Mum was saying and look at the girl on the ground in front of them in the middle of the road. His dad wrestled with the steering wheel, curving the car in a thick cloud of sickening burning rubber over to the other side of the road. The whole car wrapped itself around a tree on the driver's side. Anna could smell petrol leaking onto the ground. Jack's dad was unconscious. His mum was hidden in the crushed back end of the car. The space she had been sitting in no longer existed, her body flattened to nothing by sheets of crumpled metal. As Anna watched a cloud of steam lift from around the vehicle, she saw Jack hanging from his seat belt. His door had flown off and the seat, partly broken, had swung around to face the outside. He dangled grotesquely a few inches from the ground.

She thought they were all dead when she turned and ran away, but halfway down the road she heard a sickening wail, pain rupturing from Jack's throat as he swam up from unconsciousness to gasp a few seconds of air. Anna couldn't tell if he was crying for help, fighting for his life, or dying in loud painful death roars. She didn't turn around. She didn't even look back. The sound of her heels banging against the ground and her breath scraping the inside of her throat followed her all the way home like a pack of angry dogs she couldn't outrun.

Why had she even run away from home in the first place? It wasn't something she had ever done before, had never even thought about. Her mum used to, when she was young, she had said.

'I'd flounce out of the back door and over the fields, vowing I would wait for at least a day before I came back, and really make them suffer.'

'Where did you sleep?'

'I never got that far. I always got hungry after about two hours and had to come home for a sandwich.'

She didn't usually fall out with her parents. She wasn't difficult. They had never had feuds. Why had she chosen that evening to try and shake things up? She had wrecked her parents' marriage and ruined Jack's life. Jack had said that his parents died instantly, that the force of the impact had killed them both by the side of the road. Maybe he had insisted on sitting up front with his dad. If he hadn't, his mum would probably still be alive now, still grieving for her boys somewhere in a new life.

Anna didn't force herself awake, she didn't have to in the end. Nausea heaved its way to the surface, and pulled her eyes apart while her hands reached for where she knew the waste-paper bin was, below her bedside table. She pulled it towards her and vomited.

Of course she recognised Jack; she had killed his parents.

# PART 3

# CHAPTER TWENTY-FIVE

The terrible noise that Jack made, guttural and agonised, followed Anna from the memory and into her bedroom, where she woke up to the crack of her dream web ripping from the wall. The Blu Tack had finally given up, grown brittle and dry after weeks cemented between paint and paper, and the weight of the long thick sheets of grainy parchment had dragged them away from the wall. It took a few seconds to work out what was happening; her head reverberated with Jack's ear-splitting cry, and then this. At first, Anna thought the ceiling was falling in, or the house was crumbling to its foundations. Then the paper collapsed onto the floor in long curls, writhing out from behind the bookcase, like a slain animal across the carpet. Everything fell silent.

She poured her vomit down the toilet, her arms so shaky and weak that even lifting the waste-paper bin high enough to tip it out was a challenge. In the kitchen, she dropped it into a large carrier bag, tied it carefully, and took it to the industrial bin on the pavement outside. Nobody woke up when she slammed back into the house. It was almost dawn. The thought of dragging her numb body across the city to work made her want to throw up all over again. She climbed back upstairs, washed, got dressed, and sat on the edge of her bed waiting for the sun to rise as details from her buried memory began to grow clearer in her mind.

She had come home in the dark, covered in rainwater, her cold skin smelling of soil and dirt. She had thrown her trainers away because they were mud-soaked and torn, and picked the tiny pieces of gravel from red grazes in the soft heels of her hands, washing the sharp stones away in the basin in the downstairs toilet. Then she had stripped naked, dropping her sodden clothes on the bathroom mat before climbing into a steaming shower. The water was so hot it turned her skin bright tomato red. The next morning before school she heard about the accident. Either she had seen details of it on the morning news, or she had heard her parents remarking on it sadly, shaking their heads at the local tragedy while they read the papers over breakfast; she couldn't remember which. But she did remember bolting up from the kitchen table, soggy cornflakes still floating milky and soft around the inside of her mouth, and doing exactly what she had just done this morning, heaving her guts up into the sink.

She remembered her parents crowding her, concern on their faces, her mum putting the back of a hand on to Anna's clammy forehead and breathing in sharply. 'You poor thing; you're burning up.' She had lain on the sofa under a blanket while her mum telephoned the school, and then called her office, explaining in a low apologetic voice that she was going to have to work from home, that her daughter was very unwell.

*I suppose I am*, Anna had thought, as she threw up again into the silver cake bowl on the floor next to her head.

Her mum said she must have caught a chill from running around in the rain with no coat on. Anna could see that both her parents felt guilty about it from the looks they kept giving each other, shocked that their decision to break up had made her physically ill. Her head hurt from crying, and the more her mum did for her, buying her cherry drops and magazines from the corner shop and making her waffles for lunch, the more Anna cried, convinced that all of this was surely going to disappear and change, now that she had lost her family. So she had chosen to believe what her parents said, that she was in shock, that she had caught a fluey cold when she had run away from home, and nothing more.

It was bizarre how by the sheer brute force of private denial, you could completely alter your own history. Memory wasn't fixed, it wasn't a factual and accurate record of the past; it was malleable, slippery and shape-shifting, dangerously subjective. When she was about eleven, playing with friends in her bedroom, Anna had got giddy with excitement and decided to dial 999 for fun. Egged on by Natasha and another girl, Laura, Anna had taken the portable handset off the wall downstairs and run up to her room with it. As soon as she had heard that calm official voice on the other end of the line, patiently listing the options, asking her whether she needed police, fire, or ambulance, Anna had chickened out and gone silent, saying nothing. It turned out she hadn't hung up the phone properly, and half an hour later an ambulance arrived at the front door, a polite but curt man in uniform asking to be let in. Her dad had found the handset under the duvet in her bedroom and his face darkened, ready to get seriously angry, to make an example out of her in front of her friends. Anna insisted they hadn't done anything. The phone had an emergency dial setting on the handset; it must have been pushed by accident; no, she hadn't noticed that it was even in her bedroom.

Eventually, Anna had convinced her dad, but even stranger than that, she had come close to convincing herself too. Her lie was so plausible that she was almost unsure of her own memory. She could remember her feigned shock and surprise as genuine emotions, when her dad peeled back the covers to discover the telephone sitting under there, 999 in its most recent call list. That moment was sharper and clearer than the memory of stealing the phone and dialling the number. She had replaced a fact she was ashamed of with a fiction she could stomach, misdemeanour with myth, to the point where it was difficult to summon up the truth even when she tried. It was too alarming to accept that you could do something similar with an event this huge, and this damaging.

As soon as it was nine-thirty, Anna called work and told them she was sick. Poppy didn't question it. She could hear the exhaustion in Anna's voice, the nausea that she had to grit her teeth to speak through. Anna wasn't even sure that it was a lie. She was ill and panicky, emotional trauma creeping over the borders into physical illness, infecting her body with guilt, a real contagious disease.

If what she had just remembered was true, if it had really happened like that, then all the wildly imaginative, magical possibilities she had indulged in for the past few weeks shrunk into nothing. Reality got smaller again, a room with its walls closing in.

Only, so many of her dreams had turned out to be completely untrue; what if this was another false memory, like Natasha's birthday party, or Jack's cruel ability to manipulate her mind? She had woken up from dreaming about the birthday party and been absolutely convinced that she was going to find hard evidence tucked inside that box of photographs, showing her and Jack sitting just a few feet away from each other as children. And she had shouted at Jack in front of a whole crowd of people, had tried to force him to confess to something she had only seen evidence of while she was asleep. She needed to make sure that this disaster was real, before she tried to work out what to do about it.

She waited for the girls to leave for work, her back stiff from where she had sat bolt upright for the past few hours, going over everything frantically in silence. She left the house but she didn't want go past Jack's front door, to risk seeing him or one of his housemates leaving for work, so she deliberately walked the wrong way down the street, doubling back on herself along the main road to get to the train station. She took the tube to Victoria station, and jumped on the first train to Brighton. It was the stopping service, crawling past every station, painfully slow, and Anna's anxiety grew in her chest until every breath hurt, each bubble of air pressing against her ribcage while she fiddled with her fingers and tried to remember to keep breathing.

On the train, she called the Records and Archive Office to check it would be open and to find out exactly where it was. The man on the end of the line sounded relaxed, pondering, like he might be a volunteer. His speed of thought was even slower than the train she was stuck on.

'We're up at The Keep, dear, on Woollards Way. It's a rather striking white building, Modernist-style I suppose you might say.' He confirmed that yes they did have newspapers, obituaries, wills, burial records, and then he started to pick up steam, launching into a proud spiel about how exemplary the East Sussex Records Office was, how it had information dating back nearly a thousand years.

He hesitated. 'Might I ask, what exactly are you looking for? Are you travelling far? Over eighty per cent of the information is online now, you know. Are you a member?'

Anna grimaced for a moment at the thought she could have done all this from the comfort and safety of her room, alone, warm under her duvet. But it was better to be there, in Brighton where it had happened, and where she and Jack had lived side by side as children.

She took advantage of the man's offer of help, signing up to be a member over the phone, telling him that she was interested in looking at copies of the daily local papers from Friday 21st January 2000 until the following Friday. He tried to keep the curiosity out of his voice. *Ask me*, Anna wanted to say. *Ask me why I need to see them*. At that moment she would have told him everything, just for the awful thrill of hearing the words come out of her mouth for the first time, flooring the nice man with the horrible reason for her journey, sitting back, waiting for him to struggle for a response.

As soon as she got off the train, she took a taxi to the address he had given her, holding the seat belt between her hands the entire time, a few centimetres away from her body, looking down at it like she had never seen one before. It would never have occurred to her that the ragged red line across Jack's body could have come from something that was meant to save your life. His scar was too violent and extreme; it looked angry, personal, as if it had been caused by rage or hatred. She had no idea that a seat belt could make that kind of mark on a person.

She found The Keep, its white walls glowing in bright sunlight that made her feel dazed, and logged on to the digital newspaper archives inside. Everything slotted into place instantly. It was front-page news on the Saturday. The facts were inconclusive, the cause of the crash was uncertain, but it looked as though the car had swerved to avoid something on the road. It seemed the brakes had been applied before the vehicle lost control which suggested it wasn't caused by a driver error. The paper speculated that the man had been spooked by something in the middle of the road, referring to previous council meetings on road safety, where the decision had been vetoed to put up signs warning drivers that deer may wander onto the roads.

The weather was mentioned: the fact that the rain would have made an animal more difficult to spot and would have made it harder to break at speed. Traces of footprints had been found near the scene, but the police had quickly issued a statement to say that these were unlikely to be connected. Feathers lined the front bumper of the family's car. It was most likely a bird, an unlucky pheasant that had met its end when they had. A combination of speed and the angle of impact had meant that Jack's dad hadn't survived. His feet were trapped in the foot well beneath the steering wheel, a severe compound fracture on each leg had meant he lost too much blood too quickly. He was already deceased when the firemen detached the roof of the car and lifted him out. His mum had not been wearing a seat belt. Anna was surprised by the level of detail that the report went into, but maybe this sort of article always did. Maybe she just didn't normally notice, because she didn't usually know the people involved. Maybe readers liked the drama. Their son Jack, aged fifteen, was in a stable but critical condition in intensive care. By the following Friday the paper reported that Jack Bridger had regained consciousness.

Anna had become one of Truss's murder studies. It was like discovering blood-soaked knives in the back pocket of her own jeans, seeing freeze-framed CCTV footage that put her at the scene of a crime, being violently introduced to her own culpability. She carried on looking, reading through the obituaries for Anthony and Jane Bridger that appeared a couple of days later. She found the details of the memorial service, and the burial records showing that their headstones were at Woodvale Crematorium just outside the town centre, husband and wife side by side as little mounds of ashes in the ground.

She knew where Woodvale was, so she

started walking, two and a half miles along a road above the town. The time and the distance, the emptiness in her legs, didn't register on the way there. She only noticed the bright summer sun, blazing down inappropriately on the top of her head, making her squint as she walked, making her head ache. Anna approached the open gates, suddenly edgy. What if she bumped into somebody she knew? She wandered over the soft grass, up and down the sunlit paths. It was so peaceful. Her body felt like it was barely there.

Anthony and Jane's remains sat beneath a single rectangular tablet of polished black granite. It was a perfectly kept shrine, carefully arranged clouds of summer flowers blooming colourfully around the wide dark stone. Either Jack came here without her knowing, or there was a whole family of people missing them every day, wishing they were here, tending to this patch of earth every week. Anna was horrified that she had walked all the way here with nothing to offer.

They had always sounded funny and good-humoured in Jack's stories, people she wished she could have met. When he had told her about their epitaph, she had been unsure whether he was joking or not, and so nervous about causing any offence by pressing him on the subject, that she hadn't said much. He told her that they always loved Spike Milligan's idea, that when he eventually passed away, he would have 'I told you I was ill' carved into his headstone. They agreed it should be laughter, rather than tears, that rang out across the crematorium from their grave, for hilarity to be the first thing that happened when people came to pay their respects. Anthony and Jane had died two years before Spike; they had got there first. And there it was, their last laugh. Anna couldn't believe the whole family had agreed to it, had known them well enough to understand that those speculative conversations ran deeper, that this was really what they would have wanted: *She always said he couldn't drive.*

Anna sunk down on the grass beside the headstone, tired tears slipping through the corners of her eyelids even while she laughed at the joke. She curled onto her side, not sure if she was adopting the recovery position or curling up like a foetus, desperate not to have to go home and tell Jack what she knew she needed to. She just wanted the sun to warm her skin and for all the rest of it not to exist. Reeling through her mind was a slideshow – Jack's eyes when he caught her watching him outside the pub, the eyes that now followed her through her nightmares, that smiled at her when she climbed into bed. Somewhere in the middle of it all she must have fallen asleep.

When she opened her eyes the ground was cooler. The sun was still high in the sky, but it was nearly half past five and clouds were gathering overhead. A few feet away beside another grave, a couple were talking. Anna overheard them say that the crematorium gates would be closing in a few minutes. Anna jumped up and dusted herself down, self-conscious and embarrassed that she had been lying asleep on the grass in full view of other mourners, draped over Jack's parents' grave. She hadn't eaten since yesterday. Her stomach was empty, and sore from being sick. As she stood up too quickly, the sounds around her faded. Everything started to echo as though it was very far away. Black spots crept into the corner of her vision and her body crumpled forward, her eyelids closing, everything shutting down while the blood dropped to her feet.

She woke up in an ambulance on the way to hospital. The couple beside her in the graveyard had seen her go down, her head dropping out of sight between the tombstones. They had panicked, thinking they had just watched as a young woman, surrounded by the dead and buried, had decided to join them six feet underground. They had called the emergency services. They were on their way out to a birthday meal, but had left their number with the paramedics in case she needed them.

'I'm fine. I'm fine.' She kept repeating, although nobody seemed to be listening to her. 'I just had a shock, that's all. I haven't eaten enough today. I've been busy. Can I get out please?'

For a second she panicked when she tried to sit up, thinking she had been tied down, restrained, but then she realised her arms were too heavy to lift, lying like lead weights by her sides.

'We'll just get you checked over, love. It won't take a second.'

The paramedic was holding a blood pressure band around her upper arm and watching a screen mounted on the inside of the ambulance above her head.

'I'm fine honestly. Where are we? I'll get out here. Can you drop me at the train station?'

The paramedic chuckled and raised her eyebrows at the driver, but her expression softened when she saw Anna's face collapse, her bottom lip trembling like a child. She squeezed Anna's arm kindly.

'Your heartbeat's very fast. That's probably why you feel a bit trembly. You're dehydrated. Just rest up in A&E for an hour or so, and let us get you back on your feet before you head home. How old are you?'

'I'm twenty-eight. You don't need to call anybody for me, do you? Please don't.'

'Of course not, sweetie.'

They put her in one of the blue hospital beds, just like the one her mum had been in, probably the same as the one Jack had lain in while he was recovering. They wheeled her around to Majors and hooked her up to an ECG. They said her heart rate was fine, it was regular, but very fast, and put a cannula in her arm so they could hydrate her quickly. Anna hated that. The moment you were attached to a drip you were truly hospitalised, an ill person, a patient. She was trapped, claustrophobic. She wanted to rip the needle out of her hand. She wouldn't be able to take it if they tried to tie her up in one of those foul blue open-backed gowns.

'Don't worry about that sign.' The nurse had seen her eyes flickering to the Majors notice on the door as they pushed her through the corridor. 'It's just the only place we've got space right now. I'm sure you'll be out in no time.'

'I just fainted. I'm fine.'

The doctor told her that her signs were normalising, that she could go home soon, but that she must make sure to eat. She stole a look at her phone after he left: seventeen missed calls; Holly had texted her; Jack was looking for her. Anna had forgotten they were meant to be going out tonight. Holly said he had gone up to drop some clothes in her room that he had washed for her, things she had left at his house after their endless nomadic back and forths, the spontaneous sleepovers in each other's beds. Her dream charts were lying all over the bedroom floor, covered in her ideas and handwriting, showing every single detail from the last two months of her twisted nightlife. If he saw it all and worked it out, everything would be over. He couldn't find out like that. What time was it?

She had to get home. She puffed her way through the removal of the cannula, easing the long hollow needle out of her vein, forcing herself to keep her eyes open so she could see what she was doing, praying that nobody would come in and stop her. She had to stop suddenly with it halfway out of her arm when she heard her doctor having a conversation on the other side of the curtains. He was discussing another patient with somebody. After a few moments he moved off down the corridor. She pulled the metal out, and pressed down on the red spot with her thumb while she levered her legs out of bed, found her shoes in a plastic bag on the chair, her handbag behind it, and walked out of the hospital.

It would take too much energy to get to the

train station now, to navigate her way through Victoria on a Friday night and pack herself underground on a hot sweaty tube train to get home, walking past tipsy groups of friends on their way out for the night. There was a taxi rank outside the hospital, so she asked to go all the way back to Hackney. The driver checked three times: was she definitely sure she needed to go that far in a cab? He fixed her with a worried fatherly stare, taking in the smudges of mascara under her eyes, her cracked dry lips, the dark stigmata spot of venous blood on the back of her right hand. He told her it would be a hundred and thirty pounds. She nodded over and over again until he let her into the back seat.

'Just take me to a cashpoint on the way.'

She had to get home.

# CHAPTER TWENTY-SIX

'He left.' Holly looked stunned. 'He went upstairs for a bit and I sort of forgot he was there. I was making dinner,' she hesitated. 'He must have been up there for ages. And then, I was just sitting down in the front room, and he ran past and shouted that you weren't to contact him. Anna, what the fuck is all this?'

Holly was standing in the middle of Anna's bedroom when she got home, in a sea of torn paper shreds, staring while Anna surveyed the wreckage, swaying slightly against the doorframe. Holly picked a big strip up off the carpet, holding it between her finger and thumb, as though she didn't really want to touch it, a wildlife expert picking up a long thin poisonous snake and trying not to get bitten. Anna tilted her head to one side, her eyes spacey and tired, reading through her own manic lines of scrawling questions. *Why do I dream about Jack's eyes? Have they always been his eyes, or did it change when I met him?*

Anna turned around and ran after him. This room made her look unhinged. Had he worked it out? Or had he always known that she might be the girl from the accident? It had been frightening, exactly how she had known it would be, to see somebody else surrounded by her own fragmented questions, violent memories from over two months of nightmares. Coming in and finding this, Jack must have been confused and scared. It all needed explaining.

'What are you doing? Where are you going? Why doesn't he want to see you?' Holly shouted after her, but Anna was focussed on getting over to Jack's house as quickly as possible, her feet pounding every step on the way downstairs. She didn't have time to reply before she slammed the front door behind her. She had to try and sort this out now. If she left it, if she didn't find him and talk to him tonight, it would all be broken. It was probably broken anyway.

She ran past the clusters of people outside the pub, almost knocking someone over. Thick clouds of cigarette smoke polluted the air around their conversations. Their happiness felt ominous, so unconcerned, so carefree. Nobody realised how fragile they all were. Week after week people were blindly pumping their bodies full of nicotine, tar, drink and drugs, and laughing while they did it. How had it taken her so long to understand what a dangerous place this world was?

The big window in the living room at the front of Jack's house was open, and Anna could see him walking around on the other side of the low black balcony railings. She shouted up at him but he left the room, so she rang the doorbell, over and over again, until she got fed up of pressing the little round white buzzer button and started battering the door with her fist instead. She tired quickly. She had no strength left in her. She leant against the cracked white paint, her hands shaking, the brass number 42 making a dent in her forehead, and wept.

When the door eventually opened, she almost fell over, toppling forwards into the hallway. Hayley was on the other side, opening it just a few inches. She was looking away from Anna over her shoulder up the stairs, and shouting back inside at Jack.

'You have to let her in. This is ridiculous.'

'I do not.'

Anna couldn't see Jack, but she could hear him. How had he managed to make his voice sound so level, so emotionless?

'You don't know what this is about, Hayley. Just leave her outside.'

*Please*, Anna begged silently. *Please don't tell them why we're fighting. Please don't tell them what I've done.*

Eva ran down the stairs behind Hayley to the door. Of course: they would all have to be in there. Eva looked at her, opening the door a few inches wider, dressed up and ready to go out, all high-heels and fluttering eyelashes. They both looked genuinely concerned, and Anna wanted to launch herself across the threshold and hug them both on the spot for not automatically assuming that she was in the wrong, even though she was. They weren't going to let Jack leave her on the doorstep.

'Jack, we're going to let her in.'

It was Eva who shouted this time, looking at Anna while she did so, reaching out into the street to squeeze her hand.

'I live here, Eva, and I don't have to let her in if I don't want to.'

'Well, I practically live here, too, and I'm opening the door.'

'You do not live here.'

'I've paid Mark's fucking rent for the last three months. I'm opening the door, Jack.'

'I'm going upstairs then.'

Anna heard Jack's footsteps receding into the distance above them, his bedroom door closing with a bang. The girls pulled the door all the way open and ushered her into the living

301

room, arms around her, steering her onto the sofa. They left her and went into the kitchen; Mark and Chris were getting involved now. Anna was too exhausted and too strung out to be embarrassed by any of it.

'What's going on? What the fuck is this?'

'Has she cheated on him?'

'Has she met someone else? Has *he* met someone else?'

Anna hadn't heard Jack come back down the stairs, but it was his voice that replied, weary now, and unmistakably angry.

'No, I haven't met somebody else. It's too complicated to explain.'

'I don't think we should get involved Hayley,' Chris said. 'Just leave it.'

'Shut up, Chris. Have you seen her? She's distraught.'

'Which is precisely why we should leave them alone. It's none of our business.'

Hayley ignored him. 'Jack, why is she crying?'

Arguments started to break out between the other two couples, conversations frayed and turned to bickering. Hayley and Eva had been drinking since before the others got home from work, and Chris suggested to Hayley that she sit down and have a glass of water; it didn't go down well.

Trystan crossed the hallway past the living-room door and looked in on Anna, raising his eyebrows to ask if she was OK. She nodded quickly, remembering the night when he had caught her frantically scribbling down the details of her visions in her little notebook, curled up in the same spot she was sat in now, looking guilty. She sensed that out of everybody, Jack was closest to Trystan. If Chris had known about Jack's nightmares, that meant Trystan probably did too. He hovered by the door, looking like he knew there was more to all of this, before he sloped off to the kitchen.

'Jack,' she heard him say, 'if we all go off to the pub, will you two at least talk? We'll be just next door if you need us.'

Jack walked silently into the front room and sat down opposite her. He said nothing. Anna sat on her hands to stop herself from jumping up and reaching out to hold him. The others all left in a line, trooping past the doorway, casting anxious glances back as they went, looking nervously from Anna's tear-stained cheeks to Jack's blank face. The door closed. Everything inside was quiet. Outside, the occasional siren peeled up and over the houses from the main road; murmuring laughter and clinking glasses floated through the window from the pub beer garden behind the flat.

Jack stared at her. His hatred was less

exaggerated than in her twisted technicolour nightmares, but so much more painful for being real. The difference between how he looked at her now and how he had smiled at her yesterday morning in bed, his eyes creasing at the corners in happiness while he stroked her sleepy cheek, felt like grief.

'I wish you hadn't done that.'

'Sorry.' She was trying to stop crying, fed up of swallowing salt water.

'When did you work it all out?'

'A few hours ago. This morning.'

Jack looked shocked. He took it in.

'Oh.'

'Oh my God.' Panic rose in her chest. 'Did you think I'd known about this for ages? Did you? Of course I haven't.'

'It looked like you had been thinking about it for a while. How could you not know?' He blinked. 'What's that on your hand, and your wrist?'

She had forgotten to take the white plastic hospital band off her arm. The wound from her hastily removed cannula had opened up again, spotting dark drops of red onto her jeans. Anna rubbed her eyes, giving herself a couple of seconds to work out how to explain.

'I went to Brighton today.'

'What?'

'I don't understand any of this either. But

maybe I turned everything that night into a nightmare instead of remembering it all for real because I didn't want it to be true ... that I'm a murderer.'

He flinched. 'You're not. It's sadder than that.'

Anna sniffed. 'Last night I realised where this was all coming from, all the dreams. But I've had nights like that before, where I've seen something in my sleep, decided it's true, and then it turns out to be something I invented, some hallucination or false memory that's completely meaningless. So I went to make sure.'

'How?'

'I checked the local papers, from the next day. It really happened. I read everything about it. In the crematorium—'

'—You went to see their grave?'

'Maybe I shouldn't have done that.'

Jack was quiet.

'I'm sorry.'

Anna hung off a cliff, waiting for him to pick her white knuckles up off the rocks she was clinging to and fling her over the side. But when he spoke again there was emotion in his voice at last; she could finally hear Jack behind his words, instead of somebody strange, calm and empty.

'When I found everything in your bedroom,

305

it was like I had no idea who you were.' He closed his eyes. 'And then you weren't there, and I couldn't get hold of you. I started to think that you'd known about this for ages, that maybe you'd even been keeping it from me deliberately, that Norway was just some kind of sick joke. I know. I know how that sounds.' He held up a hand to stop her from getting upset, looking at her properly at last. 'Thank you for going to see them. It still doesn't explain all that though.' He pointed at her hand.

'I fainted. I don't know how. Someone called an ambulance for me. I'm fine.'

She had been saying that a lot today. She wasn't fine at all. Jack looked like he wanted to come and sit beside her, to put his arms round her, but he didn't. It was awful, sitting there, wishing he would hold her, and painful to watch him convince himself not to, staying firmly put and keeping his distance. She should be looking after him. He put his head in his hands.

'I still don't understand how you didn't know.'

'But, how did *you* not know? We were both there. You saw me that night, too, didn't you? I was right in the middle of the road. You stared right at me.'

Jack shook his head, confused by everything

that he was discovering, spreading his hands hopelessly in front of his face.

'I saw … something. At first I did definitely think it was a person, a girl. But then everything got confused. When they carried me out to the ambulance it felt like just a few seconds after the crash, only it couldn't have been. I must have passed out for a while, but it seemed immediately the flashing lights were there and I was on a stretcher. I even thought that the ambulance had been waiting on the road for the accident to happen, it was so quick; nothing felt right. I looked around and I couldn't see anything there, she – you – had disappeared. So, I decided I'd imagined it.'

'But you were staring straight at me?'

'When I saw all your notes lying on your floor, I knew for sure: yes, it was definitely a girl. But, at the time, everybody said it was an animal. I thought that made more sense, that I must have turned the shape of a deer into a crouched little girl. I started changing what I thought I'd seen to make it fit.'

'We looked at each other.'

'I was partly staring at myself too. The angle of the car when Dad lost control, it made everything tilted, skewed. I could see my own eyes reflected in the rear-view mirror. I looked so terrified. I didn't recognise myself. I kept staring, wondering if it was really my face. It must have all taken about three seconds, but it lasted so much longer in my head. Time went strange, really slow and detailed, every millisecond like one long journey to the next one, only with huge big black chunks missing too. But then ...'

'What?'

Jack shivered. 'I did hear footsteps. I heard the sound of somebody running away. I thought I screamed for help, but maybe I imagined that as well.'

'You did scream.' Anna's voice cracked. 'I didn't turn back.'

'I thought it might have been my own heartbeat in my ears instead, or me wishing that I could jump up out of the car and run away. Everything's out of sequence, all muddled. I heard you running after I was carried out of the car, but it must have happened before. I did hear your footsteps then,' he repeated to himself. 'I listened to them all the way down the hill. Your feet were splashing on the wet ground.'

'I should have told you when I saw your drawing; I should have said that I saw the same thing in my sleep. I don't know why we never spoke about the details.'

'I can't be bothered to talk about what should and shouldn't have happened. None of this should have happened. But it did. It has.'

'Is this why we met?'

'How many times do I have to say it? There is no *why*. None of this is pre-ordained. There's no reason behind any of it, no such thing as fate, no huge spinning concentric circle of closure: it's just bad luck, really bad, fucking horrible luck. It's bad luck that you were there; it's even worse that you remembered. It would never have mattered to me, if I'd not known. But I do know, and so do you, so here we are.'

'What do we do now?'

'Why are you asking me?'

He stood up. Anna was close to grabbing him by the hands, kneeling on the floor and begging him to tell her that everything would be OK, only she couldn't move properly, couldn't feel her legs. It didn't feel like something she would do. It would have been too dramatic, theatrical. She stood up instead, balancing on her shaky legs in silence.

'Please go home. I can't do this now.'

'When will you be able to do it?'

'I don't know.'

Anna left. The air between them was hollow and silent when she stepped past him into the hallway. He didn't reach out to touch her as she went; he didn't even look like he wanted to. This was Jack's decision. This had happened to him, to his family. She couldn't tell him how to feel about it, or try to convince him that he could get past it. She didn't want to force him to sit next to her, to have to watch his eyes as he struggled to look at her face without seeing their death. What had she expected when she ran over here? Did she think she would be able to make everything right again, immediately? It was like her parents all over again, the world repeatedly finding ways to show her that love was never enough. Because she did love him. She knew, even as she admitted it to herself, that this was the worst time to realise it, when she had already lost him.

As soon as she was back on the pavement outside, weaving wearily down the street towards home, she was so consumed by the urge to run back inside and try harder to make it bearable for him, to fix things, that it was difficult to keep walking in the other direction. She was an addict, twitchy and terrified now that she didn't know when she would next see Jack, craving the way it had felt yesterday to wake up beside him before any of this existed, wondering if she would ever be able to make him feel good again.

# CHAPTER TWENTY-SEVEN

At home, Anna attacked the shredded rolls of wallpaper liner, bundling them up, and carrying the whole mess down to the cast-iron bucket outside on the garden path. She soaked them in firelighter fluid from the cupboard under the kitchen sink, the kind they usually used to get barbecues going on sunny Sunday afternoons, and dropped a handful of lit matches on top of it all. Anna slumped back on the garden bench. The fire danced into life. She sipped vodka from the bottle, reaching out to dribble a thin stream of it down over the paper shreds, making the flames spit, leaping higher. She opened her lips and breathed alcohol fumes out into the evening air, wondering if the fire might find its way into her mouth, set her tongue alight and burn her head from the inside out.

She could feel Holly's eyes on her from the kitchen window. Out of the corner of her vision, she saw Fran and Libby join her for a few moments, the three of them leaning against the sink and staring out into the garden, before Holly shooed them away and came out alone. She opened the back door quietly, slipping her flip-flops on at the bottom of the garden path, shuffling across the grass towards Anna. She walked carefully, trying not to make Anna jump, like she was a horse who needed to be approached slowly, calmly. Holly held her hands out in a gentle gesture, in case Anna got spooked and kicked out in fright.

She was going to have to explain it all now, to say it out loud for the first time. At least Jack had worked it out. At least she had been saved from having to go through the details, to find words for what she had done. She closed her eyes for a few seconds. Orange sparks flickered around on her eyelids. The inside of her head was dark like the sky.

'Can I sit down? We don't have to talk if you don't want to.'

Anna jerked her head, halfway towards a nod, enough permission, for now, for Holly to take her place on the bench in the twilight. Anna squinted at the long flames.

'It's all over.' Even the air she let out of her mouth trembled, shivering in a little whimper like she was crying again, even though she wasn't, not yet. Holly didn't speak. 'The whole thing: me and Jack, my nightmares. It's done.'

Holly held her hand.

Anna kept looking dead ahead, focussing on the flickering white hot petals of orange and red.

'I was on the road when Jack's dad crashed their car. I was thirteen.'

Holly's face twitched round to look at her. Anna rested the palm of her right hand softly against her chest, above her heart, willing her pulse to slow down.

'I've been dreaming about it ever since, bits of it, never the full picture. It's like I forgot it, only I didn't really. Meeting Jack made me face up to the fact that I was there that night. Or the fact that I was there meant that I met Jack. I don't know which.' She swung round to look at Holly. 'I recognised him, the very first time I saw him. I told you that, didn't I?'

Holly squeezed her hand. 'You said he lost both his parents when he was younger, in an accident. Was that it? Was that how it happened?'

Anna nodded. Holly took the bottle of vodka from her hand and gulped down a mouthful.

'Why were you on the road?'

'We had an argument at home. I ran out of the house. It was January; I don't know how late it was but it was so dark, and so cold, and it was raining the whole time. I lost my footing

313

in the middle of one of the roads up to the Downs, and I fell over. I couldn't get up in time. It's so weird, there's this sense that I remember from that moment, this feeling that I still get in all my dreams.'

'What feeling?'

'I knew I couldn't move, but I could see the car coming. I stopped trying to get up because I realised I didn't have enough time, and I just looked at the car instead, just prayed that it would change direction, that it would swerve away from me. And then it did. And they died.'

'Anna, you didn't move the car with your mind.'

'I know I didn't, but that's what it felt like, me lying on the road stretching my fingers out towards the crashed car with these dead people inside, like I could pull it back into the road, reverse what I'd done, have it kill me instead. That's what it always feels like even now, in my dreams: I wish for something to happen, and it does, and then somebody dies and I realise what I've done.' She could feel her face threatening to crumple, to fold around the words and stop them from coming out. 'It doesn't matter anyway. The end result is still the same: they died, and it was my fault.'

Holly passed the bottle back to her, fixing her with a stare that had the burning fire reflected in the middle of it.

'This doesn't change who you are.'

It was the nicest thing anybody could have possibly said to her at that moment.

'Why didn't I work out what was going on? Why did I block it all out?'

'Nobody would want to remember something like that.' Holly fiddled with the vodka bottle, screwing the top on and then off again, taking a sip and shuddering. 'You know, I stopped eating almost completely when I was younger, much younger.'

Anna turned to look at her. Holly had never told this before.

'How much younger?'

'Nine. Ten, maybe. Nobody could work out why. My poor parents, they had all the other kids running around needing looking after, and me just getting thinner and thinner and more and more ill. I would cry at the dinner table, but hysterically, like I was in pain. They tried everything they could think of. Eventually Mum took me to a counsellor. I had to sit through these terrible hour-long sessions while this creepily calm woman in a pale blue suit told me over and over again that I must be repressing a trauma. Mum came in with me for one of the sessions, and suddenly piped up with how I had almost choked to death a few months before on a boiled new potato.'

'You nearly died?'

'It was lunch, at the weekend, I think. Tom made me laugh while I had a whole one of those little potatoes in my mouth. I breathed it in, and it just got stuck. It wouldn't go down. I couldn't find the right muscles to cough it up. I went red. Then I went blue. Joseph did the Heimlich manoeuvre, badly. He cracked one of my ribs, but it didn't work. In the end Dad stood on a chair, lifted me upside down by my feet and got the others to hit my back while he shook me like a rag doll. It sounds funny, but it was fucking terrifying. I was barely conscious by the end of it.'

'It doesn't sound funny at all.'

'My point is, it was as if none of us could remember it, even though we'd all been there, we all knew it had happened. Nobody had even thought to connect it to why I had stopped eating.'

Anna tilted her head back, the orange glow of the city an industrial halo stretching far above them into the darkness.

'I never realised just how fickle memory really is.'

'As soon as we started talking about it, it was so obvious that that was the reason: I was scared of choking again. But that journey home after my fourth appointment, when Mum drove me back in the car, that was the first time we'd spoken about it to each other since it had happened.' Holly waved her hands in front of her face for a second. 'I know this isn't the same, at all.'

Anna laughed. It sounded odd after all the crying.

'Thank goodness it's not. I hope nothing like this ever happens to anybody else, anywhere, ever.'

'I just want you to know that I understand. We're all playing tricks on ourselves, all of the time, erasing things we wish weren't there, especially things that are a threat to our happiness.' She put her arm around Anna's shoulders. 'It can be your fault, without you having done anything wrong, don't you see?'

'Even if, by some miracle, I manage to forgive myself for this, Jack never will.'

# CHAPTER TWENTY-EIGHT

'This is the longest we have gone without speaking since I first saw you.'

Jack lifted the curtains aside slightly, peering down the street. He was unsettled, fidgety, checking whether anybody had seen him walk over to her house, even though it wasn't that sort of street. There was nobody home at Anna's to care or to worry anyway. He was standing by the window in her living room while she sat on the sofa wishing he would stop stalking around on the other side of the room, that he would come and sit down next to her. He had said he was ready to talk.

'I miss you,' she tried.

Jack just twitched. He didn't reply.

'Do you want a drink? I could make us a cup of tea? A glass of wine?'

For a second his face softened. He made a strange half smile with his mouth, but then he shook his head, moved the curtains again. That was when Anna knew it wasn't going to be good news.

'I have thought about this non-stop, believe me. It's all I've thought about.'

He leant back against the wall. She drank his face in, every little detail, everything she'd been missing for the past two weeks as she lay in bed late at night, hating herself for not taking more photographs. It was all right in front of her again. Why would his features not stay still, safe and fixed in her mind? How had she recognised him after fifteen years, but now found it impossible to remember what he looked like when he wasn't there?

At night she put her hands over her eyes to deepen the darkness, to help her concentrate as she tried to focus on his features. She only saw details: the edge of his mouth, a smile at the corner of his eye flickering for less than a second, his collarbone, the skin behind his ear. When she tried to stand back and see the rest of him he disappeared like sand through fingertips, a fractured half-remembered dream, vivid but invisible, thwarted by the strange fluidity of her memory once again. If this was it, if he was about to tell her that it could never happen, walk back out through her front door and not come back, then she had to store this moment somewhere safe. So she looked and looked, until her eyes stung, until he turned away.

'I've gone down all the roads that lead away

from this point. I always come back to the same decision, to it not feeling the same, to me spending an age waiting for it to all to slot back into place, trying to love you but never getting there.'

Anna looked down. 'I don't ever want you to have to try to love me.'

'I don't see how this can ever be what it was. Do you?'

'It's not my place to say. If you think we can't get past this, then we're as good as finished.'

'It's not that I'm not trying. I am.'

*Well try harder*, she wanted to shout at him. But she wanted to shout at herself, too, to ask why she had wasted so much time and energy getting to the bottom of something that she should never have got to the bottom of. Why had she been so obsessed with working it all out? If only she had known that every time she took a tiny step forward towards clarity, she was closer to destroying everything.

'I'm not angry. You didn't do anything that makes you a terrible person. It's all so much more hopeless than that.'

'Please don't say that it's hopeless.'

'But it is.'

'Are you honestly saying that you will be happier, that life will be easier for you, if we stay apart?'

'The second one.'

'What?'

'Life will be easier. I won't be happier.'

'I wish I didn't know any of this. I wish I hadn't remembered.'

Jack shrugged. 'We would have worked it all out sooner or later. It was better that it happened now, before we had got to a point where we couldn't live without each other.'

His words were like a wasp sting. Acute, painful, but worsening as they sunk in and the poison started to throb. Had she accelerated past him, sped up ahead somewhere more intimate without waiting for him to catch her up? Was she out here on her own with her limbs cut off, or was he feigning detachment to hurt her? She didn't know which was worse.

Jack sat down in the soft armchair by the television, leaning backwards, closing his eyes and squeezing the bridge of his nose between his fingers. He looked up, a little brighter.

'One good thing has come of all of this: I haven't had a single nightmare since we found out. It's like I've been absolved of a crime. The haunting's evaporated.'

'Absolved, because it's my fault they died and not yours?'

'You're still having them then?'

Anna was stunned. A whole fortnight of blank nights. She hadn't even noticed, like somebody had switched the loud background music off in a busy bar, and you couldn't quite put your finger on why the atmosphere had shifted because you'd been tuning the noise out for hours. She was reliving that disaster in her waking moments now anyway. It was no longer haunting her nights.

'No. No I'm not.'

'I wasn't saying that it's your fault. It's the opposite.'

'What do you mean?'

He leant forward. It was the first movement he had made since he had arrived to shrink the space between them, to get closer to her, even if only by a few inches.

'I've beaten myself up for everything I did that day, for everything that happened. It was me who wanted to sit up front with Dad. It was me who dropped my watch in the footwell and had to turn the light on to look for it, so Dad couldn't see properly when we drove out of town. It was me who insisted on going to Design Club after school. It was me who was late out, so Dad had to pick Mum up from the gym first, had to drive the other way home. It was all me. Everything was my fault. Every single decision I made that day led to their death.

'But you being there too, and me knowing everything that was going on that day in your life, just reminded me how many factors there really are at play in all of this, how big the world is. Everything that happened for you to be on that exact road, at that exact time, that you fell over, that Dad didn't see you, they're all meaningless little moments that added up to something catastrophic. I've finally realised how many infinite moving parts there are, how many millions of things have to combine and coalesce to create every single situation we find ourselves in. I'm not important enough for it to be my fault. Neither are you.'

'So you can sleep easy now?'

He nodded. 'It's good. It's good that you remembered.'

'Not if it means I can't be with you.'

'Maybe that's not what this is though.' He gestured to the air between them. He must know that he was hurting her, twisting a knife in somewhere deep. 'It could just have been recognition that sparked between us. Maybe somewhere underneath it all I did know it was you.'

They climbed upstairs and out onto the flat roof together, to say 'goodbye'. Jack went out first, reached back for her hand and helped her up. Music was playing in someone's flat next door, the melody rising through the dusk and up towards them. She had barely lived here and not known him.

He was in every view of London, every smell that got carried past her on the air. It all reminded her of him. The damage that one short moment in her childhood had done to his entire life only made her more sure that she would never find anything this powerful with anyone else for the rest of her life, for better or for worse. Was that what Jack wanted, to back away from the intensity, to give up and settle for some pale, faded normality with someone who would never quite understand what he had been through?

They swayed together to the song from next door, Anna's tears soaking into the fabric of his jumper, holding onto him tightly like she was bobbing far out at sea. He gripped her harder and she felt his shoulders shake.

'I wish it hadn't been you.'

Anna screamed as if somebody had died after he left. She had never been heartbroken before.

It didn't feel like it had anything to do with her heart. It was all in her stomach, her head, her limbs. It was panic, sheer white blind panic, like someone was peeling back her eyelids and shining a hot light in her eyes, forcing her down onto her knees on rocky ground, her own feelings squashing her, rubber bands around her windpipe, her body temperature all wrong. Should she be fighting for Jack? Had she let him walk away?

Holly found Anna up on the flat roof at two in the morning, sobbing, her throat raw. She pulled her up to standing in the cold air, and bundled her through the window and upstairs into bed, whispering, 'I know, I know,' and rubbing her back whenever Anna tried to speak.

# CHAPTER TWENTY-NINE

For weeks, Anna dedicated herself to sleep. She rediscovered the endless silent hours of darkness she had missed, coming home to a distant friend after too long away. Her sleep was heavy. It pulled her deep down like the dead weights on a diver's belt, her body resting gently on the bottom of the ocean floor, calming dark waters pressing in over her head. The sounds of the busy world around her carried on, muted and far away above the bubbling surface of the waves. Each morning she swam back up for air, celebrating that she was finally good at this. She was stacking up great big slabs of dreamlessness, paying back her sleep debt with interest.

She retreated, coming home from work and going straight up to her room where she burrowed under the covers and watched television on her laptop, or read books and magazines like a reclusive teenager. She ate snack dinners on the way home, or bought takeaways, carrying them up to her room so she didn't have to make food. In the mornings she showered and left without breakfast. The rest of the house disappeared. She forgot about the living room, the kitchen and the garden. She barely spoke to the girls; if she heard them moving around downstairs she shut herself away until she was certain they had all gone to bed before creeping out to brush her teeth.

Occasionally she still had dreams, short flickering visions of Jack crying, the briefest of intimate moments that quickly bled into a murder or a death. They had sex that became violent or deadly, her hands accidentally gripping him too hard so that her nails punctured his skin, Jack falling in an unnatural crooked way and breaking his neck. It didn't matter too much. She deserved them, and in the absence of speaking to him or seeing him, at least they were still connected, at least he was still in her life. It was the moment when it all stopped that she feared, worried about, didn't want to arrive. Then she would have nothing of him left.

September came. The days lost their heat faster in the evenings but grew more beautiful, the air fresher, long golden evenings that stretched out for hours. Gradually, Anna began to return to the land of the living. The others were kind and gentle to her. They invited her to events and parties, took her out for dinner, suggested slow Sunday morning walks along the canal. When they were in, Libby or Sophie would cook, everybody sitting around the kitchen table eating stews, stir fries, or roast dinners, and beaming with relief each time they made Anna laugh at something. In the evenings they asked her what she wanted to watch, instead of just sticking something on, and every time the plot of a film veered towards a traumatic break-up or a tear-stricken heartbreak, she could feel them collectively hold their breath, hoping she wasn't going to get up and leave the room. She had become the youngest child in a family of caring sisters.

She knew how it looked from the outside, though. Holly was the only person she had explained everything to, and it appeared Holly had finally learned how to keep a secret. The others were patient, but they couldn't understand: her relationship with Jack had only lasted for two months; why couldn't she get over him? Why did they all have to go to the other pub now, sit in the other coffee shop? There had been an unspoken decision that she would leave certain places free for Jack to enjoy. He had lived there for years before Anna moved in; it was his territory. So she had shifted her life slightly further west, avoiding the hairdressers she liked, her favourite cafe, the pub nearest his house. She walked further up into Dalston now on her way home to go to the supermarket, or she stopped off on the other side of the park to avoid bumping into Jack in the corner shop. She was discovering another London, a place that had less colour, brought less joy, a different city from the one she had known with him.

Her work flourished and thrived. It was the only thing she could muster any enthusiasm for, so she threw herself into it, harder than she had done in years. It paid off quickly. She had been so consumed by her nightmares, she hadn't noticed how much of a back seat the gallery had taken. As soon as she started concentrating on it again, things started moving, developing. She remembered how much she loved this work, that she was good at it. Those hours from nine-thirty to six-thirty became the most valuable part of her day, the outlet for her creative energy, her ambition. She started extending them, staying as long as possible, coming home when it was already dark, pride swelling in her chest at what she was achieving. It didn't take long for Alexei to notice. He asked her why she had turned up the heat.

'Has someone broken your heart? You don't want to go home in the evenings now, is that it?' he joked, when he looked in and found her still there in the darkness, her face blue in the bright light of the computer screen. Anna laughed loudly.

He started making noises about a promotion. He was changing the structure of the team: two curators working below him, each with an assistant, instead of four assistants. He said that legally they had to advertise, but it was more likely that two people within the current team would be promoted, than an external applicant would get the job. When Anna sent him some new work she was exploring by Chinese artist Sháo Mei, he responded immediately, forwarding her an invitation that he had received to attend the private view of Sháo's *Gunpowder Green Tea* installation at Flowers Gallery on Kingsland Road. He suggested Anna join him.

The exhibition was packed when they arrived on Thursday evening, everybody enjoying the intriguing novelty of being served small clear glass bowls of loose leaf tea instead of the usual red or white wine. Sháo Mei was a textile maker, pattern designer and seamstress, trained in traditional cotton weaving, but she incorporated her hand-sewn materials into more modern, striking pieces. Her first solo exhibition in Shanghai's young and noisy OV Gallery had been deemed politically incendiary, cause for the whole place to be shut down for nearly a month and the works modified before it was allowed to reopen. The gallery had closed permanently more recently, but its founders were already working on a new project that Alexei had been tipped was set to open very soon. Anna initially noticed Sháo Mei's work for the simple reason that she had never seen anything quite like it before, with its combination of subtle, exquisite skill, and clever shock factor.

*Gunpowder Green Tea* was a living breathing installation, involving two actors who took part in a Wedding Tea Ceremony on a raised white stage encased between four high clear glass walls. They enjoyed the ritual privately, as though they were not being watched. In its rawest form, it was a political statement about the modern day, still-developing aftermath of the Xinhai Revolution, which took place a little over a century ago. Sháo Mei's family ancestry was half Manchu, half Han, her blood created by a union between the two warring factions. The document they were given at the gallery explained that the Manchu minority in China was, today, technically the fastest growing minority in the entire world. It wasn't down to population growth or birth rate; it was happening as the stigma attached to being Manchu lessened. It was no longer shameful, or

331

dangerous, to reveal that you were descended from a group of people who had been so spectacularly and completely overthrown. Manchu were altering their nationalities officially in droves.

In *Gunpowder Green Tea*, Sháo Mei celebrated the coming together of the opposition through love, just as it had happened in her family, when her Manchu great-grandmother had married her Han Chinese revolutionary great-grandfather. On the stage, a table was dressed with a traditional cloth made by the artist, covered in an ornate turquoise and pink pattern. Traditional tea sets, mugs and plates, all designed and painted by Sháo Mei and cooked and glazed by hand, were laid out across the cloth. In the centre of the table were two large glass jugs of hot water, one filled with actual gunpowder to represent the physical violence and the weaponry, the fighting that had taken place, and the other filled with deep sea-blue pearls in homage to the Chinese name for the tea 'Zhu Cha' which translated as Pearl Tea.

Every few moments the woman offered the man some 'bobo', a type of steamed cake typical of the Manchu cuisine. Each time, the man accepted with a loving smile. The woman was dressed in a traditional Manchu Cheongsam one-piece dress, with pins in her hair and beautiful jewellery in her ears. The man wore a smart Zhongshan suit, as instructed by the Republic, a neat high-buttoned collar with a floral design sewn diagonally across his chest. There was so much to admire in the quality of the sewing and the silks, the incredible patterns that covered every material Anna could see, the detail in the carpet that was rolled out underneath their feet, and the beautiful gold-rimmed porcelain that the woman held daintily in her hand. But with the work as a whole, Sháo Mei had elevated her ability, moved it forward somewhere bigger, so that it cast a spell.

If Anna hadn't spent the past few days reading about her, finding interviews with her online and examining the strange absence of detail to any of the press coverage that her controversial OV exhibition had received, she would not have known that it was Sháo Mei who stepped into the gallery, shaking the late summer rain from the ends of her blue-black hair and blushing to herself at the crowd of people gathered around her handiwork. She was difficult to age, but couldn't have been older than about thirty-five. The girl who served her tea clearly didn't realise who she was, so Anna walked over before Sháo was captured in conversation, and introduced herself, explaining she was working with Alexei at the Whitechapel Gallery.

'It's wonderful to meet you. I didn't realise you would be in the country.'

'Any excuse I get to come to London, I take.'

'This piece is incredible, really.'

It was an inadequate appraisal and one she must hear often, but Sháo Mei smiled graciously, her eyes closing and her cheeks going pink.

She leaned in to Anna, holding a hand up to her mouth and whispering, 'One of the actors is ill. That man up there now, that's my older brother. He lives over here. He is not a big fan of me today.' She raised her glass tea bowl to the man on stage in thanks. He didn't react, staying in character. She winked at Anna. 'He shouldn't be so good. I might ask him to do it all the time.' She frowned. 'I'm a little concerned about whether this will all be as strong when it changes to mannequins next month.'

'I think it will work well. It will be different, of course, but it might be powerful in another way. I don't think anything will get lost.'

Sháo Mei nodded enthusiastically. 'Bravery is currency in art over here; I was quite concerned it wouldn't be bold enough, or rather that its courage would go unnoticed, but it seems to be going down well. Even people who don't know anything about Xinhai are finding things to enjoy, the designs maybe, the novelty, I don't know.'

'Maybe the fact that it isn't only about the Revolution.'

Anna hesitated, nervous about imparting her own interpretation of a piece to its creator, and even more apprehensive when she felt Alexei walk over to stand next to her. Sháo Mei nodded for her to continue.

'It's about something more universal too, surely: forgiveness, healing, learning to love again after terrible crimes have been committed, however private or public. That's bravery in any language.'

If Anna could have painted what forgiveness would look like for her, right now, it would show her and Jack sitting opposite each other just as the man and woman were up on the stage, Jack holding one of her hands tightly across the middle of the table while she poured him a cup of tea with the other.

Sháo Mei beamed at her words.

'You must come to my studio, visit my team at Moganshan Lu.'

'I'd love to.'

'I'm serious.' She turned to Alexei. 'Anna should come and visit me. I'm setting a big new project at the moment that might interest you both. Does that sound like the sort of jaunt you might be able to fund, Alexei, or are you too tight for that these days?' She was teasing; Anna had stopped being surprised by the rapports, the existing relationships, the shared in-jokes that were revealed when Alexei met an artist or gallery owner at one of these events.

'You should go to Shanghai,' he said later when they went next door for a drink before heading home.

'Are you serious?'

'Sháo's work is interesting. She's special. But aside from that, Moganshan Road would be a good place for us to visit right now – for you to visit. It can't be anything extravagant; we can pay for your flights, but I know somebody who I'm sure would be happy to put you up, if you wouldn't mind being a guest in somebody's home.' He wagged a finger at her. 'Any wild nights out are on you, though, I'm afraid.'

Anna raised her eyebrows and looked down at her drink, still half-full. 'I'm not in the market for wild nights out any more.'

He laughed. 'You sound very old.'

Anna jumped at the chance to leave the country, to spend a week in a city where she wasn't walking home tense, anxious not to bump into Jack. It was the last week of September when she travelled out; Shanghai would still be hot, an extension to her summer season. She had enough meetings planned over there to keep her busy every day, and free time to wander up and down Moganshan Road or along the Bund, to do some shopping and take a riverboat cruise. As they landed at Svalbard she had gripped Jack's hand, frightened by the flight, the feeling of still being so far up above the ground when the plane's engines started to die down. She was less scared on the way to China, less desperate to stay alive.

Alexei had told her not to expect anything extravagant, but he hadn't properly explained that Ai Cheng, the friend she was staying with, was one of the chief directors of the Minsheng Art Museum, a business and cultural heavyweight known all over Shanghai. He sent a glossy black car to collect her from the airport and, although he was out most of the time she was there, lavished kind hospitality on her through invitations and access to events taking place around the city each evening. Some mornings he was just getting ready to leave when she came into the kitchen to have breakfast, his shirt sleeves flapping without their cufflinks, bare feet poking out from the bottom of his crisply pressed suit trousers. He made sure she found the cupboard his housekeeper had filled for her, a treasure trove of Western snacks: peanut butter, cereals, jam and white sliced bread. Ai asked her what she had planned for the day, quickly eating his steamed baozi standing up and nodding politely to her reply, even though she could tell he was in a rush. She had never seen anyone work such long hours, or live a life that was so entirely focussed on their career. She was heading fast in the same direction.

It wasn't the solitary ambling discovery tour that Anna had envisaged at all. Instead, she rushed around to fit all her appointments in, and spent the rest of the time at talks, exhibition openings, private views and gallery events. She visited M50 almost every day, a re-purposed factory space out on Moganshan Lu home to over twenty-five contemporary art spaces, all surrounded by public graffiti walls, their colourful spray-painted illustrations stretching up and down the industrial concrete. Ai arranged a viewing appointment for her at Eastlink in the M50 building. Although it wasn't active any more as a public walk-in exhibition, Eastlink still held one of the most impressive collections in Shanghai.

Anna spent two full days with Sháo Mei in her studio, poring over Sháo's new project *Love or Duty,* which examined over fifty case-study relationships of soulmates, people from all walks of life who had been together for more than forty years. Sháo Mei looked at genetics, history, disposition and values. She was working with a research laboratory, making detailed genetic comparisons between partners, family medical histories, the profiles of their natural body odour, the success of their parents' relationships, their professions, and the way they answered a series of central questions about life. Sháo Mei spoke to her about her early thoughts for how to present the findings, how to make it a personal experience for a gallery visitor, something that would involve them so completely they could apply it to their own lives. She was still laying out the design for the tapestry piece that would introduce it all, using the finely woven silk threads of su xiu. Sháo wondered if there was a clear controlled comparison she could make between these dedicated monogamists, and a free-spirited self-sufficiency. Anna offered herself up as the control, much to Sháo Mei's amusement.

'You are too young to be so jaded. A beautiful successful girl like you must be beating them away with sticks.'

'That's where I'm going wrong: I need to put down the sticks.'

It was an expensive project, and one that would take months, maybe even a year, to come to fruition, but Anna could tell that Sháo had already made up her mind: it was duty rather than love that bound people to one another for decades rather than years.

'Love doesn't last a lifetime. Duty never ends.'

Anna found the dim sum bar she liked the most, and eventually learnt how to eat xialongbao, the delicate soup-filled pork dumplings, without squirting hot liquid clumsily all over herself. She grew accustomed to toilets that opened when you approached them, to seeing more buttons down the side of a bathroom wall than in a plane's cockpit. She practised her 'XièXiè', surprised at how soft and delicate Mandarin sounded, and bought fresh flowers to fill Ai's flat by way of thanks. She ran out of business cards, her own purse so full by the end with tokens from everybody she had met that she had to spread them out between the inside pockets of her rucksack.

It should have been a freeing experience, surrounded by new sights and smells, disconnected and adrift from all the pain back home, but it wasn't. Shifting time zones upset her sleep patterns again for the first time since the night when she had remembered everything. She was jet-lagged. She lay awake when she got back each night, sleepy at first, her brain gradually kicking into gear and waking her up the later it got, until she was sitting up at the dark wooden desk in the corner and making notes about things she needed to do the next day, conversations she needed to have, people she must make sure she spoke to. She became anxious. There was a weight of responsibility on her shoulders out here that she hadn't appreciated when she boarded the plane. Alexei was trusting her to make connections, to look out for artists, to spot the next big thing from China. It was a test that she had to pass; work was the only thing she had left.

Towards the end of the week, a couple of nights before she was due to fly home, Anna came back earlier than usual to find Ai Cheng sitting on one of the bamboo chairs out on the terrace, enjoying a whisky. He shook the bottle at her through the glass windows when she came in, beckoning her over, pointing towards the cupboard for her to bring another glass out with her. His tie was unknotted, the top two buttons of his white shirt undone, and he had taken his wristwatch off, lying it out on the glass table in front of him. He rubbed his hand across his face as she sat down. He looked tired.

'I am going to bed. I thought maybe you would like one of these? You do not seem to sleep.'

Anna blushed. He put a tiny blue pill on the palm of her hand and poured a generous inch of thick amber liquid into the tumbler.

'Have I been keeping you up? I'm sorry.'

He swallowed, shook his head. 'Last night you came home at two. I had just got back. I saw your light still on when I got up at six. You must try to lie in darkness so your body adjusts, even if you do not feel tired.'

'I know. I keep thinking about things I need to do.' She yawned.

Ai shrugged. 'It doesn't matter now. It's too late; you will be home soon. This will help you get some sleep though, or you will become ill. Alexei will think I have not treated you well.'

He looked stern, caring. He tapped a finger onto the cardboard box on the table as he left, so she could see the packet it had come from.

'Thank you for the flowers. Goodnight.'

The Xanax made her eyelids droop before she was halfway through the whisky. Anna stayed sitting outside on the bamboo chair in the night breeze until she was so dreamily comfortable she had to force herself to get up. She couldn't spend the whole night dozing outside. She tottered barefoot down the darkened corridor to her room, her body tipping sideways slightly, smiling at what a sure thing sleep suddenly was, dancing easily within soft-fingered reach. There was no need to set an alarm. Her first appointment wasn't until midday, at the James Cohan Gallery, one of her favourite spaces for local artists in New York that now had a new branch on Yueyang Lu. Anna sank onto the bed, her muscles melting like warm butter, her eyes closing before she had even pulled the sheet over herself. She should cash in that tranquilizer prescription when she got back to London; this was fun.

Her eyelids didn't flutter open again until the force of the daylight shone through them too fiercely to ignore. She was lying half out of the duvet in the sun. The blinds were rolled up near the top of the window, the bedroom door slightly ajar. Elegant tapering branches of bright pink cherry blossom tapped softly against the glass in the breeze. Her skin felt delicious, warm and sensitive, and even though she knew she must be dreaming when Jack walked in, she felt so keenly awake that seeing him standing there a few feet away from her made her shiver. She had never dreamt like this before, more awake than asleep, knowing it wasn't really happening, knowing exactly where she was, but enjoying the sensations, indulging in the fantasy. She could feel his skin under her fingertips. When he kissed her she could taste him. Occasionally the scene shifted for a few seconds and she saw the world again, the room empty around her, darker than in her sunlit vision, no bright-pink cherry blossoms outside the window. But she pressed ahead, guiding Jack inside her, gasping at how real it felt, how wonderful, how she had missed him.

Her face was wet with tears when she surfaced. The room was empty and the blinds were down. She was lying in navy blue darkness, just a thin strip of yellow light like a stripe across the painted white floorboards, where the daylight sliced in underneath the bottom of the fabric. It was like losing him all over again. It was worse. She scrunched the sheet up around her hand and shoved her fist into her mouth, biting down on it, crying into the freshly washed cotton.

How had she let herself get so numb? Why was she on the other side of the world alone, without him? Everything she had kept silent was welling up inside her, and she didn't know if she would be able to hold the weight of it back. Anna grappled with herself, trying to find the button to shut this feeling down, the one she had had her finger pressed firmly down on for the past month. How was it possible to feel this way about somebody, that you were as good as dead if you couldn't love them? It was oppressive and frightening, to see life stretching out in front of her, a hostage on an endless black journey to nowhere. She should have made herself wake up. She shouldn't have taken it so far.

# CHAPTER THIRTY

'Do you think we'll be able to keep it warm enough in the winter?' Anna crossed the bare concrete floor of the warehouse. The windows were so big she could step up onto the thick breeze-block sills and stretch her arms out without touching their edges.

'This is the underfloor, that you're standing on now.' The estate agent assured them. 'There'll be hot-water pipes laid into these grooves, and another flooring layer on top, so the whole place will be heated from underneath. I expect you'll still want to get some curtains for the windows though, to keep the heat in.'

'When did you say it will be ready to move into?' Holly asked.

'Four weeks. Just before the end of October. I'll be outside when you're done; I need to make a call.'

Holly and Anna were looking round an old factory building in Bow that was in the final stages of being converted to a series of cavernous live-work spaces. The bedrooms were tiny afterthoughts, square boxes that would be squeezed completely full once a double bed and a wardrobe had been shoved inside, but the rest of the place was like a vast concrete cathedral. The double height ceilings hung above a main space that would fit the living room, a little painting studio and art office for Anna, and a production area for Holly to work from. The kitchen was spread along one wall, underneath the mezzanine floor that had the bedrooms and bathroom above it. The air inside had a metallic tang; the whole place smelt of masonry dust. The dishwasher, oven and fridge were still all covered in plastic, their shiny instructional leaflets in a pile on the corner of the work surface.

Anna stayed standing on the window sill, looking out at the view. The factory towered over the end of a pretty tree-lined residential street. White terraced houses ran along each side of it, every one with a different-coloured front door. From this side of the building you could look down the entire street, all the way down to where it met the main road, fifty houses away. A young mother with a baby in a sling and a toddler holding onto her arm shuffled out of one of the houses and down the steps to the pavement. The little boy pointed up at Anna, jumping up and down to show his mum that there was a lady in the window, that the building wasn't empty any more. She turned around and smiled briefly at Anna, taking hold of the boy's waving hand to steer him down the street.

'What do you think?' Anna said over her shoulder to Holly. 'Fancy being the Gilbert to my George? The Morecambe to my Wise?'

'Those are two very different propositions.'

Holly was pirouetting diagonally across the floor in her scruffy trainers, her head thrown back to look up at the roof.

'I love it, don't you?'

Anna had come back from Shanghai to crisp cold October weather and bad news: their landlord had decided he wanted to move back in. He had found a buyer for the smaller flat that he'd been living in, and planned to return to his old family house now that he could pay off the rest of the mortgage. He wanted to live somewhere large enough that all his children could come and stay with him again for long weekends. He turned out not to be the London property mogul that Anna had imagined or assumed, but a family man who was desperate to have his young grandchildren running around him at Christmas, especially now that his wife was no longer alive. He had given the girls three months' notice instead of the required thirty-day minimum, but after ten years there, for the others, it was a huge blow. Libby decided to go abroad. The jewellery business was expanding and now that she was a director, she had the chance to go out to New York for six months and oversee the set-up of a new branch. Fran and Sophie started looking for four-bedroom flats, but Holly and Anna agreed they were ready for it to be just the two of them again, ready for fewer people and less noise, for a tidier, more settled home.

Anna crossed the room to the back window. It looked down over the canal. Leafy green weeping willows trailed their branches down past the windows and across the murky surface of the water. There were houseboats moored up in a gently floating line on the other side of the canal, and the occasional shrill tone of a bell rang out as bicycles slalomed around one another in opposite directions along the towpath. It was two miles away from Jack. It would be the final cutting of the thread, if that hadn't already frayed and snapped in two. They hadn't spoken, not since he had suggested it was recognition rather than love that had brought them together, and left her crumpled on the flat roof.

She had imagined no words for them to exchange, when they slept together in the Shanghai morning sunlight. It felt like that was the last time she had really seen him. She had even picked up her sleeping-pill prescription, months late, in the hope that maybe she could drug herself into another of those delicious lucid dreams. The pharmacist hadn't looked at the date on the paper; he just handed them over. She had tried them twice, but they only made her mind fuzzier, her brain dull and foggy. They hadn't brought Jack back to her, not even for a few minutes.

For a week Anna hovered, anxious about making any decisions. Holly got stressed; she was the one dealing with the letting agents. The flats were going quickly. The whole factory was nearly taken. Anna got annoyed every time Holly told her that. How could people be so desperate for a place to live here that they were signing up to rent somewhere that wasn't even finished?

'Can't we wait and look round it again when the floors are in?' she pleaded, stalling, when Holly came off another panicked call, reassuring the agent that their holding deposit was on its way. Holly put the phone in her mouth and almost bit down on it in exasperation.

That weekend, though, as Anna was walking home, she saw Jack leaving the pub next to his house with a woman she had never seen before. He was holding the door open for her to step

349

down onto the street, and they looked happy. She couldn't sense chemistry. There was no obvious flirtation, no physical contact; there was no reason to assume it was a date or a romance. But the woman was beautiful, with shiny dark hair, olive skin, and dark red lipstick. Her slenderness was dressed casually in black jeans and a loose T-shirt, comfortable trainers on her feet. She held her hand up to her face to shield her eyes from the low sun while she laughed at something Jack said. They might be friends, but Anna didn't know her face. It was a powerful punch in the gut, a message on bright display that Anna knew nothing about his life any more, or who he was spending his time with. She dropped her bag on the hall floor more heavily than she needed to when she got in, making the floorboards creak, her hands shaking with trembling rage that had no outlet. Holly stuck her head out of the living room.

'I thought you'd fallen over.'

'I think we should definitely take that flat.'

They moved in, for the first time in their lives paying a removal company to do the heavy lifting and driving. They bought huge second-hand rugs to roll out over the bare concrete floors. Anna found some cheap thick black cotton material that she bulk-bought in huge rolls to turn into curtains. She sewed pale grey silk liners into the back of them to help keep the heat in, wishing she had Sháo Mei's fine weaving skills every time she pricked herself painfully with the needle. She borrowed a ladder from someone who had just moved in next door and looped the holes that she had sewn in the curtains over the thick polished iron poles that ran above each window. They arranged sofas in a square over one of the rugs in one corner of the living area, and found a coffee table to go in the middle of it. They cooked meals together, spent evenings working side by side in their studio areas, and they talked more, now that their bedrooms were too small to spend any real time in.

The only time Holly mentioned what had happened, was to remark on how much more relaxing Anna was to live with, since she had started sleeping properly.

'I sleep better too,' Holly said, surprised. 'I was always worried about you at night; every little noise would wake me up. And you looked so tired all the time; your face is completely different, so much brighter. You've got more colour in your cheeks now.'

*Now that I'm unhappy*, Anna thought. She had never had to censor what she said so much before, aware how many of her instinctive responses to things would sound bitter and out of character. Her well-rested face betrayed her ragged heart; would everybody start expecting her to have recovered, assume she was completely healed?

It had felt so DIY when they looked around, an empty rubble-strewn conversion still halfway between abandoned and liveable. But once everything was inside, Holly's production area laid out along one wall and Anna's exhibition notes spread across her big white drawing table overlooking the river, it was more like home than anywhere they had ever lived.

Anna had noticed, just a couple of times since they had moved in, that Holly had started mentioning somebody called Ben. It was infrequent at first; occasionally she peppered a conversation lightly with his name, the flicker of a smile as she did so. But then she went to meet him for dinner one night, and she didn't come home. Anna was struck by the wave of selfish panic that rolled over her as she lay in bed awake, straining her ears for the noise of a key in the lock downstairs. What would she do if Holly found someone?

The clocks changed the weekend that they moved in. The evenings grew shorter, wintry and dark. It was more of an effort to stay out late as the cold crept into her fingers and the rain started to fall. Instead of meeting up with people on green parks and terraced bars, they ate dinners in cosy restaurants, drank tea in steamy cafés, and went over to each other's flats. Anna watched it all as though through a pane of murky glass, not feeling a part of anything. She had heard about Seasonal Affective Disorder, how some people developed real clinical depression as winter set in. She had never understood it until now, until this year. The seasonal shift was so personal, such an accurate mirror for her descent from happiness to hopelessness. She had had a summer together with Jack; everything since then had turned cold and dark.

Holly pressed ahead with decorating, with making their new bolt-hole homely. It was in good-enough shape after the first week that she suggested they throw a Bonfire Night party, a little reunion for people to make the winter frost more bearable. They waited until the day after, the 6th, so that it was on a Friday. The external renovations of the factory hadn't quite reached the roof yet, and although nobody was supposed to go up there, Anna had found an access stairwell over on the opposite site of the building that led up to a door out to the top of the factory. Maintenance workers were in and out; sometimes it was closed and sometimes it was open. On the Friday morning before work, Anna went up to check that they would be able to get out there and found the door unlocked and swinging in the wind. She wedged a brick in the doorframe to stop it from closing during the day, peering out across the grey concrete geometry of the rooftops below.

That night, the air smelt of Christmas. Everyone's breath swam smokily from their mouths into the cold. Winter had arrived. They launched fireworks off the roof, Holly and Anna sharing out rocket responsibilities between them, while everybody stood around in a circle stamping their feet up and down and rubbing their gloved hands together. Their little group of spectators let out appreciative shrieks and squeals of delight each time the sky exploded with colour and the noise of crackling spraying gunfire. They stood around in a circle writing their names in the air with sparklers. Fran tried three times to write fast enough to complete her full name, Francesca, but never got past the 'c'. Every time a door slammed downstairs, or a car pulled up outside, Anna wondered if a neighbour or a council officer had come to tell them off, but it seemed nobody noticed or minded their brief pyrotechnic display.

There were more people than Anna had expected, as everybody piled loudly down the echoing concrete stairs and across the linking corridor to their flat. Sophie and Fran had brought a few of their university friends, and a couple of people from Sophie's work. Anna had invited Poppy, who showed up with her husband Alex, and a dog-eared cardboard box full of brilliantly underwhelming indoor fireworks that they set light to on a china plate in the kitchen. Everybody crowded around to watch the show, tiny worms made of coloured chalk writhing around sleepily until they collapsed, blackened, onto the porcelain.

'I remember them being much more exciting than that,' Poppy said, her face falling.

Eventually Anna began to relax, reluctantly admitting to herself that Ben was lovely when he popped in for a few hours to see Holly. But the moment Sophie introduced Anna to Chris, she tensed, immediately sensing that everybody had designs for the two of them, that this was a tentative matchmaking exercise. She caught a glimmer of expectation in the looks that flew from person to person as Chris shook her hand, and said that he'd heard a lot about her. She tried not to mind, tried to muster up some effort to be curious and interested, reminding herself to ask him questions and listen properly to his replies. He was attractive in a nice way, with fluffy brown hair, a friendly smile, and a smart shirt on that he had unbuttoned slightly in an attempt to make it casual; he was the sort of man who you instantly knew was close to his mum. Her chest sagged slightly when he said he was an artist. Maybe the girls hadn't thought they had compatible personalities at all, they'd just made an easy link between his profession and hers, or worse, between his profession and Jack's. They had a good conversation. He was probably interesting; but it was frustrating and distracting to be talking to somebody while wishing they were somebody else.

As it got later, a couple of things Chris said made her worry that she had been introduced to him with some kind of warning, 'careful, she's just had her heart broken', or, 'Anna's been through a lot this summer'. And so, perhaps to prove to him that she wasn't delicate or damaged, hung up on somebody else, or maybe to convince herself that she could still go about things in precisely the same way that she might have done before she met Jack, she sat down next to him on the sofa, refilled his glass of wine, and tried to remember how to flirt. She didn't do a particularly good job of it, but her clumsy out-of-practice attempts went down well. Chris moved a bit closer, so that they were touching while they talked. He leaned in towards her whenever she said anything, using it as an excuse to put his hand lightly on her leg. Eventually Anna asked if he wanted to stay the night.

It was bizarre. Her body didn't seem to

work properly. It was like trying to remember one of those complicated choreographed dance routines that her and her friends had taught themselves when they were teenagers. She could hear the song, could remember short sections of the routine, the way her body should feel during a certain sequence, but she couldn't put it all together in one flowing performance. It was flavourless, detached. Chris had her left breast in his hand and she was watching it with a strange indifference, not really feeling any of it. She wanted to tell him to move his fingers slightly, to prop herself up on her elbow so she could free her leg from where it was trapped, her toes tangled in the bedsheets, but she couldn't find the words, or she couldn't be bothered. Her chest tightened. The memories of Jack were too vivid, her feelings for him too real and perfect when unwittingly thrown into sharp and painful relief beside this crude imitation of intimacy.

Anna knew she thought about Jack all the time, that he was constantly there even when he softened into the background while she was at work, became the wallpaper when she was pottering around the flat with Holly. Paying attention to it was like tuning into the ceaseless beating of her own heart, unwavering, relentless, vital. She hadn't realised what it would do to a moment like this, or worse, what a broken-hearted attempt at fresh romance would do to his memory. It made everything wrong and inappropriate. Chris was a stranger, but now, sickeningly, she had made Jack feel like one, too. She didn't even recognise herself when she clicked the light on in the bathroom and leant back against the wall, just to get a few seconds to herself once Chris had fallen asleep.

She could never recreate what she and Jack had shared, or erase the pleasure of his memory, not with anyone. She shouldn't expect someone else to know how to touch her like that, shouldn't take a man back to her bed simply to hold him up alongside Jack, knowing for certain he would fall so short. If she had to sit this out, to wait patiently until she was over everything instead of knocking the heartbreak out of her with the body of another, she had no idea how long it would take, or if it would even be possible. It might be a life sentence to solitude.

Holly padded down the stairs while Anna was making breakfast in the kitchen, after Chris had gone home. She hung her head when they sat down on the sofa together with their coffee.

'I feel like I've been unfaithful. I've got that sick panicky feeling when you know you've done something wrong, something that doesn't feel right.'

Holly didn't reply with anything obvious, didn't point out that it was so soon, that Anna didn't even know Chris, that she couldn't expect it to feel natural and good right away. There was no need.

Instead she said, 'You have been unfaithful in a way. You love Jack.'

Anna watched the last loose leaves of autumn blowing around in the air outside.

'He doesn't want to be with me.'

'I don't think that's it at all. I think he can't be with you, not at the moment. It would be too hard and confusing. He needs time to think it through, to talk to his parents about it – in his head, I mean. I'm not trying to give you false hope, and I'm not telling you to wait for him. I know he may never come around. But you shouldn't force yourself to forget him.'

'I can't wait to go home for Christmas.'

# CHAPTER THIRTY-ONE

Her dad collected her from Brighton station on December 21st, trundling her suitcase for her over the frosty ground on the walk back to his. He glanced at her a few times on the way home, and Anna waited for the inevitable commentary to ensue, the same surprised compliments she was receiving constantly in London, ever since she had stopped having the nightmares: 'You look so well. Have you dyed your hair? Have you been on holiday? You're skin's glowing.' He didn't say anything. Instead, he waited for her to unpack her suitcase in the blue room upstairs, showed her quietly around his studio in the outbuilding behind the lawn, admitted sheepishly that he had really let the garden go, and sat her down at the kitchen table with a firm expression on his face, as though he was about to interview her for a job.

'Sit there. I'll make us a hot chocolate, and you can tell me why you've got a look on your face like the world's about to end, which I suppose it might be. Maybe you know something I don't.'

She hadn't even been there for an hour. It was an instant relief to know that she wasn't going to have to pretend everything was OK. They could tackle this together right from the start, and for the rest of the week her dad would dutifully shoot her conspiratorial looks of weary irony each time a well-meaning relative wished her a Happy Christmas. He stirred cocoa powder and brown sugar into a pan of milk, like he used to do when she couldn't sleep, and Anna coughed when she tasted her first mouthful. She didn't like hot chocolate any more.

'Is this what I used to drink? It's so sweet.'

'Oh thank God. I only used to have one to keep you company. I tried to ignore the parental negligence I would be accused of when you eventually developed diabetes. Shall we have a coffee instead?'

He was silent when she told him that her romantic recognition had been real, both parts of it, the love and the familiarity. But he jumped in shock when she explained the full story, his mouth falling open for a second. His movements were usually slow and contained, measured; it was unusual to see him rattled.

'I did wonder,' he pondered, anxious. 'I

thought you might have seen something.'

'Seen something?'

'The accident was all over the paper. You ran away that evening, came back with mud all over your trainers, couldn't stop throwing up, shaking with a fever even though you'd been perfectly fine when you left. Upset, sure, but not unwell. I read about the footprints. I thought perhaps you'd seen the crash, that you'd witnessed something horrific and were in shock. I never dreamt that you had been directly involved in any way.' He looked down. 'I should have asked you. I'm sorry.'

'I don't think I would have accepted it even if you had.'

'I did mention it to your mum. She thought I was trying to deflect, to make it about anything other than our divorce. She said I needed to accept we were both accountable, that we had upset you.'

'Please don't tell Mum.' He stared at her, understanding. 'It's not a personal thing: I don't think I can take everybody in my life knowing.'

He nodded.

'Has Jack cut all contact?' He held her hand. 'Do you know, I don't think I've ever seen you heartbroken before. You looked so different when you got off the train today: lost.'

She loved him for noticing, for being brave

362

enough to talk about it.

'It is a little difficult to see the point of things at the moment. And nobody understands why Jack and I stopped seeing each other. They've even been trying to set me up with people, with a person actually, an artist called Chris.'

He winced at the accidental insensitivity of her friends, and then he saw her face. 'You've ... actively tried to forget Jack then?'

Anna laughed out loud at that, the most indirect, roundabout way that a dad could possibly approach the subject of sex with his only daughter.

'I've tried. It was really lonely.'

'Nothing makes you feel more alone than being with the wrong person – not even being alone.'

It was overwhelming being back at home, reading books in her old blue bedroom while her dad tinkered away in his studio out behind the apple tree. Anna opened the window an inch so that his Radio 4, clinking paint pots, and occasional cheerful humming drifted in over the lawn, keeping her company. The pace of everything was too slow here to ignore the heavy, tugging sense of loss that enveloped her more completely now, without the noisy London distractions of work, Holly, friends, parties, even housework. She untucked her duvet and pulled it up over her feet to keep her toes warm.

Christmas Eve unfolded as it always did, with reassuring routine. They got up slowly, Anna shuffling round the house in her old slippers sipping coffee and watching the frosty little ice crystals melt from the edges of the window pane as the house warmed up. They ate lunch together at the kitchen table with the papers spread out around them, comparing half-formed political opinions that they each shied away from as soon as things got too detailed, eventually pulling their chairs together to tackle the crossword. When the faded winter sunlight gave up outside, and the house was filled with yellow electric bulb light instead, they settled down in the front room to watch Nine Lessons and Carols from King's College, before disappearing into their own bedrooms to wrap the other's presents. They always filled a stocking for each other, delivered with an unceremonious lack of secrecy, passing one another on the landing at night to lay them at the foot of each other's beds, laughing as they stumbled clumsily round corners and shushed each other for no reason. The first thing Anna always heard on Christmas morning was her dad's loud and overdone exclamation of shock as he pretended to discover the weight of all those carefully wrapped surprises weighing down his duvet when he woke up.

'What's this? Anna come in here! Do you know anything about this?'

Anna's mum joined them for Christmas Day, along with her paternal grandparents and her dad's younger sister. The aunts and uncles tended to rotate Christmases between the Caldwells and their spouses' families. This year seemed to be a quiet one, which was a shame. Anna could have done with the complicated bustle of multiple conversations, distracting wine spillages and alcoholically compromised rounds of charades. It was difficult to focus on what people were saying when she felt this sad. She drank too quickly before the meal and spent the next hour speaking self-consciously to her aunt about work, waiting for somebody to notice she was drunk and make a joke out of it.

She saw her parents clearly for the first time, realising what an incredible decision they had made to live apart. They should be Sháo Mei's free-spirited control group, detaching themselves completely from any misguided or detrimental sense of duty to think only about the here and now, bravely admitting that they weren't happy and managing to change things but still remain friends. She had spent fifteen years resenting them for being apart rather than celebrating the fact that they were both alive and both happy. Even though she saw and understood the possibility of an eventual fading out of intense love, and the necessary decision to carry on regardless or to separate, she craved the possibility of a long, enduring, duty-bound future with Jack. She floated up and away from the cranberry-stuffed turkey, the greasy pigs in blankets, the thick pasty bread sauce, and imagined a settled old age together, a dedication to one another long enough to know what the other one was thinking, as well as what they were about to say, the joy of becoming bored of one another, irritated by each other's foibles, falling out and making up with an intimacy so familiar they could make each other laugh with a look.

'Anna?' her mum interrupted. Anna jumped, spilling gravy down her dress. There were five pairs of eyes on her, waiting for her to reply to something.

'Sorry, I was miles away, what did you say?'

But her mum had jumped up and gone next door to answer the telephone, evidently hoping that Anna was going to do it since she was closest to the door.

'It was for you,' her mum said, sitting down. 'Somebody called Jack. I told him you'd call him back later.' She put her hand up like she had thought of something. 'Was *that* the Jack you wanted me to try and think of. Do you remember? Ages ago, when you had that funny

366

dream? Did you work out who he was?'

Her dad was staring at her now. Anna shook her head at him as imperceptibly as she could, willing him not to bring anything up at the table.

'That's odd isn't it?' Her grandmother piped up. 'A friend calling at this time on Christmas Day? Everybody will be enjoying their dinner.'

Anna jumped up. 'I'll call him back now.'

'No you will not. Sit down. We've only just started. We haven't even set light to the Christmas pudding yet. Grandpa's made brandy butter. Why aren't you wearing your cracker hat?'

Anna looked at her dad pleadingly but his face was impassive. She couldn't cause a fuss at the dinner table without having to explain what was going on. She bent to the will of the enforced festive jollity, putting the gold paper crown on her head and reading out a joke about chickens that was so bad it made her want to scream. She struggled to swallow the rest of the meal. Her stomach had clamped up, her taste buds dulled by her racing mind. The turkey was floury, dry and chalky white meat that wouldn't go down.

In the brief lull while the main was cleared away and her mum went to prepare the pudding, her dad shot her a look. She pushed her chair back, mumbled that she was going to the toilet, and ran upstairs to find her mobile. She tried calling Jack, but it went straight to answerphone. She texted him. There was no delivered note like there usually was, to show that he had seen it. Had he changed his number? Anna remembered the constant stream of teasing between his friends, how this was the longest he had kept a single phone running. He was always losing them, breaking them, flushing them down the toilet.

'Did Jack leave a number?'

She ambled into the kitchen under the guise of helping carry the bowls and dessert spoons, trying to sound casual. Her mum was flustered, trying to lever the Christmas pudding out of the oven without burning herself.

'No, I think he tried to give me one. Sorry, love. I assumed you had it. I might have been a bit brief with him. I was very distracted. I'd only just served up the food.' She stood up, her face shining in the heat of the kitchen. 'I'm sure he'll call you back.'

'Not if you told him I'd call him back!'

Anna dialled 1471 but her mum shook her head before she could even lift the phone to her ear.

'Aunty Joyce just called. I think you were

upstairs. It'll be her number on there now then, won't it?'

Anna tried to put the phone down without slamming it onto the side.

As soon as pudding was over she stalked out for a walk through the cold, trudging up and down Clifton Terrace for an hour, back and forth down the icy pavement, wondering which one had been Jack's house. There was no reason that he would still have the house here, on the street where he grew up. Was Jack spending Christmas in Brighton? He could be eating turkey a few hundred yards away surrounded by the same people who put those beautiful fresh flowers on his parents' graves. Perhaps they would all be out for a late afternoon walk in the early winter dusk. Anna started staring at families she passed, looking for a familiar nose, big green eyes, messy dark hair, anything that might indicate somebody was related to him. It was exasperating that they had managed to bump into each other by accident almost every day when she moved to London, but now that everything depended on it, Jack had become invisible, elusive.

A man down near the seafront asked her if she was OK.

'Have you lost something? You need help looking?'

He was out walking his dog, bracing himself against the cold wind. She must look odd, wandering along slowly on Christmas Day and peering at people. She shook her head and ran home.

Her mum was the last to leave in the end, when they shooed her out of the house insisting she let them clear up, since she had done all the cooking. Anna helped her dad move the table and chairs back to their usual positions. It took over an hour to wash everything up and put it away, past midnight by the time they sat down in front of the fire, now a pile of blackened sticks and softly glowing embers.

Her dad poured her a whisky and let out a long sigh as he sank back into his favourite armchair.

'How do you think he got this number?' Anna asked, swirling the glass so a little circular current spun in the middle of the liquid.

'It's on my website.'

Anna had told him all about *Kaamos,* had showed him the few photographs they had remembered to take together in Longyearbyen.

'I don't think he's got the same number as before. I tried his phone but it's not switched on. He was always losing them. I don't understand why he hasn't tried to call back here?'

'Can you imagine how your mum would have sounded? He was probably terrified calling in the first place, having to work his way up to it, and then a very stressed out Christmas cook picks up the phone and fobs him off, panicking that her broccoli's over-steaming in the kitchen next door.'

'Don't say that.' Anna put her head in her hands. 'It was a bad time to call.'

'He'll get back in touch. If – when – he's sure he wants to, it won't be hard for him to find you, I'm sure.'

'Don't you think I have to try as well, though? Shouldn't I get hold of him? I didn't say enough, the last time I saw him. I didn't tell him how I feel.'

'I think you have to give him space, but yes, you should let him know how you feel. Right now, though, I think you need to go to bed and get some rest. You're over-tired.'

Anna smiled at him. It was what he always said when she was little, when she got irritable and short-fused in the evenings but refused to go to bed. She would stand facing him, hands on her hips, and reply precociously, 'I am not over-tired. If anything, I'm *under*-tired. I expect it will be at least another hour before I'm even nearly a bit tired.'

Anna returned to London earlier than planned.

It was too tense, sitting at her dad's waiting for the phone to ring. It never did. He assured her that if he heard from Jack he would put them in touch immediately.

She went back up to his parents' grave before she caught the train home, with a brushed copper vase of winter flowers, blue thistles and snowdrops, fir, wild pine and crimson poinsettia. New flowers had been laid. A miniature false Christmas tree on its own stand was strung with a set of battery-powered fairy lights that still twinkled, not yet out of power. Somebody must have been up here recently. She was torn. She wanted to speak to Jack so desperately that she would have waited here all night just to see his face, but she was worried about what would happen if he found her here, looking like she had adopted his tragedy as her own, that she was trying to share a pain that wasn't really hers.

Anna dropped her bag back at the flat in Bow, and unpacked her bag of presents onto the drawing table, boxes of paints, beautiful expensive new brushes that she would never have been able to justify buying for herself, and a set of cheap plastic paint pallets, because her Dad knew she always threw them away instead of cleaning them. He had tied a tag onto each gift. 'Because you're colourful' on the paints, 'Because you're classy' on the brushes, and 'Because you're terribly lazy' on the pallets.

She had written a card to Jack that she now tucked into the big square inside pocket on her winter coat. She grabbed her keys and jumped down the stairs, light-footed without the heavy bags, and walked all the way along the canal towards London Fields and across the park to Jack's. Nobody was home; she had expected that. She slipped the card through the letterbox and walked back. She hadn't written much inside, only what was needed.

*For me, it wasn't only recognition.*

She included her new address, *if you ever need Arctic Anna.*

# CHAPTER THIRTY-TWO

Anna didn't hear from Jack, and her false sense of resolve veered between unreasonable hatred of her mum for putting the phone down on him at Christmas, and violent anger towards Jack each time she imagined him arriving home, reading her card and throwing it away, leaving her to wilt. She agreed to go for a drink with Chris, and the week after for dinner, until she could no longer bear the fact that she was using him and wasting her own time on strange, short, unenjoyable dates. It wasn't just that she was going against the good advice of Holly and her dad, but that she was battling herself, too, for no good reason; she just needed to be on her own. How could Chris be interested in spending time with this version of her anyway, a sad and distracted person who worked too hard and pulled away whenever he tried to get close? Jack wouldn't have fallen in love with this Anna.

She got claustrophobic sometimes, while she

was sitting on her own in the flat. If she had to focus on her computer screen or an exhibition catalogue for any length of time, the room shrank around her, making her eyes hurt and her arms and legs tingle, a black cloud of anxiety hovering over her head. When it got too much she took herself up to the roof and stood there in the wind, a few inches away from the edge, looking down at how far away the ground was, wondering whether it would even hurt if she fell. She flushed the rest of her sleeping pills down the toilet to stop herself from fantasising about swallowing the whole packet. She had no desire to die, no wish to end everything. She was just curious, considering ways she might be able to make the sadness lessen, wondering how long it was possible to miss somebody this intensely before you just stopped, bored of feeling bad, and got over them.

Together, Anna and Holly worked through the January freeze, wearing woollen fingerless gloves with the huge black curtains drawn shut and all the lights blazing. Anna was setting up the spring exhibition. She had been made a curator, along with Poppy and now worked more closely with her own assistant Ruth. Alexei said it was his New Year's gift to the best team he had ever had, which was as kind as it was probably untrue. On Fridays she worked from home, but the rest of the week she spent on site at the gallery, often having to go in for a few hours on a Saturday, or attend an event somewhere on Thursday evenings when most of the openings or private views were held. It was busy and chaotic in the office, but at least it was warm.

As the 20th came and went, the anniversary of Jack's parents' deaths, Anna became increasingly jittery about her birthday, looming imminently on Thursday 28th.

'I keep remembering this conversation Jack and I had at Libby's party that night in the old house,' Anna said to Holly when it was finally Wednesday evening and she couldn't hold it in any longer.

They had both arrived home late, shattered after working hard to make up for the morning off they were about to take so they could enjoy Anna's celebratory birthday breakfast at leisure. They were each spread out over a sofa, reading magazines, and dipping their hands alternately into a big bag of crisps and a bowl of carrot sticks. Holly said the carrot sticks meant that they were growing up.

'What conversation?' Holly rolled over onto her front and propped herself up on her elbows.

'We talked about what we were going to do for my birthday this year. Well, Jack asked me

376

what I wanted to do, like he just assumed we'd spend it with each other.'

That whole night pulsed loudly in her head still, the fact that she had immediately started expecting disaster, her face turning red when she remembered the anger she had inflicted on him a couple of hours later in the garden, in full view of her guests.

'It was such a lovely thing to say and I thought, even then, "famous last words", like he had jinxed it by assuming that everything would be fine and we'd still be together.'

'Don't let all this ruin your birthday.'

'He put the date in his phone calendar, and set a reminder for the day before so the alarm would go off today. I'm pretty sure he's lost his phone, but I keep thinking, what if he hasn't and the alarm goes off? I put a note through his door, when I got back to London the other week. Did I tell you that? I never heard from him. He's not online anywhere. All his profiles have been inactive for weeks.'

'Maybe he doesn't want to speak over the phone.'

'I gave him our address too.'

Holly sat up quickly and clapped a hand to her forehead. 'He's been away, Anna.' She said it like it was the answer to a difficult problem, something that had just struck her out of the blue. 'He's been travelling.'

'Jack has? How do you know?'

'Ben and I were having drinks last week, and this guy came over, all confused, saying he had definitely met me before, it was really bothering him, and could I work out how I knew him? It was really awkward at first; I couldn't place him at all and poor Ben was just sitting there like a lemon while we went through all the options. But then I told him what my name was and asked his, and it was Trystan, Jack's friend.'

'Where was this?'

'Hackney Road, at The Looking Glass. I'm sorry, I didn't completely forget, but I didn't realise that you had tried to contact Jack. I wasn't sure whether you'd want to hear about what he was doing, whether that would be a good thing.'

Anna shook her head. 'It's OK, but I do want to hear. He tried to get through to me on Christmas Day, called my dad's house just as we were sitting down to dinner. Mum picked up the phone and pretty much fobbed him off, told him I'd call him back.' Holly grimaced. 'I know. She doesn't know what's going on, though. I tried to find a way to get back in touch but his line keeps going straight to answerphone.'

'He must still be away. Trystan said it was a last-minute decision. He's with his cousin,

Olivia. They're really close, apparently. Did you ever meet her? Trystan said she lives round here.'

Jack had mentioned Olivia a lot, but she had been away for most of the summer at various fashion weeks. She was a model. Anna breathed a knot of tension out of her chest: the girl at the pub in October.

'When did they go?'

'Just after Christmas. Apparently she had just broken up with somebody, and they met up at a family thing and neither of them had any work booked in January, so they just took off, pretty much finished their turkey and drove to the airport. I can't remember where they went.'

'How long did you talk to Trystan for? Sounds like you covered a lot.'

'He bought us a drink each in the end, to say sorry for interrupting our date. It was nice; he's been looking after Jack, I've been looking after you. We had stuff to talk about.'

'Did he say how Jack's doing?'

Holly squirmed a little.

'It's your birthday tomorrow. I don't want you to get your hopes up, or tell you things I shouldn't. I don't really want to get involved – with the stuff in between you two, I mean.'

'Please. This whole thing is just dragging on and getting more painful because we're not talking and we don't know what the other person's thinking.'

Holly took a deep breath. 'Trystan was very clear about it. This isn't a question of strength of feeling, or of whether Jack wants to be with you; he doesn't know whether he can be. He definitely wants to see you, but I think he keeps talking himself out of it.'

'Seems like he's never going to be sure.'

'It's not just about him: everyone else in his whole family lost somebody that night; at some point he'd have to introduce you to all his relatives, knowing who you were, even if they didn't.'

'I thought I'd looked at this from every angle.' Anna closed her eyes. 'I hadn't thought of that.'

Holly started flapping, worrying that she had made Anna morose, had let her go to bed on her Birthday Eve in a sombre mood, but when Anna climbed into bed and turned out the lights, she found a little glimmering buzz of hope had sparked back into life, a firefly floating around her in the dark bedroom. Had Jack called her at Christmas to tell her he was going away? When he hadn't got through, had he just decided to leave it until he got back, to wait until his head was clear? He probably still hadn't read her card.

She visualized it sitting unopened in his

kitchen in a pile of post that Trystan was keeping safe for him, or up in his room. The envelope was golden and just had Jack's name on it, handwritten. Trystan would know it was important.

It was so different from how she used to force things around jerkily in her old haunted dreams, making things happen through lucid force of will. This was gentle, positive. She was making a birthday wish. If she saw it over and over again, watched it happen as she drifted off, she could imagine it becoming reality just a couple of miles away down the river.

Jack dropped his rucksack in the hall. Trystan handed him his post. Jack opened the golden card first, or maybe he left it until last, but either way he opened it in the end. He read her note. He turned his phone on for the first time in a month. He saw the reminder: "Anna's Birthday".

# CHAPTER THIRTY-THREE

Anna woke up to the smell of pancakes, and the sound of Holly humming to herself while she flipped the pools of batter in the frying pan downstairs. She had surpassed herself this year, making a stack of blueberry and vanilla ones, and a plate of wafer-thin French crêpes that she was drizzling with lemon juice when Anna wrapped a dressing gown around herself and stuck her head over the side of the bedroom mezzanine. There was a bowl of red fruit on the table, jars of chocolate spread, peanut butter and maple syrup, coffee bubbling away on the stove, and fizzing champagne flutes next to each plate.

'Happy Birthday!' Holly dropped the last pancake onto Anna's empty plate and smothered her with a hug as soon as she got to the bottom of the stairs. Anna squeezed her tightly in thanks.

'I'm still waking up. This has to be the best one yet. This is incredible.'

'I was up at five,' Holly yawned, pouring coffee out. 'Your dad was driving up to Scotland to see a friend and wanting to drop something off for you on the way.'

Anna looked around, expecting a painting to be propped up against the brick wall, a conspicuously wrapped champagne bottle in among everything else on the table.

'I didn't hear anything.'

They clinked glasses. She followed Holly's pointing finger over to the breeze-block window sill at the back of the flat. Holly had parted the curtains to sit Anna's presents and cards on it. The sky outside was bleached and grey, a cloudy dawn creeping slowly from the horizon up.

'What is it?' Anna asked. It looked like a tree, a sculpture of some kind.

'He said because you didn't have a garden any more, he'd tried to make you an indoor one, for every season. One you wouldn't have to water. It's your family tree. He's funny, your dad,' Holly spoke through a mouthful of food. 'He made me make him a pancake.'

'I can believe that.' Anna covered the one on her plate with strawberries and maple syrup, and carried it over to the window sill to have a closer look.

The tree was beautiful, the delicate whorls and knots of its trunk carved into a soft wood that her dad had painted, parts of it stained gold, parts of it blackened. Names and dates were etched into each branch, as though they had been carved with a compass, the private personal graffiti of a love-struck young teenager out in the woods alone. Green shoots and buds sprung from her younger cousins' branches, little closed blossoms that were yet to open and flower. Her mum's name was written on an elegant tapering twig, a thick cloud of purple and blue flowers blooming along its length, different from the yellows and pinks on the rest of the tree. The branch looked as though it had been cut off, separated from her dad's branch, but was now tied to it tightly with a sparkling golden thread, a supporting splint for a growing sapling.

Anna found herself there, her name and birthday carved in golden grooves on a piece of silver birch that sprung from where two roots met, one from her dad's branch and one from her mum's. A heavy hanging blossom that looked a little like a lotus flower dropped from the tip of her birch branch. Her dad had written Jack's name on its petals. She took the rest of the masterpiece in blurrily, happy tears swimming across the surface of her eyes. Her grandparents, in the autumn of their years, were covered in feathered orange, red, and yellow leaves, like fire. Anybody who had passed away was all the way up at the top, on the spindly bare skeleton tree branches of midwinter, their names written in silver instead of gold.

Holly sat down on the other side of it, tracing a finger over the names, reading the "Happy Birthday" tag that was tied around its trunk. She picked one of the cards from the pile, a bright blue tissue paper bundle sellotaped to the back of it.

'Your dad's kind of stolen my thunder, but try and look excited.'

Anna laughed, opening a card from Holly, and a beautiful golden necklace. The chain poured out of the tissue paper into her hand like water, thin and delicate, with a tiny paintbrush charm hanging at the bottom. Anna tried to hug her, to gush about how beautiful it was, but Holly got embarrassed by things like that and batted her away.

'It's nothing. I'm glad you like it.' Holly jumped up to attend to her mobile on the table, buzzing insistently against her coffee cup. She was in the middle of editing a film at work, and Anna knew it had been difficult to take even a few hours off. Holly read something on the screen for a second and gave Anna a sheepish look.

'You need to go in to work, don't you?' Anna sat back down at the table. 'It's fine, don't worry. I'll go through the rest of the cards, eat my bodyweight in pancakes, maybe even finish this bottle of champagne, and have to pay someone to roll me into work. Go.'

Holly was already wiping her mouth, darting round the table to kiss Anna on the forehead. 'Thank you,' she pulled her shoes on, checking through her bag for her keys. 'I'm sorry.'

Anna stood up to hand her the things she needed, like a couple who have lived together for long enough to turn leaving the house into a choreographed routine. She stood out on the hard stone floor at the top of the stairs, watching Holly run down to the door at the bottom, shouting 'goodbye' and 'happy birthday' over her shoulder as she went.

It was nice to be alone. She would be able to go into work before lunch if she needed to. She returned to the window sill, coffee in her hand instead of champagne. There was a silver envelope with no address written on it, nothing except her name in graphic black biro swirls. She put her coffee down. Her hands were shaking. Jack had put this in her letterbox. He hadn't posted it; he had been here.

She opened it, trying to empty her head of expectations, making her positive birthday wish again with eyes closed as she pulled the card out from inside. It was the picture of

Arctic Anna, folded up, the one he had drawn in Svalbard and promised to give to her. She turned it over, searching for a note, for a sign within the drawing. There was nothing written on the back, no evident changes to the sketch. She opened Holly's card again, read what she had written. *It's going to be a good year. I can feel it.* The air went very still. Holly never left in the middle of a birthday breakfast. Anna walked over to the front of the building, stepping up onto the wide sill and opening the curtains, the air cooling as she got closer to the glass.

She knew it was Jack immediately, at the very end of the street. You never forgot how somebody walked when everything about their body was interesting to you, when you had studied the way they moved, when they had walked towards you over and over again in your dreams. She squinted through the beautiful winter morning, the light low and bright. He was hesitating, moving slowly.

Last night, Holly had spoken about all the doubts Jack must have, and Anna had said he may never be sure. He didn't look sure now. He was hovering. The silver sunlight followed him from behind, turning him into a silhouette as he trod the pavement, blurring the edges of his body like the undefined shivering lines of a mirage, a shape cut messily into the morning sky behind. Anna narrowed her eyes, but without knowing for certain which way he was facing, it was impossible to tell whether he was leaning purposefully into the wind on his way to her, or hunched over in defeat on the way back home.

She didn't wait to find out. She flew across the floor, through the door, and down the stairs. The ground was hard and freezing, the soles of her feet aching painfully in the cold. She ran across the entrance hall and out to the big glass external doors at the front of the factory, shivering in her pyjamas as she threw them open wide, just in case, to wait for him.

# ACKNOWLEDGEMENTS

A headline and heartfelt thank you to my dear friend and agent Imogen Pelham at Marjacq. Imogen's belief in and support for *Waking* has kept me afloat, and her ability to tread the line between friend and agent with ease and elegance continues to mean a great deal to me. Thank you.

Thank you to the very brilliant Rebecca Lloyd, my wonderful editor. It has been a giddy joy to work with somebody who so perfectly understands my words on the page, and thus my imagination, my intent for *Waking*. Thanks too to Kate Ellis and Karen Bultiauw, and the team at Accent Press. I feel hugely fortunate to be a part of what you do.

Huge loving thanks to my husband Christian, who offered invaluable and constant encouragement, and who paid the bills while I shut myself away amongst the fragmented debris of Anna's nightmares.

Thanks to my parents Mary and Ian, who also supported me financially while I was writing, and who read *Waking* critically, honestly, and with occasional(!) compliments. Although it may seem crass to discuss the uncertain personal economy of debut authorship, I believe it is important to mention it. So many valuable new works and new writers are given a voice in part by the financial support offered to them initially by their loved ones.

Thank you to Sandy McPhonenix, for being the English teacher of dreams, and for being the only adult who ever admitted to us that 'life is more fun when you're a grown-up'.

Thank you to Naomi Annand and her harmony of angels (invented collective noun) at Yoga on the Lane, for keeping me sane and centred.

Thank you to my best friend Olivia for your love and belief over many many years, and for reading and enjoying *Waking*. You are an inspiration.

Thank you to my brother Mark, who has always been and will continue to be my creative sounding board. Talking through an idea or a problem with Mark always helps me find my way to a solution or a breakthrough. Mark, this book is for you. In return, please expect more awkwardly timed and confused phone calls.

There is no real map or guide for writing, only a deep and inescapable compulsion that many of us inexplicably feel. It is a need, not a want. It is a part of our autonomic nervous system, like our breath or our pulse. The bubbling source of this urge is so often the nourishment, education, and transformative insights that we have experienced by immersing ourselves in the writing of others. So a final thank you to the writers – far too many to list here – who I have read, studied, loved, disagreed with, submerged myself in, and been changed by.

# ABOUT HELEN RICHARDSON

Helen Richardson works as a producer, making short films, documentaries, and commercials for channels, charities, and brands all over the world. She writes fiction, as well as poetry and essays on her blog, *Read Me Softly*. Helen lives in East London with her yoga mat and her husband (not necessarily listed in order of importance) where she devours books of all kinds, and hours of house music.

Blog:**www.readmesoftly.com**
Twitter: **@helen_r_writes**
Instagram: **@helen_richardson_writes**